AN OUTSIDER AT THE HIGHLAND COURT

CELESTE BARCLAY

OLIVER
HEBER
BOOKS

Published by Oliver Heber Books

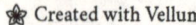 Created with Vellum

THE HIGHLAND LADIES

SUBSCRIBE TO CELESTE'S NEWSLETTER

Subscribe to Celeste's bimonthly newsletter to receive exclusive insider perks.

Subscribe Now

PREFACE

The Highland Ladies series is a spinoff to my first series, *The Clan Sinclair*, and follows the lives of ladies-in-waiting at King Robert the Bruce's court. If you are a fan of Highlander romances, then you've surely encountered the time that spans the Wars of Scottish Independence, along with the rise and reign of Robert the Bruce.

While I was intentionally vague about the time and royal couple in *The Clan Sinclair*, there is little way to avoid the history of Robert the Bruce when this series takes place predominantly at Stirling Castle after he was crowned king. I have taken creative license in a number of areas, especially the creation of characters such as our hero and heroine, but the events and clan dynamics are true to history.

In the following story, I created the feud between the MacLarens and MacFarlanes, but the clans were historical rivals. It was the MacLarens who also had a contentious relationship with the Buchanans. But you will discover in this tale that neither the hero nor the heroine care for the MacLarens' troublesome neighbors. I didn't find records to inform me about what caused the discord or to what degree it ever escalated, so what you will read is a product of my imagination.

I mention *Creag an Tuirc*, "the Boar's Rock," which was an ancestral rallying point for the MacLarens. That wasn't fiction, and today there is a memorial cairn at the steep hill's summit. The clan gathered there in Balquhidder, the region from which the MacLarens hail and where the lairds' families lived at Edinample Castle. Balquhidder has a famous local hero, Rob Roy MacGregor. His life and fame (infamy) came a few centuries after my story takes place. But visitors can view Rob Roy's grave in the Balquhidder churchyard.

As I researched Clan MacFarlane, I discovered they were notorious reivers. They frequently rustled cattle from Clan Colquhoun, and it was said that on a full moon, they lit "MacFarlane's Lantern." The metaphorical lantern was thought to be the full moon, which lit the raiding parties' way. Our heroine, Catherine, mentions this tradition and the clan's infamy. The term is so intertwined with the clan's history that you can find restaurants by that name. The clan's newsletter is entitled *MacFarlane's Lantern*, and a band used it as a song title, and there's even a Scottish country dance that bears its name.

Both clans had ties to Clan Stewart of Appin. Clan Stewart inherited the Earldom of Lennox in the 1400s. The MacFarlanes claim their descent from the original Earls of Lennox when the title was created in 1154. I didn't discover how the MacLarens' ties to the Stewarts began, but I suspect it was in part because of where both clans lived. Despite their inability to get along with one another, the MacFarlanes and MacLarens were staunch supporters of Robert the Bruce, and they fought alongside one another with the Stewarts in the 1460s and later in the 1490s. I can only hypothesize.

But when the earldom passed to the MacFarlanes because a daughter married a Stewart heir in 1425, it did little to improve the fractious relationship with the MacLarens.

I refer several times to Clan MacGregor encroaching upon MacLaren land after Clan Campbell dislocated the MacGregors from their former homes. I took creative license to move these events nearly two hundred years earlier than actuality. Much of the incursion happened in the late 1400s and early 1500s, rather than in the early 1300s. I mention this event, Robert the Bruce giving MacGregor territory to the Campbells as a reward for their loyalty, in both *A Hellion at the Highland Court* and *A Harlot at the Highland Court*. The MacGregors' attempt to annex MacLaren land caused strife between the MacLarens and the Campbells. One Campbell laird offered the MacLarens aid if they acknowledged the larger and more powerful clan's feudal superiority over them. That was an undesirable arrangement for the MacLarens, so they refused. Consequently, the MacGregors plundered the MacLarens' land. Interestingly, the MacLarens lost more of their lands in Balquhidder in 1500 when James IV of Scotland granted lordship to Janet Kennedy, his mistress.

James "the Black" Douglas has a cameo in this story, but I think he deserves mention here. He was one of the most influential commanders in the Wars of Scottish Independence and was a longtime ally to William Wallace then Robert the Bruce. His maternal grandfather was Alexander Stewart, 4th High Steward of Scotland, which connected him to the Earls of Lennox, who both the MacFarlanes and MacLarens supported. He earned a formidable reputation as both a tactician and a warrior, keeping the English at bay in the south. This is where the story grows rather gruesome. As one of the early combatants to side with the Bruce, Douglas became known for his mobile attacks. On Palm Sunday, 1307 (possibly 1308; there is some historical dispute), he gathered his men and some villagers from near his own Douglas Castle. The British controlled the keep, and when soldiers gathered at the church for the holy day's service, the Black led a charge. It was the first recorded use of the war cry "Douglas! Douglas!" He and his men swooped in, gathered the soldiers, took them back to the mostly empty castle, and sequestered them in the cellar where the troops stored most of the food supplies. He ordered the prisoners beheaded, stacked in a pile, and set alight. The locals dubbed the event "the Douglas Larder" and earned him the moniker, "the Black."

My final historical point is about the Highland Gatherings I mention throughout this book and in both *The Highland Ladies* and *The Clan Sinclair*. Historians think what we now call the Highland Games dates back to Ireland in 2000BC. When many Irish migrated to Scotland (Alba) in the fourth and fifth century, they brought the tradition with them. The first record of the Highland Gathering, or the Highland Games, was during the reign of King Malcolm III, around the mid-to-late 1300s. Legend says he ordered competitors to run up Craig Choinnich as a test to find his royal messenger. It was a traditional time for the clans to gather —clan politics aside—and celebrate summer. There were feats of strength, endurance, speed, agility, and all things warrior. Clans engaged in usually good-natured rivalry and showcased their best warriors' abilities. What we can spectate now at Highland Games around the world is a Victorian version, which restored the games after the Highland Clearances and the Jacobite

Rebellion. If ever you have a chance to visit a local Highland Games, they are events to remember.

I hope you enjoy *An Outsider at the Highland Court* and come to love Catherine MacFarlane and Rab Mac-Laren as much as I have.

Happy reading,
Celeste

CHAPTER 1

*R*ab MacLaren shifted yet again as his backside complained about another day in the saddle. Rab tried not to wriggle too much, but his backside ached, and his upper thighs were numb. He'd been riding patrol along the MacLaren border near Campbell territory for more than a fortnight before setting off for Stirling Castle. When King Robert the Bruce requested an audience, both Rab and his father, Laird Caelan MacLaren, understood it wasn't an invitation but a summons. Rab and half a dozen MacLaren guardsmen were once more on horseback. Their home in Balquhidder, at Edinample Castle, was three days' ride behind them.

"You can stop squirming. I spy the battlements from here." Cullen clapped Rab on the shoulder as the senior warrior grinned. Rab scowled as the rest of the men chuckled. But he'd seen them trying to find more comfortable positions for the past two hours.

What should have been a two-day ride had stretched into a third when torrential rain and gusty winds threatened to knock both man and beast from their feet. Rab and his guards sheltered amongst forest trees to avoid the storm. Being soaked and cold didn't

1

help any of their discomfort. But as Rab strained and stood in his stirrups, he returned Cullen's grin. The men spurred their horses toward the town gates. It was market day, and the town roads were congested. Rab was certain he heard more than one of his men groan. It was his turn to chuckle.

Once they arrived at the castle gates, the entire party's mood shifted, as if another dark cloud hovered above them. As Rab announced their arrival, the MacLarens watched the guards narrow their eyes, and their posture became defensive. The royal guards practically snatched the swords from the MacLarens' hands as the latter turned them in to be stored in the armory. Rab struggled not to curse a blue streak, knowing he had his cousins to thank for the clan's ruined reputation and the meeting with the Bruce. Much like when they were children, Rab's cousins caused trouble, then left Rab to clean it up. Except this time, Rab was alone to face judgment while his cousins' souls were in hell. At least that's what Rab hoped.

The MacLarens collectively sighed as they led their horses into the stables. It relieved them to be off their mounts and to have made it through the gates without confrontation. None in the group had been certain how people might receive them or what news about their ongoing feud with the MacFarlanes had spread. It was clear plenty of people were aware, and opinions weren't in their favor.

Rab dropped his saddle to the ground and pulled a curry brush from his saddlebag. He intended to lead his horse to a stall when he finished and shovel a mountain of hay for the trusty steed. He rolled his neck as he tried to ease the tension that seemed to compound now that they'd reached their destination. He heard the high-pitched voices of a group of women pass just outside the stable doors and grimaced. His head ached without having to deal with the inevitable gaggle of ladies-in-waiting who attended the evening meal and who moved throughout the castle.

"Perhaps some of them wish to chatter in ma ear," David, another MacLaren guard, jested. "Who kens, mayhap they might even look in yer direction once they're done ogling me."

"There's only one thing I wish for a woman's mouth to do, and it's nae talking." Rab grunted as he rose from squatting and checking his horse's hooves.

"And there's only one thing a mon needs to do with his arse, and it's not riding." A feminine voice echoed in the now silent stable. "Your saddle doesn't belong in my way. Perhaps those muscles could move it. Please."

Catherine MacFarlane grinned at the men who faced her, but the man to whom she'd responded still had his back to her. Her gaze passed over the men, but none returned her smile. Instead, they all peered past her shoulder. She glanced back at her cousin Andrew and the other MacFarlane men who joined Andrew and her on their ride. She shifted her attention back to the MacLarens as the mountainous man she'd teased turned toward her. The blood drained from her face through her body and surely pooled around her feet.

"Kitty?" Rab's hoarse whisper was barely audible, but Catherine watched his lips move. She suspected her voice was just as soft when she responded.

"Rab?"

"MacLaren." Andrew Óg MacFarlane stepped forward, reaching for Catherine's arm, ready to move her behind him. But Catherine pulled away and stepped forward. She hesitated to take another step, but her heart urged her to keep moving until she found herself in Rab's embrace, her own arms wrapped around him. Andrew repeated himself, the warning sharp in his voice. "MacLaren."

3

"Aye. I ken." Rab released Catherine, but neither was in a hurry to step away. He took in the more worldly face he'd once known as a young man. The mischievous spark that he'd seen when he first turned around, the one he knew from before she arrived at court to become a lady-in-waiting to Queen Elizabeth de Burgh, had made her eyes gleam. Now there was caution and maturity. As Catherine moved back to stand beside her cousin, Rab turned his head to speak over his shoulder. "Leave."

"What?" Cullen spluttered. "Nay."

The MacLaren men watched their clan tánaiste in disbelief. They weren't about to abandon him in a stable to their clan's most reviled enemy.

"I didna ask." The authority rang in Rab's voice, and the men knew they had no choice. They edged toward the doorway, watching the MacFarlanes rather than Rab. Once his men were gone, Rab raised both his hands, palms forward. He moved to the closest hay bale and, keeping his left hand up, he used his right to pull a dirk loose from his belt. He placed it on top of the hay, then removed a knife from his boot and drew up his plaid to remove one strapped to his thigh. When the three knives lay on the hay bale, he raised his right hand and repeated the process on his left side. "Catherine, I need ye to wait outside. I need to speak to yer cousin."

Catherine's eyes widened as she shook her head. She feared what Rab's men did: Rab would wind up dead.

"Kitty, this is the only chance I'll have without a hive of gossips buzzing around or the king interrupting." Rab's gaze shifted to Andrew and remained there even as Catherine spoke.

"Interrupted? Mayhap intervene."

"Nay. I'd speak to Andrew without others deciding

4

what they wish to hear and interrupting. Please, Kitty. This isnae something I wish for ye to hear."

Catherine nodded, understanding to which topic Rab alluded. She longed to listen to what he had to say, but she doubted she would like it. She knew Rab asked her to leave, not to be rude or to discount her value because she was a woman, but because he was doing it to protect her. She could only imagine what he planned to reveal. With a brief glance at Andrew, she walked out of the stables. Rather than leave, she moved to stand to the right of the door, where she could still listen.

"Leave," Andrew barked. His men prepared to disagree, the same as the MacLarens had, but they knew Andrew's authority as their clan's tánaiste was as unwavering as Rab's was with his men. Rab continued to hold his hands raised until there were no guardsmen from either clan left. He suspected Catherine hadn't gone far, but he seized the opportunity to make his position known. He walked toward Andrew but stopped where they were still two arms' lengths apart, each barely out of reach of the other.

"Óg." Rab addressed Andrew with the diminutive "lesser," which meant younger in Andrew's case, since he shared a given name with his father. "I'm sorry."

Rab's directness surprised Andrew. He was unprepared for Rab to apologize.

"My father and I never sanctioned that raid." Rab shook his head. "It never should have happened. I'm sorry for the heinous way ma cousins treated yer mother and sisters. I'm sorry for their deaths and the assaults on yer clanswomen. I'm sorry that I wasna there to stop them before they even left Edinample."

"Sorry? That's what you wish me to know?"

"Nay. But I wanted to start there. Ma apologies dinna bring back anyone or undo what ma cousins did. Ma father passed judgment on them and banished them. I carried out his sentence and ensured they will forever remain banished. It's nae possible for them to return."

"You executed them?" Andrew watched Rab, wary of his enemy but still shocked that not only had Rab started the conversation and then apologized, but he admitted he'd killed members of his own family. "Your father only ordered them banished."

"And he sharpened his dirk the night before and handed it to me the morning we rode out." Laird Caelan MacLaren never ordered his son to kill his nephews, but both Caelan and Rab knew it was the only remedy. Neither liked nor trusted the men, and it had been the ultimate sin on the three young men's long list.

"Why'd you do it? Why you?"

"It was ma job to punish them, but it was ma choice how I carried it out. They will never harm another innocent."

"That doesn't explain executing them. Why?"

"Because it could have been—" Rab peered toward the doorway, but Andrew finished his thought for him.

"Catherine."

"Aye. She could have been there like yer mother and sisters were. She would have been a boon for them."

"But she wasn't. She was here," Andrew countered.

"That matters nae to me. It could have happened, and I willna live with that risk."

"She's here to find a husband, MacLaren."

"I ken. They would have made her a target to stop any alliance her marriage makes. Is she betrothed?" Rab feared choking over the last word.

"She was close, but it fell through." At Rab's cocked eyebrow, Andrew fought not to grimace. "Laird Edgar Gunn. It fell through because of his involvement in

Lady Campbell's abduction. Brodie didn't take too well to it."

"And perish the thought that the MacFarlanes insult the great Clan Campbell." There was little love lost between the MacLarens and the Campbells, but the Campbells' numbers dwarfed the MacLarens. The two clans kept their distance. Rab glanced at Andrew's wrists. "I'm surprised to spy ye still have both since I heard ye had a hand in that."

"Hardly my finest choice. Needless to say, my father opted not to pursue the match. I'm here to secure her marriage." Andrew crossed his arms.

"And redeem yerself," Rab added. Glancing once more at the door, Rab lowered his voice, hoping Catherine couldn't catch the last of his admission. "They suffered the same brutality they committed when they assaulted yer mother and sisters. I disemboweled them, then it was by my hand that they were drawn and quartered. I left their remains to the wild."

Andrew flinched. The reminder of finding his mother and sisters raped and murdered, compounded by the image of the three men with their arms and legs ripped from their bodies and their intestines strewn around them, made him want to vomit.

"They chose violence, so they died by it. Let their last thought be of the pain and indignity of having their bodies violated by someone stronger." Rab's tone held the raw anger and hatred he still harbored. But it softened once more to a whisper. "I dinna want her to ken that side of me."

Andrew nodded, unable to speak, still choked by emotions crashing over him. There wasn't a day that passed that he didn't envision the destruction he encountered as a small band of MacLarens swept through his home. Rab's three cousins and a team of men scaled the walls at sunset from a boat bobbing in Loch

Lomond. They only targeted women, leaving his mother and sisters dead but other women to live with the disgrace and trauma. They stole the women's dignity and spat in the faces of the men tasked to protect them. Andrew and his father had returned from hunting as the alarm went up. The MacLarens had a man at the postern gate, having killed the MacFarlane guard, and another outside with a boat to carry them the short distance from the tiny Inveruglas Isle to the shore. The MacFarlanes killed a handful, but all three of Rab's cousins escaped.

Andrew stared at Rab, neither speaking. Swallowing several times, Andrew finally nodded. "I willna tell her." The raw emotions Andrew fought to contain made his brogue slip through, making him sound as much a Highlander as he and Rab both were.

"I'm here to accept whatever the Bruce decides. To others, I'm here to pay our taxes. But from the way the men glared at us coming through the gates, I'd say most will ken the real reason." Rab watched Andrew, unsure of his reaction. The penance was likely to be costly, be it coin or forfeited livestock and land. The MacLarens could afford neither, but Rab nor his father could argue with the king's edict. "I needed to say ma thoughts to ye in private. I need ye to ken that nay matter what the king orders, I ken it will never be enough."

"Thank ye."

There was nothing more for either man to say. Backing away, Rab returned his knives to their sheaths and lifted his saddle bags over his shoulder. His horse, trained to be patient throughout battle, hadn't moved since the conversation started. Rab led him to a stall, knowing Andrew watched him. He carried his saddle and swung it over the wall that separated two stalls. Rab and Andrew exchanged one last look before Rab walked out of the stables.

Looking to his right, it didn't surprise Rab to find Catherine standing there with her guards. His gaze shifted to find his men milling around a few yards away. He wanted nothing more than to speak to Catherine, to share his apologies with her, but it wasn't possible. Andrew came to stand in the doorway as the MacFarlane guards encircled Catherine, their height nearly blocking him from her view as she strained to see Rab.

"Good day, Lady Catherine." Rab walked past and joined his men. The MacLarens left the stables, leaving the MacFarlanes to stare after them.

Catherine struggled throughout Rab and Andrew's conversation to catch what she could. She suspected both men knew she stood beyond the door and strained to listen. Rab's lack of surprise when he spotted her confirmed her suspicion. It made her even more curious to know what they discussed, what Rab said, since he'd chosen to keep her from hearing, both by asking her to leave and by keeping his voice down.

She was certain it was about his cousins and her aunt and cousins. She hadn't been with her clan during the raid, and it was Andrew who had to inform her when he returned once more to court to arrange her marriage. After he told her what happened, neither had spoken. Andrew had the foresight to have them ride away from the castle. He'd led them to a copse of trees, where they spoke in private. It appeared to anyone watching that Andrew offered her comfort as she sobbed, but he'd cried along with her as they embraced.

Catherine's parents—Shamus and Adaira—died when she was young, leaving her an only child to be raised by her aunt and uncle. Andrew Óg, Fia, and

Greer were more like her siblings than her cousins. While she still had vivid memories of her parents, Andrew *Mòr*, the elder of the two Andrews, and Aveline had raised her as their own for most of her life. Her aunt's death was like experiencing her mother's for a second time. It had traumatized Catherine even more than losing her cousins.

She knew Rab's presence should repulse her, even make her pray for retribution, but she'd known from the start that he played no part in it. As Andrew Óg recounted the events in halting and stammering words, it was he who reassured her that Rab hadn't been there. When she recognized him in the stables, it hadn't been her family who she thought of. It had been the summers when she'd seen Rab at the Highland Gatherings that came to mind. It was a time before the MacFarlanes' and MacLarens' feud become so violent. All clans suspended their animosity in the spirit of the gatherings, the brief time each year where the Highlanders united in their love of their traditions. While the feats of strength were competitive, it was just as much a showcase. It reminded all present why Robert the Bruce had depended on the Highland warriors to carry him to victory and his throne. And it had been a time for young Rab and young Catherine to grow smitten with one another.

It had been three years since Catherine last spent time with Rab, but in the brief moments he embraced her, it was as though no time had passed. The feel of his arms wrapped around her still held the same rightness as they had when she was seven-and-ten. It was a secret she intended to carry with her, like she had the depth of her feelings toward Rab.

As she stepped toward her cousin, she tried to guess his thoughts, but his impassive expression let on nothing. Catherine marveled at how much Andrew had changed since that raid. She'd once been able to read his thoughts merely by looking in his eyes, but he kept his own counsel now, and at times, it felt like she encountered a stranger.

"Do you still wish to ride?" Andrew's question was cautious, but Catherine caught the concern.

"I'm all right, Óg." Catherine steeled herself against looking in the direction Rab walked and forced a smile. "I think it would be nice to escape the castle for a while."

Andrew nodded, relieved to be leaving a place he loathed on the best of days, but was now a place where his memories haunted him in his waking hours. He couldn't cast his eyes on Rab without picturing his mother and sisters as he helped lower them into the ground at their burials. He guided Catherine into the stables and helped saddle her horse before tending to his steed. Once he helped her mount, the MacFarlanes clattered across the bailey and out through the castle gates.

Catherine watched Andrew from the corner of her eye, his somber expression only creating more curiosity among their guards. She'd ordered the men, with her eyebrow cocked and lips pursed, to stand at a distance from the door. The men had known better than to test her, all familiar with her renowned stubbornness. It was the best Catherine could do to offer Andrew and Rab privacy, even if she didn't include herself in that. She prayed Andrew might confide in her once they reached a place to let the horses rest.

CHAPTER 2

"atherine." Andrew swept his gaze over the riverbank and the men tending their horses. He guided Catherine a few yards upstream, his back to the guardsmen, both to ensure their conversation didn't carry and because he trusted the men to protect them from anything approaching from behind. He spared a moment to lock eyes with Catherine before continuing to survey their surroundings. "He apologized."

"I know," Catherine admitted.

"You listened. How much did you make out?"

"Most, I think. Sometimes he was too quiet to even know if he spoke, but I'm guessing he did."

"He asked me to keep his confidence, and I will. Even from you, so you can cease thinking you will get me to tell you." Andrew watched as Catherine scowled. While she hadn't appeared eager, he understood how her mind worked, and he knew she was desperate to know. He'd seen how the pair gazed at one another, and he'd sensed the tenderness in their embrace. He remembered the brief time when even he had hoped something might come of Catherine and Rab's friendship. It was those memories and his concern for his cousin that kept him from sharing the gruesome parts

12

of Rab's confession. "He was right to ask you to leave. I don't fault him for not wanting you to know. I will say that he ensured his cousins met the end they deserved, but I won't tell you any more."

"Does that mean you forgive him?"

"Catherine, I never blamed him. He has never been the type of mon to do what his cousins did. That doesn't mean I don't hold him and his father responsible. That he carried out his father's sentence, even to his own blood, may speak to his honor. But where is that honor in the rest of his clan? That is a failure in his and his father's leadership. That any member of his clan dared go against his father's orders speaks louder than words."

"You're a hypocrite."

"Catherine—"

"Nay. Your sins weren't as heinous as those Mac-Larens, but you defied your father, our laird, and you know it. Mòr is still angry at you for your part in that bluidy bet. Should your choices reflect on me since I'm your kin any more than those men's choices reflect on Rab? You acted of your own free will, as did those beasts."

"And where is your loyalty?" Andrew seethed, angrier at Catherine than he had ever been. "You'd side with him."

"I side with my family as much as you do, but Mòr didn't think he needed tell you not to help kidnap Laurel, but you did. I doubt Caelan or Rab thought they needed to tell their kin not to rape and murder our family."

"It's not the same. Not even by half."

"I didn't say it was the same, but it is similar. You're a hypocrite to hold Rab responsible when you don't hold your father responsible for your shite choices."

13

"My shite choices didn't get anyone killed!" Andrew barked.

"They nearly did. Laurel and I were never friends. I don't even like her, and I doubt she likes me. But I still learned how close she came to being poisoned by the MacDougall brothers and then murdered when the Lamonts attacked. You had a hand in that." Catherine glanced down. "Rab's right; I don't know how you came away with both of them still attached."

"You're defending him. That's unconscionable, Catherine."

"Him. The single mon. Not his clan. Not his father. Not what *they* did to our family." None of the MacFarlanes spoke the names of the three men who devastated their clan and their lives. It was a tacit agreement, and Catherine didn't even want to think about them. "Does your piss-poor choice make Mòr a failed leader, a laird unable to control his clan? No. No more than it means Caelan is a failed laird and Rab is a useless tánaiste."

"And because I am our clan's tánaiste, you hold me in contempt, even though you can only claim the "could haves" and "might haves" to my choices. We know what *they* did."

"Óg, I have never held you in contempt. I don't. I'm hurt and angry, too. Blood might say Aveline was only my aunt and Fia and Greer were only my cousins, but my heart has always felt they were my mother and sisters. I have prayed many nights for God's wrath to wipe those men from the earth. But even without running into Rab again, I didn't blame him or Caelan. God gave mon free will, and it is each of us who chooses our own sin. My fear is the retribution you and Mòr plan. You will never tell me, but I can't help believing it will come." Catherine stepped forward, wrapping her arms around Andrew's waist even though he didn't return her embrace. "I don't want to lose you and Mòr. I would have no one left in this world who I love as I do my family. I just want you to realize that you can exact a pound of flesh from the MacLarens, but you can't have it all. I'm scared, Óg."

Andrew embraced Catherine, and they both sighed. They didn't always get along, but he understood what she meant. And he understood her fears. He knew Rab was right about what could have happened if Catherine were home at Inveruglas Isle during the attack, and his father had nearly died trying to reach his wife. Had Catherine and his father died too, it would have left him in the very position Catherine described.

"You say what I need to hear but rarely want to." Andrew kissed Catherine's forehead. "I will wait for King Robert's judgment. I respect Rab's decision to speak to me and his decision to carry out his cousins' punishment. But seeing that plaid only reignites anger and pain that may never go away."

"That's all I want, Óg. Wait for the king. Don't wage a war against Rab. Let the Bruce pass his judgment on the clan rather than you doing it to the mon."

Rab refused to think that he took the coward's way out, but once he reached his chamber, he decided to take a tray there rather than go to the Great Hall for the evening meal. He soaked in a much too narrow and short tub until the once steaming water chilled him. He ate his meal alone and in blessed silence. He'd been around other men with no reprieve for more than two moons, so he relished the solitude. He didn't wish to admit that he neither looked forward to facing the scrutiny that was inevitable whenever Highlanders came to court nor the inevitable fallout from rumors that already swirled around the court. He'd seen how people glared at him as he moved through the passage-ways. He could only imagine what version of the truth was circulating. He didn't take Andrew for being a gossip, and he was certain neither Andrew nor Catherine volunteered to discuss the attack.

Rab also knew he didn't want to face Catherine. He wanted to see her, to hold her, but standing before her made his heart pinch. He prayed she hadn't overheard him describe his retribution against his own family. His rage had been so consuming, that even three days after the raid and even though his cousins spent that time cramped together in the oubliette, he'd barely been able to see straight when he and five guards rode out with his cousins. The culprits taunted him, reminded him of Catherine, and that was what ultimately sealed their fates. He might have merely hanged them, but when they boasted of the violence they'd intended for Catherine, he lost all sense of humanity and mercy. He'd shocked himself with his capacity for cruelty, but he couldn't dredge up any remorse, which shocked him even further. He didn't want Catherine to learn of that side of him. He wished for her to remember him as the young man he'd once been before the real burdens of being tánaiste settled on his shoulders. Instead of facing her and the rest of the royal court, he hid in his chamber.

Rab laid in bed, staring at the canopy over his head. He'd laid in his own bed at Edinample, staring into space countless times, his thoughts as they were that night. He wondered how Catherine fared during her years at court. He wondered if she remembered half of what he did, and if she did, did she remember them as fondly as he? He recalled the year the Mackenzies held the Highland Gathering as though it were yesterday. He and his brother, Douglan, planned to filch apricots from the orchard. They were teasing one another as they walked through the gates, only to find a gown and two feet hanging from a branch. Without warning, the branch shook, and the woman's body swayed. Down came a handful of apricots, followed by the woman who seemed to be after what Rab and Douglan intended.

Rab could never forget the unrepentant expression Catherine shot the brothers when she turned around and found them staring. She had the audacity to pick up two apricots, chucking one at Rab and one at Douglan. The petite brunette had prepared neither brother for the force that came with her throw. As they watched her in shocked silence, she gathered four more apricots, which she stuffed in her arisaid, and walked past the brothers. She'd cocked an eyebrow and pointed over her shoulder, telling them they'd have to go further into the orchard since she'd already gotten the best ones from the tree she'd scaled.

She didna even blink when we caught her. Granted we were there to steal fruit too, but nae a moment of remorse or even fear. Happy as ye please, she walked right past us. I should have kenned right then and there. She's nae easily cowed. She may have admitted later that Douglan and I terrified her, but neither of us would have ever kenned. She is a woman meant to be a partner and helpmate to a laird, a woman who can lead when her husband is away. God help the mon or the clan who thinks to cross her. How could Mòr and Óg even consider that toad Gunn?

Rab hadn't known who she was when they met, even though he recognized the MacFarlane plaid. The MacLarens and MacFarlanes had been on tense terms back then, but Catherine hadn't seemed to care about, or even notice, their plaids. He could tell from her plaid's pattern that she was part of the laird's family, but he didn't know if she was Andrew Mòr's daughter or someone else. It was clear the brothers wearing the

MacLaren laird's plaid failed to impress her. It was that same mischievousness that he'd seen for a moment that afternoon before they recognized one another in the stables. She'd been three-and-ten, and he was barely eight-and-ten. He encountered the young woman he considered a woodland nymph throughout that gathering, but it was the following year that their friendship began in earnest.

Rab had marveled at the difference a year made in her appearance when he stumbled upon her at Castle Varrich, home to Clan Mackay. She hardly resembled a girl and appeared far more like a woman. At nearly nine-and-ten, he assumed he had little in common with the young woman, but he spoke to her often because she was Andrew Óg's constant companion. Rab and Andrew weren't nearly friends, instead often fierce competitors. But they were the same age, putting them in the same groups for the various races. He discovered Catherine had a wicked and off-color sense of humor from spending too much time with Óg and his friends. She eschewed being stuck inside sewing with her cousins and escaped the keep whenever she could during that year's gathering. It didn't take long for Rab and Catherine to realize they shared the same favorite color and favorite foods.

She's the only person I ken who could happily feast on Arbroath smokies for days. Nay one else I ken likes haddock that much. Yet she and I both do. She may have laughed when she noticed me pushing aside all the neeps and keeping the tatties, but she didna fool me. I watched her do the same. Turnips are hideous. She didna even flinch when I pulled the eel from the basket when the Sinclairs hosted at Dunbeath. She asked how much I'd share with her at the evening meal. Cheeky. She still owes me an apricot tart.

For the next two years, they sought one another at the gatherings and when they both attended the same weddings. Their friendship had always had a charged air of attraction, but the year Catherine was seven-and-ten, Rab thought he might ask her uncle for her hand. However, it was during that gathering when Clan Ogilvy hosted that an argument erupted between Caelan and Andrew Mòr. The clans had raided one another off and on for years, but the explosive disagreement threatened to derail the entire gathering as other clans took sides. Rab didn't learn the cause until after he'd returned home. Each laird accused the other of being dishonorable and liars when they denied being the culprit to the other clan's missing cattle and razed fields. It was that year that the feud escalated.

Three years later, it came to a violent head when members of his own family murdered members of Catherine's. It shocked him when she even spoke to him in the stables rather than spitting in his face. It further shocked him that Andrew didn't plunge every dirk he carried into Rab. While his attraction to Catherine hadn't waned, his hope of a joined future had. That hope surged back to life the moment she stepped into his arms. But knowing he must speak to Andrew and remind them all of why he was at court crushed that hope. Now as he laid alone in his chamber, everything ached—his head, his body, and most painfully, his heart.

The sooner I can leave, the better. If Óg finds her a husband while I'm here, I dinna think I can keep from running the lucky bastard through. I ken I'd wish her happy and be lying with every word. Ma chance with her might be over, but that doesnae mean I have to like that her time with someone else may be just starting. If the Bruce doesnae take ma head from ma neck, then I will do what I must and ride out before I watch her swear to join her life with someone who isnae me.

CHAPTER 3

*C*atherine struggled against the yawn that insisted upon reminding her that she'd barely slept the night before. She'd been so restless that she was certain she'd kept her roommate awake by constantly shifting and rolling over. At first, she told herself that she merely couldn't get comfortable, but it was her mind that found no comfort. The initial excitement of encountering Rab wore off during the evening meal when she realized he wasn't coming. Remembering that even if he came to the Great Hall, they couldn't dance together—they couldn't even speak to one another—compounded her disappointment. The castle was abuzz about both Rab and Andrew Óg being under the same roof. While Catherine knew they'd brokered their own sort of truce, at least while they were both in Stirling, no one else knew. The possible entertainment of two massive Highlanders tearing one another apart spurred the gossip.

As she laid in bed that night, her mind was more restless than her body. She couldn't cease thinking about Rab's expression when they recognized one another. She wondered how she hadn't recognized his voice since it played in her mind most days of the week.

Something she caught sight of or did would trigger a memory, and her heart pinched. But it no longer stole her breath like it had her first year at court. When she was both homesick and pining for a man she knew her uncle would never consent to marry her. After the combustible tension at the Highland Gathering three years earlier, Catherine never dared mention her interest in Rab to her uncle. She feared he'd have an apoplexy and banish her. She recalled the scent of fresh air, pine, soap, saddle leather, and a hint of wet wool that she inhaled as they embraced. Not that unlike from what Andrew smelled like, but the effect was vastly different, eliciting an entirely separate range of emotions.

It was the wee hours of the morning before Catherine fell asleep, and her eyes felt like someone rubbed them with sawdust when they opened to the sound of her roommate preparing for Terce. Catherine dragged herself from her bed, then from her chamber and into the castle chapel. She kept her head down as she made her way down the aisle, but her eyes skimmed over the gathering congregation until they met a pair of ice-blue orbs that locked with her own cornflower blue irises. She nearly missed a step, and the lady-in-waiting behind her stepped on her hem. But even that didn't break the moment between Rab and her. They watched each other until Catherine entered her pew and too many heads blocked them from gazing at one another.

It was as though she moved in a trance, resisting the need to yawn with each "amen," mouthing the liturgical responses. But all she was aware of was Rab's physical nearness, and all the things that set them a world apart. She wished for nothing more than to go back to bed and pray for God's mercy that she might fall asleep. Alas, no such divine intervention came. She trailed after the other ladies and the queen as they made their way to the Great Hall to break their fast. Catherine was used to the other ladies tittering when new Highlanders arrived at court. It was a mixture of moral condescension and physical inquisitiveness. She'd listened to women speak about her cousin much the same way as she listened to women speak about Brodie and Dominic Campbell, the various Sinclair brothers, Kieran MacLeod, and even the shy Ronan MacKinnon. They all wondered if the rumors were true about what lay beneath the heathenous plaids that many of the Highlanders refused to relinquish, despite most men wearing breeks and doublets at court.

"Who's that?" Evina Murray wondered. "I haven't seen him before."

"Who?" Blythe Dunbar asked, but she shrugged when her gaze followed Evina's outstretched finger. "You would think after all these years here, I might learn the plaids, but the Highlander ones look so much alike to me. Dark. Do they think they're coming to court to hunt down wives? There are no woods to blend into within the castle. They stick out more than ever."

Many of the ladies-in-waiting were Lowlanders, unaccustomed to the frequent wearing of their clan plaids. While several young women over the years hailed from the Highlands before they came to court, most assimilated to the Lowland customs to keep from sticking out. Catherine was one such lady, losing her burr on the way to court. Her aunt had warned her it would do her no favors to sound like the savages most Lowlanders believed them to be. She only wore her arisaid on days that were too brisk to go without the extra layers of wool but not yet cold enough for her fur-lined, sealskin cloak. She cared not what the other women thought since they nearly froze during the queen's morning constitutional. An excursion the queen expected all ladies-in-waiting to attend whether the weather was fair or foul.

"That's a MacLaren," Catriona Douglas whispered, a darting glance at Catherine. The latter recognized apprehension in Catriona's eyes, and it made her wonder how much her relatives told her the last time they visited court. Representing various branches of the powerful clan, there were always at least two Douglas delegates at court besides Catriona as a lady-in-waiting.

"His name is Rab." Catherine hoped the nonchalance she attempted came through. "He's the clan's tánaiste and heir."

"Oh, dear." Lady Margaret Hay's whiny voice held no sincerity. It was pure mocking, and Catherine wanted to drive her fist through the woman's teeth. She could barely tolerate Margaret, but she despised the woman's younger sister, Lady Sarah Anne. The younger Hay sister had a cruel streak to her that made anything the legendary Madeline MacLeod or even the shrewish Laurel Ross did, seem meek. Catherine learned quickly to keep her distance from the Hay sisters, and when she couldn't, she remained quiet most of the time. She was ashamed to admit that sometimes she was less than courteous because it was easier to appear on Sarah Anne's side than to stand against her. If it were only Sarah Anne, and even Margaret too, then Catherine would have stood up to the women long ago. But women who genuinely feared Sarah Anne, and by extension Margaret, surrounded her. If she alienated herself from the others while putting herself in Sarah Anne's crosshairs, it would make an already challenging existence at court excruciating.

Catherine remained quiet, not interested in encouraging Margaret's inevitably snide comments. When she said nothing, Margaret turned to Catriona. Catherine braced herself for whatever came next.

"You're one of them." There was no doubting Margaret meant Catriona was a Highlander. "How is he not dead for what he did?"

Catherine's stomach both clenched and roiled, a sensation she would be happy never to feel again. The bit of porridge she'd forced down threatened to spew forth as she waited for Catriona's answer.

"As best I know, the mon did naught." Catriona shrugged and turned toward Blythe, refusing to engage with Margaret. But the older Hay sister was unsatisfied, having not gotten the reaction she wanted.

"He's a butcher. He should be out at the sty rather than in here with civilized people." Margaret's eyes locked with Catherine's as she spoke. But once more, Catherine refused to acknowledge Margaret. When Margaret grew impatient, she opted to thrust the knife directly into Catherine's heart. "He let them rape and murder your family. Where is that Highland honor your people are so famous for? How can you allow him to dine in the same chamber as you?"

"Allow? Last I checked, I'm a MacFarlane not a Bruce. It is not for me to decide." Catherine turned away, but Sarah Anne joined the conversation.

"You'd break bread with the mon who slaughtered your family. You'd have been one of them if you weren't here."

Catherine slowly turned toward Sarah Anne, who sat on the other side of Evina, who was to Catherine's left. Her fingernails bit into the wood bench upon which she sat. Bile burned the back of her throat as she rapidly considered how to respond. If the Hay sisters didn't cease, Catherine would find herself on her knees in prayer until the day's end, the queen's favorite punishment for wayward ladies-in-waiting. Her temper was sliding to where she struggled to control it. It wasn't often that she lost her temper, but it put any Highland blizzard to shame with its ferocity.

"He was not there. I know that, and so does my family. If he had been on that raid, my aunt and cousins would still be alive. For all you mock us Highlanders aboot our sense of honor, you'd do well to find some. Do not use my grief and my family's loss to play your games, Sarah Anne. I promise you, you will not win that match."

"How can you defend a mon from the very clan who caused that grief?" Evina asked softly.

"Because I know Rab MacLaren, and I know his father. I know what my clan dislikes aboot them, but I also know that they are two men who do not fight their battles through women. King Robert will bring their clan to bear their punishment, as they should. But it was not Rab's fault. Gossip aboot whatever you want, but bring my family into it again, and I will make your life the worst kind of hell. If you don't believe me, ask Andrew. Ask him what I'm like when I'm truly angry." Catherine's voice remained calm, but there was an ominous tone no one missed. It was so unlike the Catherine they knew, or at least thought they knew, that the table fell silent until the meal ended.

"Are you all right?" Blythe whispered as she walked beside Catherine to the stables. Once outside and on the way to watch the royal hunt begin, the other women returned to chattering. The sound reminded Catherine of magpies. She offered her friend a tight smile and a nod. "Are you riding out today?"

"Aye. The queen requested I come. She knows I don't mind the hours of riding, and she knows I grew up hunting with Andrew." Catherine stepped aside as stable hands brought out stallions, geldings, and destriers. Among the enormous steeds were a few sidestepping and nickering mares. Catherine recognized the horses that stood alongside her own mare, and she breathed easier. Catriona, Evina, and another Highlander named Sileas Gunn, joined Catherine as the queen's attendants. Sileas was Edgar Gunn's cousin, and Catherine had once been close to becoming the woman's family-by-marriage. She liked her roommate and was close friends with Catriona, so it relieved her to know that she didn't have to watch over her shoulder for both wild animals and the fellow ladies-in-waiting.

"I wish you well, Catherine. Mayhap the fresh air and space will do you some good." Blythe offered a sincere smile and squeezed Catherine's forearm before she walked away. Before gathering her mount's reins, she found a barrel of apples, grabbing one for her horse, Timber. She'd named her mare for her coat's color, the same golden brown of freshly sawed maple wood. As she reached out her hand, palm up with the apple on it for her mare, another horse neighed before nudging her shoulder. She turned around, coming nose-to-nose with an animal she recognized.

"Bolt, do you remember me? If I'd known you'd come say hello, I would have brought you a treat too. But Timber has eaten it all. I haven't aught to offer you."

As if the horse understood, the stallion nodded several times. Catherine ran her hand along the broad nose, stroking up between the animal's eyes. Ever since she met Bolt nearly a decade ago when he was little more than a spindly colt who liked to run away from his owner, it had always surprised her that he allowed her to get so close when he was as cantankerous as an old man with almost everyone else. She supposed it was because Rab introduced her to his steed when the animal was still young. She always marveled at how the beast knew her, even with her back to him. The horse's massive head nudged her shoulder again before resting against it.

"You had better not nibble on my hair this time. Do you know how long it took me to get your drool out of it last time? Have you learned any manners yet?" Catherine teased as she ran her hands over the stallion's neck, appearing to return the horse's embrace.

"Nay, he hasnae. Nay matter how hard I try." Rab approached, but he'd been watching Catherine and Bolt since his horse turned away from him and wandered toward Catherine. He'd known it was she who Bolt spotted because there was no one else at court, not even among his men, for whom his horse so brazenly ignored him.

"I think ye like yer wee beastie just as he is. I dinna think ye've tried." Catherine lapsed back into her brogue, relishing when she didn't have to think about each word as she said them. She spoke more to Bolt than Rab, but they both knew it was to keep it from being obvious that they chatted. Rab stood on the horse's opposite side.

"Are ye hunting today, Kitty?"

"Nay. I'm to keep the queen company. I didna bring ma bow." Catherine wished she were part of the hunt rather than merely the queen's companion, but she didn't regret that she wouldn't be amid the crush of men vying for the king's attention, both in conversation and by bringing down the largest stag or boar.

"Do they fear ye will show them up?"

"I only do that to you, Douglan, and Óg." Catherine's tinkle of laughter spread heat through Rab's chest. Tall enough to peer over his horse's neck, he watched

Catherine's gentle hand as she continued to stroke Bolt's neck.

"Ye mean to say, ye've been here all these years, and nae one mon here kens ye're the best of the lot?" Rab asked with playful disbelief.

"I canna think of too many men, Lowlanders in particular, who want to be shown up by a lass, and a Highlander to boot."

"Kitty." Rab's voice grew serious, making Catherine direct her eyes at him. "If ye want to hunt, I'll speak to Óg. I'm certain he can arrange it."

Catherine's mouth hung open for a moment before she gathered her thoughts. "Ye'd speak to Óg twice in two days, and this time simply so I might have a turn hunting? It doesnae matter that much, Rab."

"If it's what ye want."

"Óg already asked, but he and I ken the queen willna allow it. If she'd wanted me to join the hunters, she would have told me to bring ma bow. I'm to ride with her. But I thank ye for yer thoughtfulness." Catherine offered Rab a tight smile before stepping toward Timber. She gathered her horse's reins as she added, "Good luck and be careful."

Catherine's expression warned Rab that the courtiers wouldn't receive him well. She'd said the same thing to him plenty of times in the past at the various gatherings, but her tone held warning rather than good cheer. He nodded before swinging into the saddle. Andrew stepped forward, startling Catherine, who hadn't realized he stood close enough to eavesdrop on her conversation with Rab.

"You play a dangerous game, cousin. I haven't said aught to anyone, and mayhap I should have. But the men have been gossiping more than a village of fishwives. They want to know when I will challenge Rab to single combat. They're trying to outdo one another with outlandish suggestions for how the king will punish him. If anyone sees you nattering on like auld friends, you will end up the subject of their speculation. Your reputation and you will not come out unscathed."

"I know, Óg. If you learned what we said, then you know he was being thoughtful, and his horse was being playful. But I understand that isn't how it might appear to others."

"Catherine, you said you didn't mind not hunting. It didn't sound that way when you talked to Rab. Do you wish to?"

"What I wish and what my duties are, are not the same. I can't, even though I want to." Catherine shook her head but grew quiet as the royal couple approached. She watched as King Robert helped his wife into the saddle before swinging onto his stallion's back.

"Lady Catherine."

"Yes, Your Majesty." Catherine dipped into a low curtsy as she answered the queen.

"Catriona's uncle is practically insisting I allow her to hunt. I don't want her alone in the mix of men. You will join her. One of your guards is coming with your bow."

"Thank you, Your Majesty. I look forward to it." Catherine dropped into another deep curtsy before glancing at Andrew, who shrugged. She caught Evina's gaze, then Sileas. Both women mirrored Andrew's shrug, both knowing they would remain by the queen's side.

"I'm looking forward to hunting, but my bluidy uncle wants me to catch a husband rather than a doe," Catriona grumbled as she maneuvered her horse beside Catherine's. "Thank the saints you're coming too."

Catherine and Catriona grinned at one another. They'd both ridden out on royal hunts together and gladly accepted one another's company. They were both experienced horsewomen, both having ridden between their clans' territories and Stirling countless times over their years of service. Catherine grew up with Andrew, who was much more like an older brother than a cousin. Catriona had four brothers of her own, two older and two younger. The two ladies-in-waiting, accustomed to male posturing, merely remained quiet during most hunts. When they tired of watching the men enjoy themselves while they remained at the back, they would surprise men new to court, and annoy the experienced courtiers, when they often bagged the most prey.

It wasn't long before Catherine had her bow slung over her shoulder and her quiver fastened to her saddle. The women rode toward the back of the pack, in the middle, flanked by family and allies. Catherine watched as Rab maneuvered himself toward the outskirts of the group, as far from Andrew as he could. It pained Catherine that she couldn't ride alongside Rab, as she had during various gatherings. Their clans might be at odds, but she missed the man. As though it were a sixth sense, she was aware of him throughout the morning, and she suspected it was the same for him. Their eyes locked more than once when the party stopped for hunters to claim their bounties.

By early afternoon, it bored Catherine and Catriona to allow the men to ride ahead of them. Neither had fired an arrow yet, and they wished for their own entertainment. The queen enjoyed the excitement of the hunt but rarely took part. It made both ladies wonder why the queen instructed them to bring their bows if they couldn't separate from the royal. Catherine and Catriona were more adventurous than the staider Evina and Sileas, who were content to observe.

Sensing their impatience, Queen Elizabeth nodded to young women. Grinning at one another once more,

Catherine and Catriona spurred their horses on. The pounding hooves of the large hunting party flushed a covey of pheasants from grass. The ladies nocked their arrows and let loose a quick succession, bringing down one bird after another before most of the men could fire their first shot.

"Well done, Lady Catriona and Lady Catherine," King Robert boomed. "Ride at the head of the group."

Catherine shot a quick glance toward Andrew, but her gaze traveled beyond him to Rab, who shifted in his saddle as he eyed the men toward the front. When their eyes locked, Catherine watched the nearly imperceptible nod, feeling assured that Rab encouraged her. She finally looked at Andrew, whose narrowed eyes told her he'd watched the pair. He offered her a more noticeable, albeit tight-lipped, nod. She turned toward Catriona and noticed she had the same silent conversation with one of her uncles and an older brother.

Andrew and the two Douglases nudged their horses to follow Catherine's and Catriona's as they jostled their way forward. Catherine once more cast her eyes toward Rab but could no longer catch sight of him. She supposed he kept his distance, but a wave of disappointment crashed over her yet again. Only a few moments passed before Catherine focused her concentration on leading the hunters. No longer could she trust Timber following the beasts in front of her. As the horses and their riders barreled across a meadow, Catherine leaned forward, squinting against the afternoon sun.

"Catriona," Catherine whispered barely loud enough for the other lady to hear her over the sounds of the hooves. "To your right, through the tall grass before the loch."

"I spy them. But so will everyone else the moment

we pull ahead. The stallions and destriers will beat our mares."

"Do you see the outcropping?"

"Aye," Catriona nodded.

"If we can get ahead before we pass the boulders, we can swing our horses around and shoot. But we must be quick, or the deer will flee. They'll bolt as soon as they feel the ground rumble."

"Are you ready?" Catriona pulled an arrow from her quiver, her bow already resting in her lap. Catherine followed suit. Both women demonstrated their experience, riding with the reins in one hand. Their mares were just as experienced and followed silent commands nearly as well as any warhorse.

"Aye," Catherine laughed. She'd dreaded coming on the hunt, fearful that it would bore her to tears. Then she'd been anxious when she whispered with Rab, wishing their conversation could carry on forever, but apprehensive someone might watch them. Above all, she'd felt reassured that Rab was among the men riding with her. She finally enjoyed herself as she plotted with Catriona.

The pair of ladies-in-waiting leaned low over their horses' withers as they squeezed their mounts' flanks, urging them on. As planned, they pulled ahead of the men and dashed toward the outcropping. They ignored the grumbles and the calls for them to fall back into the larger group. They even caught curses that they were ruining the hunt. Neither woman cared. As they passed the cluster of four boulders, their horses scrambled over the uneven terrain as the women drew back their bowstrings. With near synchronicity, their arrows imbedded themselves in the necks of two stags. It was only a moment later that they felled two does. The bucks staggered several feet in opposite directions, but the does landed where they were shot.

"Bluidy hell, Catriona," bellowed her uncle, Maxwell Douglas. "You might have given us some warning."

"So you could claim our prizes? I think not, Uncle." Catriona cocked a challenging eyebrow at the older man, a smugness that no other person dared with the savvy politician and renowned warrior. "If you don't wish for me to hunt, you never should have taught me." Catriona held up her bow. "And you never should have given me this."

"Lass," Maxwell warned. Catriona offered him a beguiling smile before dismounting near the loch. She and Catherine led their horses to the water and let them drink as they walked toward their kills. They perfectly aimed both arrows, causing neither doe to suffer. They looked around as men went in search of the stags they also shot.

"Your daredevil ways are still as strong as ever." Andrew came to stand beside Catherine. "He might have been proud of you, but I'm waiting for you to break your bluidy neck."

Catherine darted a glance to where she noticed Rab stood with his horse, surprised to see Maxwell Douglas approaching him.

"Aye. He watched you like a hawk, and when I wasn't doing the same, I watched him."

"Do you fear he's going to do something to one of us?" Catherine doubted Andrew believed that, but she didn't understand what he was trying to say. She'd stopped watching Rab when she pulled ahead of him. Andrew couldn't be blaming her for Rab's attention, even if she secretly appreciated knowing he watched over her.

"No. But I fear someone else will kill him. It's no secret that I'm here to find you a husband. You come with a hefty dowry for the size of our clan, Catherine. You know that. Between his clan's reputation and your hand still being available, it would take little for someone to read his attention for what it is. If you don't want him dead to be out of the way, you'd do well to keep your distance."

"And you suddenly care? Yesterday, you wanted him to be held responsible for it all. You wanted the Bruce's anger to rain down on him."

"I care because if you're with him, you might wind up dead too. At best, a ruined reputation and a spinster."

Catherine snorted. "How reassuring. And why would I be with him for anyone to find us together?"

"Because it doesn't take much to recognize the attraction between you two. I don't know who I wish more hadn't come on this hunt." Andrew mumbled his last thought to himself.

"Well, we're both here, and there is naught any of us can do."

"But I can keep you away from him," Andrew countered.

"You've warned me more than once, Óg. As much as you tell me being with him puts me in danger, the opposite it true too. I won't risk his life because someone sees me looking at him or talking to him."

"Aye. Don't forget stags and fowl aren't the only things being hunted." Andrew looked pointedly at Catherine's left hand as it stroked Timber's neck. She scowled, disliking being likened to prey, but she supposed that's what the marriage market really was: a hunt to bag the best bride. While there had been few men looking in her direction ever since the debacle with Edgar Gunn, more would pay attention if they believed not only could they gain themselves a bride but cast Rab asunder. Catherine nodded and offered a tight smile before Andrew moved to tend to his mount. The fun was short-lived.

CHAPTER 4

*R*ab watched Catherine throughout the hunt, not at all surprised when she and Catriona took off and then claimed the largest prey as their own. He'd noticed the bow she carried. It was the one he'd given her at their third summer meeting at a Highland Gathering. It had been his first bow when he was barely more than a boy. He was far too large to use it, even by then, but it still was a perfect fit for Catherine. As she shot the pheasants, he noticed her arrows' fletching were the same he'd taught her to make. He knew both Andrews and her father taught her to hunt, but he'd encouraged her to enter the women's archery contests once he gave her his bow. She'd done well, tying with both Mairghread Sinclair, who was now Lady Mackay, and Mairghread's cousin Blair Sutherland, who was now Lady Cameron.

Pride surged through him as he observed her riding alongside Andrew. He'd ground his teeth when the Bruce ordered the women to the front, frustrated that he could no longer ride parallel to her and distrusting the surrounding men not to let their larger horses push Catherine's smaller mare aside. He'd breathed a sigh of relief, even though he observed Andrew tense and rise in his stirrups, when Catherine pulled ahead. He knew her plan, having thought the same thing, but assuming he'd have to fall behind to make his way around the boulders. It didn't surprise him, like it did several courtiers, that Catherine and Catriona were expert marksmen. He'd known Catriona longer than he had Catherine. His mother and Catriona's were friends. He knew the two ladies-in-waiting were cast from the same mold.

As the riders brought their horses to the loch's edge to drink, Rab wished for nothing more than to congratulate her, but he kept his distance. No one had spoken to him since he joined the party in the bailey. He supposed it was better to be ignored than being accused of being a rapist and murderer as he'd heard three ladies-in-waiting say that morning as he left the chapel. He'd forced an impassive expression, pretending as though he hadn't listened to them, when all he wanted was to scream from the rafters that he hadn't been there. That he'd punished the culprits in a way likely to send his own soul to hell for eternity. He wanted to speak to Catherine and apologize, as he had with Andrew. Instead, he kept to himself, only Cullen riding out with him. The experienced warrior rode close to his tánaiste, but he knew Rab was in no mood for banter.

"MacLaren."

Rab wanted to cringe as Maxwell Douglas walked toward him. While he didn't mind the man, he preferred not to have his name broadcast for all and sundry to hear. He held his horse's halter and waited for the burly man to make his way to Rab's side.

"Douglas." Rab nodded, unsure whether he should extend his arm. When Douglas glanced down but didn't extend his, Rab was even more uncertain if the other man had expected them to grasp forearms.

"You're a brave mon to ride out with so many arrows that could wind up in your back." Maxwell's smile hardly appeared jovial.

"I suspect that's what the king hopes will happen, so he doesnae have to deal with me." Rab found no point in trying to hold up the pretenses that he was at court to pay his clan's taxes. The raid was widespread knowledge.

"That's most unfortunate." Maxwell pinned Rab's gaze in place as the older man assessed him. "A wee birdie told me you carried out your cousins' sentence."

Rab fought the temptation to glance at Andrew, furious that the man shared with Maxwell what had been told in confidence. Rab merely stared at Maxwell, unblinking for so long that Maxwell shifted his gaze.

"The king already knows, MacLaren, as you know. Mayhap the birdie wasn't quite so wee." Maxwell nodded before glancing back over his shoulder to where the Bruce stood with Maxwell's nephew and Andrew.

Rab released the tension in his jaw, not pleased that anyone other than King Robert, Rab's father, and the handful of men who accompanied him that morning knew what he'd done. But it relieved him that Maxwell hadn't learned it somewhere else. Hadn't learned it from Andrew.

"You should know before—"

"Why?" Rab interrupted. Maxwell's brow furrowed. "Why should I ken what ye ken? Why should ye tell me?"

"Blunt. You don't understand how this game is played at court. That's one thing you should know. You are a Highlander among judgmental Lowlanders. Bluntness might suit you well among our people, but it will win you no favors here."

"Whose favor should I curry? Yers?" Rab cocked an

eyebrow. He knew he was blunt by anyone's standards, and a small part of him found a perverse pleasure in watching the seasoned courtier shift uncomfortably.

"It certainly doesn't hurt your cause if you did. But, no. I am not the one who needs winning over. That would be the king. But you should know that it isn't the MacFarlanes who have cried the loudest. Dennis Buchanan claims your people have set their sights on making his clan next. While the king views him for the fool he is, plenty of other people are taking up his standard against your clan. I jest not when I say you should be wary of ending up with a back full of arrows."

"Ye've told me what ye ken. But ye havenae told me *why* ye're telling me." Rab crossed his arms, his muscles bulging. But they were of little consequence to the older man, whose own arms appeared like they belonged to a blacksmith.

"Because your troubles with the MacFarlanes shall get the Campbells involved. They're not only allies with the MacFarlanes but barely speak to your clan. I don't need Brodie Campbell holding any more influence than he already does. Bluidy Campbells already think they own all of Glencoe."

"That's because they do." Rab smirked. He understood there was little love lost between the Campbells and the Douglases when it came to their rivalry for being the most powerful clan in Scotland. However, as much as he disliked the Campbells as a clan, he respected Brodie and his younger brother, Dominic. However, he minded that the Campbells' incursion into MacGregor land, after King Robert gifted them a sizable piece of MacGregor territory, meant the MacGregors were encroaching on MacLaren soil.

"Either way, no one else will guard you from those who lurk in the dark shadows at court. No one else will ally with you and possibly face the Campbells."

"Other than to prove ye have a pair of bollocks, mayhap even large ones, what do ye want?"

"Like I said, I don't need Brodie Campbell and his neb stuck in the middle of this."

"Ye wish to be the one to broker the truce," Rab cut in, not waiting for an explanation after all. "Ye aspire to be the great statesmon who ends the violence and brings the MacLarens and MacFarlanes together to break bread. How excited ye must have been to discover the MacFarlanes' tragedy, to ken ye can use their misery to enhance yer standing. And that I should be so loathed will only make the accomplishment so much grander."

"You may have surmised the situation, but you haven't turned me down."

"What is there to turn down? Ye've nae made an offer, and I'm nae standing here to hear one. I dinna need to be yer pawn. I'm up to ma eyeteeth in shite. I'm nae making this disaster yer crowning glory."

"You'd rather make an enemy of me than an ally?"

Rab leaned forward, his arms still crossed. "Remember: Icarus learned what happens when a mon tries to fly too close to the sun." He didn't wait for Maxwell to puzzle through what he meant or for the conversation to go any further. If Maxwell wanted to be the king's favorite, he could find another means. Rab swung into the saddle and turned back toward the castle. He'd made his appearance, even nabbed several hares. He no longer cared who might think poorly of him for leaving without the king's permission. He figured most couldn't think lower of him than they already did.

As he rode past Catherine, he was certain she was aware of him, but she made no move to glance in his direction or acknowledge him. He'd seen Andrew speaking to her and deduced he'd warned her away yet again. He kept his eyes forward and walked his horse around the assembled riders, who were mounting once more. He was nearly clear of the group when, yet another voice called to him.

"MacLaren." Queen Elizabeth guided her horse to stand alongside where Rab stopped. He bowed over Bolt's neck and waited for the queen to speak. "How fares your mother?"

Rab was unprepared for the question, so he hesitated. He suspected his father told his mother of how he carried out her nephews'-by-marriage deaths, but she had never said as much. However, she'd changed toward him, grown more distant since then. Rab worried his mother feared him or feared for his mortal soul.

"She's well, Yer Majesty."

"I haven't seen Lady MacLaren in several years. When I was but a lass in Ireland, I traveled to the Isle of Tiree and met your mother. She was kind to me when I knew no one. It wasn't long after that her father, the auld Laird MacLaren of Tiree, betrothed her to your father. I haven't seen your mother since she became a MacLaren of Balquhidder. But my memories are still vivid and fond. I have faith she shares her kindness to all around her, especially as a mother and clan's lady. I'm certain she continues to be a worthy influence on all who know her."

Rab wanted to ask Queen Elizabeth to speak clearly rather than leaving him to deduce her meaning. With no disgust or animosity toward him, he hoped he understood her meaning. He believed she attempted to let him know she recognized him for being an honorable man, since she mentioned his mother's kindness twice.

"I am most fortunate that Nessa of Tiree became Lady MacLaren of Balquhidder and ma mother. She is a vera warm-hearted woman, and I pray some of her virtues rubbed off on me."

"I believe they did, young MacLaren. You may resemble your father, but anyone who tries will recognize your mother in you too." Queen Elizabeth smiled. "Mayhap around the eyes."

"Thank ye, Yer Majesty." Rab observed the queen as she watched him before she turned away. Rab knew without moving that she watched Catherine. He was certain of it, even though he hadn't turned to follow her gaze. He knew the queen to be astute.

"Hopefully, you can resolve all that you need to during this visit, MacLaren. Time is not on your side." Queen Elizabeth spurred her horse, leaving Rab to bow once more over Bolt's neck. He made his way back to his chamber, where he once more lay on his bed and stared at the canopy.

In only a day, I've spoken to Kitty again, even caught her laughter. I've watched the lass I kenned enjoy a hunt she didna want to attend. I've had Maxwell Douglas issue me veiled threats in the form of an alliance. And the queen—I think—means she understands I'm nae to blame for their choices, and she may ken ma feelings for Kitty. Would that ma conversation with the Bruce should go so smoothly.

If he admits me to the Privy Council chamber tomorrow, mayhap I can have the matter settled before sundown. I dinna ken what the outcome will be, but at best, I will be back on Bolt's back the morning after tomorrow and back on ma way to Balquhidder before I watch Óg betroth Kitty to someone else. As though I didna notice the men watching her today. It willna be long.

Rab closed his eyes but jolted awake several hours later when he heard the bells peeling for the evening meal.

Once more, fighting her desire to search for Rab, Catherine made her way to the evening meal. He hadn't attended the evening meal the day he arrived or the day prior when they'd gone on the hunt. Catherine hadn't seen Rab all day, but she'd listened to men talking about him. It had made her cringe at first when they described him as though he were some primordial beast, but pride swelled in her chest as she followed the men into the Great Hall. While they'd sounded disgusted at Rab's strength and prowess in the lists that day, Catherine thought about the years she'd watched him at the gatherings and how he'd only grown more impressive with each tournament.

The hair on the back of her neck rose, making her shift in her seat. As though he were a lodestone, Catherine's eyes followed Rab as he made his way to a far table with his men. They sat apart from everyone else, and Catherine wasn't sure if that was wise or foolish. She considered the distance kept them from getting into any arguments with other clan delegates, but it also made them stand out more. She wished for Rab's sake that they could merely blend in. But the niceties and formalities of court were foreign to the men accompanying Rab.

"Heathens," Rebecca Kerr spat as she glared in Rab's direction. Catherine had barely taken a seat, but she glanced toward the MacLarens. She noticed that each man had a whisky flask before him rather than a wine chalice. Three servants stood at various spots along their table while the men speared large hanks of meat from the platters with what appeared to be dirks rather than eating knives.

"I hear men as massive as they have massive appetites for all things," Evina giggled, but it died on her lips as the Lowlanders glared at her. Normally, the women had no qualms jesting about the Highlanders' many renowned strengths. But at this meal, disdain consumed them too much to even consider the men's desirability.

"Aye. My uncle says he's close to signing contracts for my marriage." Catriona announced as she reached for her chalice. "Aboot bluidy time I get back to the Highlands. He'd best have paired me with one of those braw men and not some gangly toad from down here."

Catherine watched as Catriona darted her eyes toward Rab with speculation. A stab of jealousy coursed through Catherine as she wondered if that was what Rab discussed with Maxwell the previous day during the hunt. Rab left the hunting party immediately after and didn't appear like a man who'd settled a betrothal. He'd appeared sullen and even more withdrawn until Catherine watched him stop to talk to the queen. Despite the distance, she could tell his face relaxed, even if his posture didn't.

"You'd have that criminal?" Rebecca demanded.

"'She who is without sin among you, let her throw a stone at him first.'" Catriona quoted the scripture, changing it to make her point toward Rebecca. "Your family isn't without scandal nor criminals. How fares your cousin, Brighde? Word is she's immensely happy in the Highlands with her husband and bairns. Alexander Sinclair is one of the brawest of them all."

Catherine bit her lip to keep from smirking. It was a faded memory for many that Brighde's father, the former Kerr laird, had arranged a marriage to the infamous Randolph de Soules. People knew him for being on the wrong side of morals and the law until he died for his conspiracy. Rebecca's other cousin, Mary, had once been the merciless ringleader of the ladies-in-waiting. Her reputation for cruelty matched Sarah Anne Hay's. She'd conspired with Sarah Anne's uncle, Archibald Hay, to abduct Deirdre Fraser, who married

Alexander Sinclair's brother Magnus. Mary carried on an illicit affair with Archibald until they both died for their crimes. The Kerrs hardly had a sterling reputation.

Rebecca scowled at Catriona, making it clear she wished to make a rebuttal, but nothing came to mind. She turned her attention to Catherine, who cocked a challenging eyebrow. While Catherine got along with most of the ladies-in-waiting, she had a reputation for being blunt when pushed to share her opinion or to defend herself. Rebecca opted to remain quiet, not wanting to take on both Highland women.

"Do they even chew or merely inhale their food?" Margaret Hay snarked. She had no qualms about pointing at the MacLarens, who appeared to gobble their meal. Catherine assumed they wished to finish the meal and duck out of sight as soon as they could. Their serious miens made them appear even more intimidating than their reputation did. Still using dirks instead of eating knives, the men guzzled their supper. Only Rab ate with a modicum of decorum. He took smaller bites and chewed longer, but his elbows rested on the table when he wasn't adding more food to his trencher. Catherine's brow furrowed for a moment, knowing Rab's mother had instilled better manners into both her sons. Catherine supposed it was testimony to how badly the MacLarens wished to escape the Great Hall.

"I'd run away to a convent before ever agreeing to marry such a barbarian," Sileas Gunn noted. Catherine turned toward Sileas, surprised that the reserved Highlander spoke up against one of their own. "Even by our standards, he's uncouth for a noblemon."

It took great restraint for Catherine to point out that manners did not make the man. Sileas's cousin

Edgar had sufficient manners and turned out to be as dishonorable as the day was long.

Catherine and the other ladies-in-waiting had ventured to an almshouse that morning to offer donated knitted woolens to the orphans and impoverished. While she'd tried to focus on being gracious with those who she encountered, the other ladies ignored those less fortunate than themselves, and instead spent the time discussing various upcoming weddings and matches in the making. Evina and Sileas both had men courting them, and Sarah Anne and Margaret were closer to the altar than Catherine. The two sisters' potential husbands were as desirable as the peevish women, but it was likely they could both wed by the end of the year.

Throughout the women's conversations at the almshouse, Catherine hadn't been able to conjure the image of any man but Rab. There were several handsome men at court, some of whom were even Highlanders. She knew Andrew was right when he reminded her that she had a healthy dowry, but she'd also caught the gossip among the men during evening meals, warning one another away lest they get into bed with the Campbells rather than her. While many thought it a boon, just as many feared their clans falling short of the Campbells' esteem. Either way, it left only the less honorable men to bid for her hand.

"Evina, when do you think your father will sign the contracts?" Catriona asked, bringing Catherine back to the present.

"Any day now, I think. Laird Matheson is eager to marry off his youngest son. Since naught came of the brief interest in Madeline MacLeod—er—Grant," Evina stumbled over her words. It still surprised many that the once would-be-nun and the often-recalcitrant Fingal Grant were now blissfully married. "My father

45

believes it's an excellent match for me. He is the youngest of four, so there is little chance I will ever be Lady Matheson, but he is handsome and amusing. I've met my future sisters-by-marriage before, and they seem welcoming."

Evina's cheeks grew red. There were few who didn't know the couple was smitten. There were even rumors that they'd shared more than one kiss when the young Matheson visited Evina at court, but they had set no date.

"My Liam delivered the bride price to my father a sennight ago." Margaret Hay boasted, but few were interested in her impending marriage to Liam Oliphant. He was slithery and smarmy. He'd been an instigator of the conspiracy in which Edgar Gunn found himself, thusly ruining Catherine's chance for marriage.

Catherine hadn't realized Margaret was truly only a few steps from the altar. Jealousy, much like she'd felt earlier when she watched Catriona cast Rab a speculative expression, surged through her. First, she'd been jealous that Catriona might be interested in Rab, and with no acrimony between the MacLarens and the Douglases, there was little to keep Catriona from flirting with Rab. Now, she was jealous that Margaret, who rarely had a kind word or a deep thought, was marrying soon, even if it were to a man who reminded Catherine of a toad.

Catherine had more time than she wished over the past two days to spend reminiscing about how her feelings for Rab developed. It had been slow since she'd met him when she was on the cusp of womanhood, noticing young men but not understanding the draw. It took her nearly a year and a half to realize that her emotions for Rab ran deeper than mere infatuation. She'd tried to convince herself that it was simply a physical attraction, but just as she recalled in her Stirling chamber the past two nights, she'd enjoyed her friendship with Rab since it began.

It took little for Rab to gain Catherine's trust, as they were so much alike. There had been an intuitive connection since the moment she landed on the ground in the orchard and spotted Rab and Douglan. She'd barely noticed the younger brother. It was as though a magnet in her chest drew her to Rab, and she'd been certain that the same had been true for him. The four Highland Gatherings they spent together and various weddings they'd both attended gave them time to explore their burgeoning feelings.

"Ye should talk to him," Catriona whispered in Catherine's ear as she reached for the wine pitcher. Catherine froze. It surprised her that Catriona lowered her guard and allowed her brogue to break through, and she was uncertain to whom she referred. She feared Catriona suspected Rab. "Ye keep stealing peeks at one another since the hunt. Ye will resolve naught if ye dinna talk. And ye dinna want to lose the one chance ye have."

Catherine canted her head to observe Catriona, who appeared intent upon pouring her wine. Catherine wondered if Catriona meant her one chance before he left for Balquhidder, or her one chance before King Robert punished him for his relatives' crimes. That thought was a bucket of ice water, a reminder yet again of what she'd lost at the hands of MacLarens.

47

CHAPTER 5

*R*ab sat at a table close to doors leading to the terrace. While he loathed having his back exposed to the dark abyss beyond the doors, it allowed him to watch all around him. He and his men had agreed to eat and leave the meal without dallying. None felt comfortable in the Great Hall, especially without their swords. There'd been more than one guardsman training in the lists that day who put more force into his swings than necessary. Cullen and the others sported nicks and bruises. They'd defended themselves but never went on the offensive. Rab had warned them that they would be scapegoats and targets, and he hadn't been wrong.

Rab wondered if the morbid interest in the raid was because Catherine lived at court, so it constantly reminded people of her clan. Or perhaps it was how unprovoked the attack seemed, along with women being the only target. Either way, he heard plenty of people, including several Highlanders, question his honor. He cared little for the Lowlanders opinions, but losing face and respectability among his peers sentenced his future lairdship to ruins. The MacLarens couldn't face gaining any more rivals.

Rab continued to mull over the false accusations. The Buchanans, a clan loyal to the Bruce and once seneschals to the Earls of Lennox, clamored to gain the king's attention and favor. Rab feared they searched for an excuse to engage the MacLarens in the name of self-defense. If they vanquished the MacLarens for a supposed incursion, then the court, and even the king, would deem them heroes. Rab spotted Dennis Buchanan when he entered the Great Hall; he'd found the man already staring at him, an assessing gleam in his eyes. Rab pretended not to notice as he took his seat. It wasn't hard to forget Dennis when his gaze landed on Catherine. He did what he could to ignore her and the feelings she elicited. Remembering that he'd warned his men not to tarry, he ate as quickly as they did. The meal was pure frustration as his thoughts jumped from his cousins and meeting with the Bruce to the Buchanans to Catherine and back again. When the music began and the servants cleared the tables, he prepared to make his escape.

Moving toward the doors to the terrace, Rab leaned against the wall as he nodded to his men. None were eager to yet again abandon Rab to the wilds of court, but his piercing glare told them they followed his orders and not the other way around. Few paid attention to a handful of guards leaving before the nobles began dancing, but Rab leaving with his guards wouldn't go unnoticed. Despite how he wished to flee, he refused to give anyone the satisfaction of watching him do so. The crowd swelled as people moved into place for the first dance.

"Catherine," Andrew's voice floated to Rab, who casually turned toward it, kicking himself as he was in line with an unobstructed view of Catherine's profile. The soft angles of her face were ones he'd stared at countless times over the years as they stood, walked, and sat alongside one another at gatherings and weddings. "A MacDonnell of Keppoch and a Keith approached me today. Their lairds are interested in pursuing matches with you."

"And what did you tell them? Did you say that my dowry redeems me for your poor choices with Edgar?" Catherine's eyes narrowed as she stared at her cousin. "Óg, I'm not foolish enough to think feelings between me and the mon I marry count for aught, but you really intend to marry me to a mon who has never even laid eyes on me, never once spoken a word to me? The Keith laird is auld enough to be our father. He's never paid attention to me when we've seen one another. The MacDonnell laird is even aulder and a practical recluse. What happens when neither can sire a child on me, or worse dies trying?"

"They aren't that auld, Catherine."

"Óg," Catherine snapped. "They are both sixty, if not aulder."

"And many a mon has sired a child aulder than that. Besides, they already have heirs."

"So it really is only aboot my dowry."

"Catherine." Andrew released an aggrieved sigh.

"At least Edgar was close to my age."

"Does the marriage bed really matter that much to you?" Andrew narrowed his eyes, his glare matching Catherine's.

"No. But it means something. I want a family, Óg. I want children. What happens when they die and there's no dowry left to marry me off a second time? Neither clan will keep me if I've borne the laird no children, and even if I do, there's no chance they would ever inherit. Both lairds have married sons with sons." Catherine's frustration increased with each word. Her gaze darted around the Great Hall as she searched for any excuse to escape. It passed over Rab before slowly returning. She realized he could hear the entire conversation, despite his apparent nonchalance.

"We don't always get what we want, Catherine," Andrew stated pointedly as his head canted toward Rab. Catherine realized he'd positioned them on purpose. He wanted Rab to understand he was moving forward with a marriage. Catherine's hands fisted at her side, and Andrew nearly took a step back, recognizing the near menacing edge in Catherine's gaze. He'd been on the receiving end more than once as a lad when he'd crossed the line, teasing Catherine or his sisters. There'd inevitably been hell to pay afterward.

"I'm walking away. If I stand here another moment, I will get some wicked thought in my head. And you know you barely survive when I do." Catherine caught a slight movement beyond Andrew's shoulder. Rather than looking at Rab directly, she allowed her peripheral vision to catch him nod toward the terrace. Catherine cocked a challenging eyebrow at Andrew but hoped Rab recognized it as the expression she'd always given when she waited for him to lead them on an adventure. Before Andrew could say anything, she stepped around him and entered the crowd of dancers. She moved through the people, avoiding bumping into dancing couples until she watched both Andrew and Rab without being obvious. She caught sight of the back of Rab as he eased through the terrace doors. She noticed Andrew already deep in conversation with a Keith delegate. Catherine slipped through a set of doors into a passageway, then sprinted along it until she could inch open a door that led to the bailey. She hurried through and made her way to the terrace.

"Kitty," Rab whispered. His hulking form emerged from the shadows. It would have been intimidating if Catherine had ever feared Rab a day in her life.

"Shh. Follow me." Catherine reached out her hand,

slipping it into Rab's. She led them across the bailey and into the dark gardens. When they were sufficiently far enough into the orchard on the far side of the garden, Catherine stopped. Neither knew who reached out first, but they fell into one another's arms. The embrace was fierce, each of them clinging to the other. Both implicitly knew this might be the only chance they had to share a private moment together.

As they eased their hold, their mouths sought one another. It wasn't the first kiss they'd shared, but it was the most intense, far more than a mere peck. It was as though it brought them back to life after sleeping through years of their lives. It was languid, the opposite of the ferocity of their embrace. Rab ran his hand over Catherine's back as the other wrapped around her waist. Her hands tunneled into his hair as she gave herself over to the kiss.

But a thought niggled at the back of Rab's mind, which he couldn't push aside. He drew away from Catherine but cupped her cheeks.

"I have dreamed of doing that every day since the last time I was with ye. It's always been ye." Rab straightened as he peered over Catherine's shoulder. "I want naught more than to lose maself in yer kisses until ma last breath. But I canna."

Rab stepped back and ran a hand through his hair as he debated how to proceed. He knew he was about to hurt Catherine, but he refused to keep anything from her, especially if she only learned of it later and from someone else.

"Kitty, I have a leman. In good conscience, I canna kiss ye kenning that there is someone else."

Catherine stood, aghast. The wind evaporated from her core, and her lungs burned. "You love another, but you're out here with me."

52

"I do nae love Katherine." Rab flinched and thought Catherine might bolt when she shook her head.

"She has my name. Or is it that I have hers?"

"She has yers. Kitty, I have loved ye since the day I met ye. I didna understand it at first because we were too young. But I have never wanted another woman at ma side, but I thought I would never see ye again. I thought—I assumed—ye would already be married." Rab swallowed the lump in his throat, the anguish on his face visible in the moonlight that shone upon them. "The reason I began ma relationship with Katherine is that she has the same name as ye. It was yer name I wanted to cry out. I just told ye that I've dreamed of kissing ye every day since the last time I was near ye, kissed ye. She has dark hair, Kitty. She gets what she wants from bedding the laird's son, and I get someone I can pretend is ye."

"Does she ken this?" Catherine demanded.

"Of course nae."

"How long? How long have ye been playing this woman for a fool? How long have ye let her think ye care for her? Do ye?" Catherine's brogue emerged as her turbulent emotions consumed her.

"Nearly two years. She kens we'll never marry. She kens I canna marry her."

"But she believes if ye love her that ye will, that ye might still find a way."

"Nay." Rab grabbed Catherine's upper arms, easing his grip immediately as he pulled her toward him. "I have never loved a woman but ye. I have never made her think I might feel that way. I've been clear. Over and over. She kens I must marry to make an alliance. That's ma only choice since I canna have the woman I really want."

"Would she still be yer leman after ye wed?"

"Nay. Ye ken I dinna believe in infidelity. Remember

the family ma uncle created by straying from ma aunt. His sons ran wild because neither parent could stand to lay eyes on the other, so they abandoned their children as much as they did one another." The pure loathing Rab felt oozed into every word. It chilled Catherine to listen to Rab speak of his own family. These were the same men who wreaked havoc on her own. "Whomever I marry, I will always be true to her."

"Why are ye telling me this? Ye're going to marry someone else. Why nae just enjoy this moment and keep this to yerself?"

"Because I'm nae letting ye go ever again. Ye ken as clearly as I do that we still feel the same for one another. We said as much through our kiss. But I willna pursue ye while I have another woman waiting for me. I'll set off for Edinample this eve and break things off with her. I want ye to ken it's only ye and for that to be the truth."

"Rab, being with ye is the only thing I've wanted since I was auld enough to understand what it means to want a mon, to wish to spend ma life with someone. But ye speak as though what we want is what's going to happen. Ye ken that isnae how it will work out." Catherine stepped away from Rab, shaking her head as she swallowed the threatening tears. She didn't want to have this conversation. She didn't want to discuss what couldn't be, and she certainly didn't want to learn more about the woman who shared Rab's bed when Catherine might never do the same.

"I'm nae letting ye go ever again," Rab repeated his earlier declaration. "I ken I will never be welcome into yer kin, but I ken for certain ma kin would welcome ye. Ma clan would accept ye."

"The bluidy hell they will. Yer people hate ma clan enough for men to join yer cousins and rape ma aunt and ma cousins, to kill them before Mòr's and Óg's eyes. They willna accept me any more than ma clan accepting ye. We'd only make it worse."

"Or we could force a truce. Either way, I willna give up and walk away. I will find a way to balance ma duties with marrying ye, Kitty. And if ma clan canna accept it, then ma father can disinherit me. Douglan can be laird."

Catherine puffed a breath through her nose, the derision clear. "Douglan may be a good brother to ye and even an impressive warrior, but he will never be the leader ye are."

"Aye. And ma father kens it."

"Ye'd stake yer life, yer future on that. Our future."

"I would. But if I'm wrong, I'm nae without means. I can hire out ma sword arm to another clan."

"Ye canna mean that ye'd become a regular warrior in some clan."

"That's nae what I want. But I want a life with ye more than I want aught else. I've kenned that for seven years, and the past three days have been naught but a tortuous reminder. I will always provide for ye and our family. Make nay mistake aboot that."

Catherine shook her head. "Why are ye breaking ma heart all over again? It felt as though it could never take a steady beat again when the feud erupted, and I thought I was never to lay eyes on ye again. It broke seeing ye here and kenning that naught can come of it. Why are ye saying what we ken canna happen?"

"Do ye nae wish to marry me, Kitty? Have I misunderstood all these years?"

"I told ye only a moment ago that ye're breaking ma heart a third time, and ye wonder if I ever wanted to marry ye? Daft mon." Catherine wrapped her arms around Rab as she inhaled his scent. She fought the tears, the sobs that choked her. "I'd marry ye this vera moment if I didna fear ruining more than our own lives."

"Kitty, I love ye." Rab realized it was the first time he'd ever made the declaration. He'd already admitted it while they talked, but the statement had never stood alone.

"I love ye, Rab. I always have, and I dinna think I will ever stop." Catherine sighed. "But do we love each other as we are now? Or do we love the person we once kenned? I ken I'm nae the same as I was three years ago. Can ye say ye are the same mon?"

"I'm nae. But I havenae changed that much. Who I am in ma heart is still the same. Have ye changed so much that ye canna love me, or I shouldnae love ye?"

"Nay. I havenae changed that much either. At least, I dinna think so."

"Then I'll ride back to Edinample. I will end things with Katherine and come back to ye."

Catherine stared at Rab, struggling to order her thoughts. Their conversation was moving too quickly, and it all felt too easy after years of heartache. "What will yer father say when ye ride into the bailey, visit yer leman, then ride back out?"

"He willna ken I was there. Katherine lives in a croft in the village, nae within the walls. I will meet her at night and leave before anyone kens I returned."

Catherine's left eye narrowed.

"I will nae bed her for auld time's sake." Rab guessed the thought that whirled through Catherine's mind, trying to take root. "I'll ride to a nearby village and find a priest to post the banns. Somewhere close enough to here to witness it each sennight, but far enough for word nae to reach here or our families. Kitty, I want to marry ye."

"And I want to marry ye, Rab. At the last gathering, ye ken I planned to talk to Mòr, tell him I wanted him to consider yer suit. But then everything fell apart, and I didna dare mention it." Catherine slid her hands into Rab's as she stepped back to meet his gaze. "Dinna ride back yet."

Rab objected. "I'm nae courting ye or marrying ye while a woman—a different woman—thinks I'm returning to her bed. I willna marry ye while I have a leman."

"We may have suited three years ago, but what if we dinna now? Why break things off with a woman ye must be fond of if ye've been with her for two years? If things dinna work out between us, ye'd have naught to return home to."

"Because I dinna want Katherine ever again. I dinna think I can want any woman again who isnae ye." The adamance in Rab's voice ran a shiver along Catherine's spine. She'd heard the tone before, and she knew it meant he wasn't backing down.

"Can we nae try to court first?"

Rab's mouth thinned, but he nodded. His reluctance was apparent, but he acquiesced for Catherine's sake. She stretched onto her toes and bussed a kiss across his lips.

"If ye can make yer confessions to me, then I must do the same." Catherine felt the heat creep into her cheeks.

"Ye dinna have to tell me aught."

"I want to. We may want to court, but neither of us can be certain when we'll have another chance to be alone. I feel like the sands are falling too fast in an hourglass we canna stop. I feel like we must say everything right now, lest we dinna have another chance."

"I feel the same. I hadnae planned to share all of this with ye in the dark in the royal orchard. I'd rather we took a long walk or a ride, but we dinna ken when we might have this chance. But I am determined to court ye, Kitty. Everything in me says I canna walk away from ye. It's like a voice screaming inside me."

"It's the same for me. It's like something is pushing me to tell ye everything, making me fear I might nae get another chance." Catherine inhaled through her nose as she fought to keep her mind on a single idea. "I'm still a maiden, but I'm nae as innocent as when ye last spent time with me. Ye ken I nearly married Edgar Gunn."

"Aye. I canna figure what Mòr was thinking to agree to such a match."

"It was a good alliance for us. Despite the distance, they have a large force that could come to our aid if we…" Catherine trailed off, her lips turning down.

"If we continue to feud, and ma clan attacks again."

"Aye. Edgar isnae a mon I'd choose for maself, but he was the mon I was certain I was to marry. He has a leman too. More than one, from what I deduced. It's nae that I thought I could make him give them up or make him faithful. But I wanted a home without discord, and I want a family. I thought if I allowed him a few liberties before we were even betrothed, he might believe me worth the effort to at least nae ignore."

Rab understood her logic. He understood it came from both fear and optimism. He'd resigned himself to not marrying Catherine and being forced down the aisle to another woman, eventually. He couldn't fault her for the same and for trying to protect her future.

"Rab, I let him do more than kiss me." Catherine bit her top lip, waiting for Rab's reaction. When there was none, she continued. "I told ye I'm still a maiden, but I'm nae entirely untouched."

Rab didn't want to listen to Catherine's confession any more than he'd wanted to make his own. But he'd already told her he'd been bedding someone else. He would be a hypocrite of the worst kind to refuse to listen after unloading his past onto her shoulders.

"Kitty, ye believed ye were going to marry the mon. Ye risked a great deal, but I understand why ye did. I dinna wish to think of another mon already kenning parts of ye that I wish were only for ma eyes, ma hands —ma mouth. But I made ye ken I havenae been a monk. I dinna have a right to hold any of this against ye. I dinna."

Catherine dipped her chin, trying to hide her smile.

"Kitty?"

Catherine recognized the warning, so she looked at him unrepentantly. "It's still for only yer mouth. At least the important part."

"Kitty," Rab hissed.

"I'm certain ye werenae a virgin when I met ye, and I dinna think ye played one between gatherings. I—"

"I wasna, but I did."

"What?" Catherine's brow furrowed.

"After the second gathering, I thought I was already courting ye. At least, in ma mind I was. I kenned I wanted nay one else. I wasna with another woman until more than a year after the last time I saw ye."

Catherine could only stand and blink. She never imagined Rab choosing celibacy. She'd been jealous of imaginary women, envious that they did with Rab what she wished to learn from him. It took her a long moment to gather her thoughts.

"I never—" Kitty cleared her throat, now suddenly shy to admit what she'd explored with Edgar and what she hadn't. "Ma eyes and ma hands may ken more than they once did, but ma mouth doesnae."

"Kitty, ye dinna have to tell me this."

"I ken. I'm certain ye dinna want to hear it either. I ken ye canna say the same, but I accepted that long ago.

It surprises me to nay end that ye went without a woman for so long."

"I didna want anyone else. It didna feel right the few times I considered it, so I abandoned the thought, always waiting to visit with ye at the next gathering. I pined for ye, but I didna miss it like I expected. Instead, I trained more."

Catherine chuckled and Rab joined in. "I'm certain Douglan didna appreciate that. I'm guessing he was on the receiving end of yer frustrations."

"Aye, but he caused them as much as going without did."

"Rab, I wish I could go back and—"

Rab cut Catherine off with a kiss. "I'm more than a wee jealous, but I dinna wish for ye to regret aught ye did during the time we were apart. I dinna love that I ken the mon who introduced ye to passion, but I also ken I'm nae the one who will live with a reminder just beyond our bailey wall. Besides, having a bride with a little knowledge isnae wholly unappealing."

Catherine barely caught what Rab said at the end. Her mind became mired in imagining inevitably meeting Katherine, likely running into her nearly every day until one of them died. She nodded, but Rab sensed her withdrawal.

"Kitty, do ye remember when I started calling ye that?"

"Of course. Several of us went out for a hunt on foot. Even Catriona was there. None of us foresaw the storm rolling in. It simply appeared. It drenched us within seconds, and we took shelter in that cave. I was shivering so hard I frightened ye. Ye wrapped yer plaid around me and held me against ye side. I said I must look like a drowned kitten, and ye said that ye'd tend to me well past me being a cat." Catherine sucked in a breath as understanding dawned on her. "Ye were trying to tell me then that ye wished to marry me. That ye wished to have me for years to come. I'd merely thought the pet name was wonderful. I didna understand the rest."

"I was. I knew even then that I intended to protect ye and take care of ye until ma last breath. I would shield ye from ma past if I could, and I will do what I can. But I wanted ye by ma side then, and I want ye there now. I want to make ye happy, keep ye safe, love ye."

Catherine nodded. "I want the same, Rab. I always have. I was warm and nearly dry by the time the storm ended, but ye were nearly frozen solid from giving me all yer heat. I feared ye catching the ague from being wet and cold for so long."

"Aye. I have never eaten as much or drunk as much mulled wine as I did when we all returned to the keep. Ye wouldnae cease feeding me." Rab kissed Catherine's forehead. "I thought ye were attentive by nature, but I realize now that Óg was with us, and ye barely spared him a glance. Ye were taking care of me."

"And I always will. I want to make ye happy, keep ye safe, love ye." Catherine stretched again and kissed Rab. This time the kiss drew out, once more loving as they both reminisced as much as enjoyed the present. "I ken Óg realized what was between us because I forgot aboot him."

"This willna please him. What if he signs a betrothal soon?"

"As much as he may try to seem commanding, he'd never agree to marrying me to a mon who is sure to make me miserable. He never could and especially nae now. Besides, it isnae his decision. He will have to tell ma uncle, who will decide. Óg can act on Mòr's behalf to sign the contracts, but he wouldnae dare make the agreement alone." Catherine's buoyant mood deflated as she remembered losing her aunt and cousins once again. Rab lifted her chin and kissed the tip of her nose.

"Are we in agreement that we wish to court?"

"Aye. Are we in agreement that ye will nae hie yerself off to Edinample yet?"

"Aye," Rab grumbled. "I will do as ye wish, but I'm nae happy aboot that part. It doesnae sit right with me."

"And it doesnae sit right that ye end what's been a good relationship if there isnae a reason to."

"I usually admire yer practical nature, but I'm nae so fond of it right now."

"I ken," Catherine smiled softly. "I suppose it's me trying to protect ye."

Rab nodded before looking back at the keep. "We've been out here far longer than I think either of us realizes. Someone is bound to have noticed that ye're gone."

"Aye. But—" Catherine pursed her lips and managed to turn them down at the same time. "Evina Murray is now ma roommate. She kens I slipped off with Edgar more than once. She willna ken I'm with ye, but she'll ken nae to say aught. She'll say that she didna see me awake, or that she didna speak to me. It willna be a lie, but an evasive truth. Seems she's quite good at that. I got the feeling she did it for Caitlyn Kennedy before she married Alexander Armstrong."

"When can I see ye again? I canna court ye in the open."

"True. Nay one can catch us together. Meet me tomorrow eve in the hayloft."

"Is that…" Rab didn't want to know once he began his question.

"Nay. I met him in the garden a few times but never somewhere where we could—recline so easily." Catherine squeezed her eyes shut. "I'm nae saying I suggested the hayloft so we can. But I—"

"Wheest. I understand. It was probably wise of ye with a mon like Edgar. Ye risked a great deal being alone with him. He isnae kenned for his gentleness with women." Rab straightened and narrowed his eyes.

"Before ye start, nay. He was never rough with me. It was passable, and I could have lived with it, but I never enjoyed his touch. But neither did he have to force me. He may nae fear Óg, but I ken he fears Mòr. He never risked his own life by doing aught I didna want. He's too fond of himself for that."

"After the evening meal?"

"Aye. Wait until it's nearly over. I slipped out without waiting for the queen to dismiss us. I canna leave before the other ladies-in-waiting again, or people will talk. When everyone retires, I will slip to the loft."

"Vera well. I dinna care for ye wandering the bailey in the dark."

"Ye can watch the side door I'll use from the stable's entrance. Ye can watch me."

"That makes me feel better."

"I ken, *mo chridhe*." Catherine knew it was the truth when she called Rab her heart. He was. He'd been a part of it for years, and it felt as though it finally beat strongly again.

"*Mo piseag*." Rab stroked the pad of his thumb over her cheek. "It's been too long since I called ye that." When they were in the cave the day Rab gave her the pet name, he hadn't merely called her Kitty. He'd said "my kitten."

They left the orchard in silence, holding hands, passing through the gardens and crossing the bailey in the shadows. They didn't dare another kiss when someone might catch them so close to the keep. They squeezed each other's hand before Catherine slipped inside. Rab waited a couple minutes before entering the castle and making his way to his chamber. He willed himself to believe Catherine made it safely to hers. He fell into a deep slumber once he pulled the covers around his shoulders. His recurring dream of walking through a high meadow with a little boy on his shoulders and a babe tied to Catherine's back made his lips twitch in his sleep. For weeks, nightmares of what his cousins did, or what could have happened if Catherine had been there, plagued him. He finally had a restful night's sleep.

CHAPTER 6

"*M*acLaren."

Rab steeled himself for Andrew's approach as he waited outside the Privy Council chamber. He'd been waiting in the passageway all morning and skipped the midday meal in hopes of keeping him from losing his place. It had done him no good. It was midafternoon, and the chamberlain didn't indicate King Robert intended to summon him that day.

"MacFarlane." Rab kept his tone civil despite all eyes upon the two men. Whatever Andrew had to say, Rab was certain he preferred it be in private.

"Stay away from Catherine."

Rab appreciated Andrew's directness, even if he wanted to shake the man for speaking Catherine's name with so many big ears and loose tongues milling around. He nodded and moved to turn away, but Andrew pressed on.

"I know you listened to us last night. I made certain you did. She has at least two men inquiring aboot her. Do not ruin her chance for a happy life by dragging her down with you."

"And discussing her with me isnae going to do exactly what ye warn me against?" Rab swept his eyes over the people leaned against walls and those grouped together, talking. Plenty of people watched with open curiosity. "Ye could at least keep yer voice down. I heard, and I'm nae disagreeing with ye." Rab planned to be careful not to ruin Catherine amid making her his wife.

"Hear me well, MacLaren. I know what's between you, and it will never work. My father will kill you before he ever lets his only niece marry you. Aught that's between you ends now before you're the one who gets half your clan killed."

Rab straightened from leaning casually against the wall. He stood a fraction of an inch taller than Andrew, so they still stared one another in the eye. "We've already proven we dinna take well to threats. I have nay interest in shedding more blood, enough has already been lost. But I will defend ma people just as ye will yers. Do nae bring Kitty into this and make things worse."

"Kitty? Kitty? You make it worse by using that bluidy name. She isn't your woman to speak so familiarly aboot. Stay away."

"At least pick a mon who can make her happy. She's young and has a full life ahead of her. Dinna think of it as me asking but think of her. Dinna sentence her to misery. She doesnae deserve it. She's lost enough in this lifetime. Dinna take her last chance for happiness."

Andrew's jaw set as his gaze traveled from Rab's boots to his hair. "If you love her as much as you sound like you do, then realize this is her only chance for happiness. I love her like I did—do—" Andrew flinched, unwilling to accept that Fia and Greer could never again tease him, hug him, talk to him. "—My sisters. I will do what's right for my clan, but I will do right by her too. I almost made the gravest mistake by pushing my father to betroth her to Edgar. My bad choices ended up saving her. I won't make the same mistake twice."

"How much longer until ye think the king will meet with me?" Rab nodded toward the door where two guards stood. "I dinna wish to be here when ye announce her betrothal." Neither did he want Catherine there, either. But it would be at least three sennights before they could marry from whenever the banns were first read. He knew he faced waiting at least a month to marry, and that assumed Catherine agreed after only courting for a week. Rab's belly tightened with unease, fear that time was running out, and Andrew might sign Catherine's marriage contracts before he had time to marry her himself.

"You can count on being here at least a fortnight before he sees you." Andrew upper lip curled in smug satisfaction as Rab once more became an enemy he wished to watch bleed before him. "He will drag this out so that, by the time he sees you, you will be the most hated mon at court. He will let the court be your jurors before he passes down your sentence."

"Then he could have seen me yesterday if that were his goal. I'm already the most hated and least trusted mon here."

"But you aren't miserable yet." Andrew sized Rab up once more. Anger and hatred he'd kept under tight rein for Catherine's sake, and to ensure Rab didn't tune him out, boiled over, bringing out his brogue. "Ye willna have to wait for the king if ye dinna stay away from Catherine. I will ensure ye suffer far more than the king can, even if he has his own dungeon."

"Óg, for better or for worse, I willna ever do aught to harm Catherine." Rab felt odd calling her by her given name, but he wasn't interested in antagonizing Andrew any further. Andrew nodded, regaining some calm. He didn't glance back as he walked away from

Rab, leaving the latter to stare straight ahead, hoping he appeared indifferent to his brief encounter with Andrew.

After his confrontation with Andrew, Rab opted to take a tray in his chamber that evening. He refused to miss his rendezvous with Catherine, but he decided absenting himself was wiser than making people wonder if they both disappeared at the end of the night. If he never appeared at the meal, no one would consider Catherine slipped away to meet him. He prayed she wasn't wrong to trust her roommate to protect her reputation.

It felt like hours from when he stepped inside the stables and peered out to when he caught sight of a woman leaving the keep. She didn't look around, though Rab was certain Catherine was aware of everything within the bailey. Her situational awareness had always rivaled any warrior Rab knew, and he was glad for it, knowing that she lived among a lecherous court. She hurried until she reached the stables. He drew back into the shadows once he was certain she'd spotted him. Neither lingered in the doorway, Catherine leading the way to the ladder to the hayloft. She gathered her skirts and scaled the ladder as though she were still a young woman climbing trees. Rab forced his eyes away from her shapely backside as he followed her.

Once they stood away from the edge, their kiss threatened to devour them whole. Gone was the tenderness from the night before. In its place was unadulterated passion. Having admitted their feelings, confessed at least some of their secrets, and agreeing to court, there was nothing left to hold them back. Rab's hands traveled from her waist to her bottom, cupping the round globes. While Catherine wasn't particularly tall, nor was she overly endowed on top, she was curvy through her hips and backside. Rab was certain he'd died and gone to heaven. The thought of having the right, the privilege, to touch Catherine like this for the rest of his life was heady.

Catherine's hands skimmed over Rab's chest to his shoulders before sliding around his ribs and up his back. Every inch she felt was hewn muscle. She marveled at how hard the planes of his body were as he relished how soft she was. She pressed herself against Rab, frustrated when his sporran kept her from what she wanted to feel. Edgar had worn breeks at court, so it left little to the imagination when he was aroused. It had made Catherine want to pull away the first time she felt his length against her mound, but she'd reminded herself that she started the intimacies to woo Edgar into staying in her bed once they married. Now she was eager to feel Rab against her for the sake of being closer to the man she loved.

Catherine pushed Rab's sporran out of the way, her hands gripping his hips. She pressed him toward her as she took a step closer. Her breath caught in her throat at the feel of Rab's manhood against her mons. She had only one other man to compare with, and Rab far exceeded her expectations.

"When we wed, Kitty, the first time may nae be what either of us hopes. But I promise every time after will be pleasurable. I never want ye to be afraid."

"I'm not. I'm—impressed." Catherine didn't know what else to say and wanted to swallow her tongue when understanding flashed in Rab's eyes. He knew she compared him to Edgar, but it relieved him that he exceeded the man's precedence. "Even before that, Aunt Aveline explained what happens between a mon and a woman. I think she suspected our feelings and even hoped something might come of us. I've always believed she talked to me because she wanted to prepare me to be your wife."

Their kiss burst into flames, like the last one had. Rab walked backwards until he found the pile of hay. He drew Catherine down to straddle his lap as he sat on the mound. They moved together, their hips thrusting as Catherine rode him. Both knew the layers of clothes were a blessing, keeping them from going too far, doing something that could never be undone. But they frustrated the couple, nonetheless.

"I've never been afraid of this with you. I can't say I've felt so at ease when I've pictured marrying someone else. But with you, it feels right. It feels as normal as breathing."

"I doubt I should say this, so I should stop if I had any sense." Rab tucked hair behind Catherine's ear. "Never will I have to pretend to be with someone else, to ken when I cry out 'Catherine' into the night it's because I'm with the right woman at last."

Catherine eased back and sat on Rab's lap. "You really picked Katherine as your leman because she has the same name as me?"

Rab sighed as he nodded, guilt plaguing him for the umpteenth time over the two years he'd been involved with Katherine MacLaren when all he thought about was Catherine MacFarlane. "When I decided I wouldnae be a monk anymore, I feared yer name on ma lips, in or out of bed. I canna deny she's an attractive woman. Ye'd ken it for a lie the first time ye meet her. But she has dark hair much like yers, and ye're a similar height. I felt guilty using her when I first started visiting her, but she seemed content to keep things simple. As time went by and I missed ye more and more because she wasna ye, I didna want to give up the fantasy that I was with ye. It's twisted and despicable."

Catherine wrapped her arms around Rab's ribs as she leaned her head against his chest. His steady heartbeat was a soothing cadence. "I've never had a lover, but neither was Edgar the only other mon I've kissed. It was always light pecks, naught that encouraged more. I hoped each time that I could push ye from ma mind. I hoped Edgar could finally make me stop wishing. Instead, he was a poor substitute for the mon I couldnae have. It was ye I imagined. It was ye I could taste, smell. It was yer name on ma mind and far too often nearly on ma lips." Catherine hadn't noticed that her speech lapsed back into sounding like a Highlander, but her emotions were raw as they once more confided in one another.

"Kitty, I'm nae proud of what I've done, and I dinna want to hurt her. Whether ye agree to marry me or nae, I'm riding back to end it with her. I'm nae eager to return to her, and I canna dredge up even a sliver of anticipation to see her again. It's over with her, regardless of what happens with us. I want to end it. I dinna wish to be here, falling even more in love with ye, kenning I must face her. How can I return to a woman who I dread seeing? And she doesnae deserve to find out it's over because I ride into the bailey with ye as ma wife."

"Can ye leave without meeting with King Robert? Even if ye ride as fast as ye can each way, ye will still be away long enough for word to reach him that ye left. He'll never forgive the insult."

"I ken." Rab stroked the hair that hung down Catherine's back. The silky strands with the hint of rosemary brought back waves of memories, ones that he no longer relegated to his dreams. "I will go as soon as I can. Once I have an audience with him, I can always say I must confer with Father and bring back his decision."

"Ye'd lie to the king? Ye said ye'd go to Edinample without Caelan kenning. What happens when he discovers ye lied to the king? What happens when the king discovers ye never saw yer father?"

Rab inhaled a whistling breath and sighed. "Ye're right. I canna say ought to King Robert aboot leaving, and I canna let Father ken I returned home with things unresolved. Hopefully, something will come to me."

Catherine felt her body relaxing as her worry decreased, and Rab's warmth enveloped her. "I shall fall asleep if ye continue to stroke ma hair. I dinna remember the last time I felt this content."

"I wish to hold ye for however long we have. Sleep if ye wish for the rest."

"Nay. I came here this eve to spend time with ye. Awake. I'm nae sleeping through our chance to talk. I want to ken more aboot ye and the mon ye are now."

"There isnae that much to tell, I suppose. I spend most of ma time on patrol, riding the borders. We have been on tense terms with the Campbells for years, but we keep a mindful distance. It didna help that one of our hunters foolishly delivered a message to Dominic without learning from whom it came. He was supposed to be hunting for Father's saint's day and instead thought he might earn a few coins. He came back so shaken after Dominic chased him down, he confessed all to Father. We were fortunate Dominic and Brodie were more concerned with who sent the message than who delivered it."

"I ken things must be even harder right now since we fought alongside them against the MacDougalls and Lamonts. I'm nae sure if Laurel can look in Óg's direction without wanting to spit, but he seems to have redeemed himself in Brodie's eyes with how he fought on the battlefield."

"Aye. It makes it uncomfortable, but we keep to our side of the border, and they keep to theirs. When I'm nae riding there, I'm usually close to the Buchanans. Our ties to the Stewarts of Appin are what's kept yer uncle from attacking, but it may be what makes the Buchanans finally ride for Edinample. They've razed some fields and harassed our farmers, but Dennis Buchanan is here painting a picture that they're the victims. I dinna ken what the Bruce thinks, but much like with the Campbells, we dinna stray from our land. We've caught Buchanan riders each time they cross over, but we dinna kill them, just send them back a little worse for wear."

"It doesnae surprise me that the Buchanans are trying to take advantage. Their laird is a bitter auld mon. Dennis is nay better. He's smug to everyone else while also trying to crawl so far up the king's arse that the Bruce may never sit straight again." Catherine peered in the keep's direction. "Dennis has tried to gain Óg's attention, but blessedly, Óg willna even consider him. He doesnae trust Dennis, and Mòr doesnae trust the clan."

"Keep yer distance, Kitty. He is a conniving mon and wouldnae think twice aboot forcing ye into marrying him by deed or by rumor." Rab tightened his hold around Catherine as she continued to lean against him. She laid her right hand over Rab's chest beside where her cheek rested. His silent strength reassuring her when she didn't want to admit aloud how uncomfortable Dennis Buchanan made her. Andrew was never out of reach whenever the man was nearby. But Rab made her feel safe in a way no cousin ever could.

"Things have been quiet by courtly standards of late. We had some unwelcome excitement while Alexander

Armstrong was here. I'm nae sure if ye've heard, but the Scotts wounded him in battle. He's lost the use of his left arm and has a horrible scar on his right cheek. Somehow, he didna die, but he isnae the same mon he was. King Robert ordered him and Angus Elliot to appear at court since they were both involved in the battle with the Scotts. I dinna ken the details or what the king decided, but it angered the Scotts enough to hire gallowglasses to go after Alex."

"At court? The bollocks on Laird Scott," Rab mused.

"Aye, well, it turns out it 'was Sullivan, nae the auld laird. The auld laird is dead, and Sully is rotting in the king's dungeon. His cousin is now laird, and it seems he's prudent enough to stay far from the Armstrongs and the Elliots."

"I suppose where the Armstrongs go, the Kennedys now travel alongside. Innes has been loyal to the Bruce since the king was merely an earl. After what I learned happened with Cairren and the Munros, I doubt King Robert can afford to anger Innes ever again."

"He canna. Anyway, after Caitlyn and Alexander married and left, we came to find out that a few of the gallowglasses followed Caitlyn through the keep while she was with some of us, then they chased her when she was alone. It was scary to ken they were so intent upon getting to her they followed a group of ladies-in-waiting."

"Were ye in danger?"

Catherine felt the tension building with Rab. "Nay. I dinna ken all the details, but someone or other told me the leader was originally a Highlander or a Hebridean. I dinna ken which, but he doesnae allow women to be targets. These men defied him, and I'm pretty certain they are dead for it. But it was scary kenning they were here and nearby."

"Tell me the truth, Kitty. How dangerous is it here?"

"I always have ma guard up. I dinna go many places alone, and I never leave the bailey without at least two MacFarlane men to accompany me. But that's the case anywhere but at home. Some men are too forward at times, but between how often Óg has been here during the last year and discovering I carry more than one dirk, I dinna feel in danger."

"I noticed the bow ye carried." Rab smiled even though Catherine couldn't see.

"It's the only one I use. It's both painful and comforting to have it. It hurts kenning, or rather it did hurt to believe, I wouldnae see ye again. At the same time, it was a comfort to have something that was once yers that ye gave to me. I still have the ribbons, Rab."

At each gathering, he'd bought her ribbons for her hair and for her gowns. She kept them in the false bottom of her jewelry box. She gazed at them each day, running her fingers over them to where spots were nearly threadbare.

Rab leaned back and reached into his sporran, withdrawing two ribbons. One was a canary yellow and the other a shimmering teal. It was obvious they weren't freshly cut from a spool; instead, slightly discolored spots showed where the material had thinned. Catherine recognized the cause because they resembled the ones she'd touched over and over as a comfort and reminder.

"I bought these the day everything went wrong. I'd planned to give them to ye after we talked to our lairds; one to say I love ye, and one to celebrate our official courting. Before I could, I was chasing down ma father as he bellowed for our clan to break camp and saddle up. I couldnae search for ye because ma father mounted and was ready to leave. I tried to tell him I had something I had to do, but the look he gave me told me he knew I was talking aboot ye. I was ready to argue with him, to disobey him, but then ye rode past sandwiched between Mòr and Óg."

"I stomped on Óg's foot and tried to knee him in the bollocks to get free of him and to find ye. But Mòr tossed me onto Timber's back. I considered sliding off the other side, but ma aunt's expression warned me nae to. I never imagined watching ye mount yer horse as I rode out was the last time I'd lay eyes on ye in three years. I never imagined I'd spend three years believing that was ma last chance to ever see ye." Catherine ran the back of her fingers over the bristles on Rab's left cheek. "Ye ken I planned to say aye, even if Mòr hadnae agreed under better circumstances."

They sat in silence for several minutes, both trying not to think about the time lost, but neither avoiding their thoughts.

"Kitty, Óg kens there's something between us. If he isnae watching me, then he'll be watching ye. Are ye certain this is a wise place to meet? What if a stable boy says something to him or he hears aboot it from someone else?"

"He'd likely skelp ma arse and run ye through. But I willna let him find out. I think he may ride back to Inveruglas in the next day or two. Ye ken both the Keith and a MacDonnell of Keppoch are interested in ma dowry. He'll have to speak to ma uncle before he can make any offers or accept them. Since it's aboot the same distance there as it is to Edinample, it'll take him two-and-a-half days each way. We likely have a sennight without him interfering."

"And if he returns with yer uncle's permission to sign contracts? Or worse, what if he arrives with signed contracts?"

Catherine flinched. She wanted to believe Andrew took her feelings into consideration and would tell her uncle about the men's interest but recommend that it go nowhere. However, she couldn't be certain, definitely not now that Andrew was motivated to keep her from Rab.

"Without a betrothal ceremony, they are but pieces of parchment. I willna speak any promises."

"And ye ken that as the woman ye dinna have to. Either Andrew could do it on yer behalf."

"And nay priest in Scotland will marry an unwilling woman. Unwilling is an understatement for what ma temper will be. Besides, Mòr kens what ma father wanted for me. He canna promise a loving marriage like ma parents had, but he kens Da wanted me to marry a mon who honors me and respects me. Neither the Keith nor the MacDonnell are like that. They merely want ma dowry and someone to tup. Mòr kens that too. Neither the Keiths nor the MacDonnells of Keppoch can offer much beyond a bride price. The Keith laird likely took interest to thumb his nose at Edgar since the Keiths and Gunns dinna get along."

"And allying with the MacDonnells of Keppoch will help yer uncle keep us at bay. He might ally himself with another of our rivals. Does he plan to marry Óg off to the Buchanan's daughter?"

Catherine hesitated since she'd heard her uncle suggest that very thing more than once. She hadn't understood Andrew Mòr's interest until now.

"So he has. And is Óg willing?"

"Nay," Catherine snorted, then giggled. "Óg thinks she has a face like a plow ass, is long in the tooth, and is as bright as one. Poor lass sounds like a braying ass too."

"Yer uncle might consider that MacDonnell more closely than ye think."

"He willna. Da couldnae stand the mon after he insulted Mama at a gathering. He'd haunt Mòr until his last day if ma uncle wed me to that mon. It surprises me that Óg is even entertaining the suggestion."

"Mayhap yer uncle thinks more aboot yer clan's safety than he does his dead brother's wishes for a lass." Rab's sympathetic gaze took the edge from his words.

"I dinna want to think that. I'd rather believe I'm right until I'm nae. Otherwise, it's too scary, Rab."

"I ken, *mo piseag.*" Once more they fell into silence as Rab held Catherine against him, and she brushed her fingertips along his beard. Neither minded the quiet, both lost in thought but enjoying the companionable silence. They eventually dozed off until a horse whinnied. Catherine stirred when Rab jumped. They gazed toward the window opening in the loft and noticed the dark black sky of night had lightened to the deep sapphire of predawn. Rab descended the ladder first, lifting Catherine down the last few rungs. Sticking to the building's shadows, they crept to the door Catherine used earlier that night. Without a word, she guided him to the ladies'-in-waiting floor. He watched her dash to her chamber with only a soft click of the handle to announce she'd entered. He wound his way through the keep until he reached his bachelor's quarters. Much like the previous night, his years-long recurring dream took the place of his more recent nightmares, and for the first night since he arrived, he didn't wish to ride out with the sun's earliest rays.

CHAPTER 7

*A*ndrew watched Catherine fight the urge to swipe her fingers over her eyes yet again as he approached her in the bailey. He'd seen her bloodshot eyes when they spied one another during Terce, and he'd seen her attempt to stifle her yawns during the morning meal. He'd even watched her act as though she were brushing away an eyelash, the hint that she wished to rub her eyes. On his way to the lists, Andrew decided on the detour since he needed to speak to his cousin, anyway.

"Óg," Catherine greeted him with a smile, albeit a weary one. "Good morning."

"Is it?" Andrew cast her a speculative expression and watched as she stiffened, a wariness added to her weariness.

"I slept poorly."

"Slept poorly or not enough?"

"Both. You've given me much to worry aboot. You can't deny it's enough to be troublesome both when I'm awake and when I'm asleep."

"Worry? Catherine, no one has finalized aught. I said they were interested in you. I'm obligated to

79

present them to Father, but it doesn't mean aught will come of it."

"You seemed hopeful two days ago, and I've seen you speaking to both representatives."

"Aye. I'm negotiating, but Father has the final say."

"And if he listens to you and marries me to one of them?"

"Then he won't have listened. Catherine, I'm trying to balance what's right for the clan and what's right for you. They're the only two who have stepped forward of late. I can't ignore that."

Catherine watched Andrew, biting her tongue to keep from blurting that there was only one candidate he should consider. Staying with Rab later than they intended exhausted her, and she'd tossed and turned once she went to bed, worrying about what might not work out. She was grateful that the court rose much later than people in villages and rural areas. She didn't have to appear until Terce, which was nearly midmorning. She was disinclined to argue with her cousin, so she remained quiet.

"Catherine, I'm riding back to Inveruglas tomorrow. You know that means I'll be away at least a sennight. I know you feel comfortable with him, but do you feel safe with his men around?"

Catherine cast Andrew a dumbfounded expression before scowling. "Of course I do. He'd never let his men do me harm. I can't believe you're worried aboot that or that you'd ask me such a thing. You should be more relieved that he is here and will keep me safe, regardless of what you think. It's not he who I feel uncomfortable around. Liam Oliphant has returned, supposedly because he's announcing his marriage to Margaret Hay. He makes my skin crawl. I'm not fond of Dennis Buchanan either. He'd like naught more than to trap me into marrying him to gain an alliance with our clan.

The Buchanans will do naught for us but make our troubles worse with the MacLarens. You should be silently grateful that you can travel without fear of what you'll return to."

"Och, I fear plenty of what I will return to. As long as you two are together here, I trust neither of you to have the sense God gave an ant. Neither of you can see the woods for the trees. You will only make the strife worse if word travels back to Father or Laird MacLaren."

"Then be sure that it doesn't, Óg. Do not redeem yourself at my expense."

"I never would. That hurts." Andrew whispered the last two words, and Catherine recognized the genuine emotion in his gaze. She'd seen it before when he thought of his mother and sisters.

"I'm sorry. I shouldn't have accused you of that. I don't envy your position any more than you envy mine. Just please don't mention Rab and me to Mòr. I know you'll have to say he's here, and Mòr is no fool. He'll know I'm aware Rab came to court but use discretion."

"I will. But in turn, please don't jeopardize your actual future with hopes of one that can never happen." Andrew wrapped Catherine's arm around his as he escorted her to where the other ladies-in-waiting were awaiting the queen and their morning constitutional. "I want you to be happy, Catherine. I can't promise it, but I will do what I can to help you marry a mon worthy of you."

"Thank you, Óg. I love you too." Catherine grinned as she kissed her cousin's cheek, then grimaced. "And if you want to find a lady who will come to your bed without being paid or screaming the roof down, shave this bluidy beard. It's like kissing a boar's arse."

"I shall miss you too, Cousin." Andrew returned the

kiss, rubbing his beard against Catherine's cheek on purpose. She swatted at him. "Save me a dance this eve."

"I will, Óg. Now go train. You can at least swing one sword today, if not both. And don't tsk at me. I got my sense of humor from you and your friends." Catherine released her arm from Andrew's and offered a genuine smile before he turned away. While she thought they might have made some progress toward Andrew not recommending the Keith or MacDonald lairds with any sincerity, she couldn't be certain. He'd matured as a politician since his debacle with Edgar and the Mac-Dougall brothers. She wasn't certain she could read him as well as she once had.

Catherine fell in step between Sileas and Catriona, but she wished she could walk at the back of the group once she heard Agnes Buchanan's voice. She was the lady her uncle suggested her cousin might marry. Her voice did remind Catherine of a braying donkey, loud and nasally. The young woman glanced over her shoulder at Catherine several times as she gossiped with Evina. Catherine knew where the conversation headed since the woman took an interest in Catherine.

"Did you notice him and his men this morn? They shoveled their porridge like a farmer shovels shite. Uncouth beasts."

"They may not fit in well, but they've kept to themselves," Evina hedged. "Other than table manners, or their lack of them, they seem like ordinary Highlanders come to pay their taxes."

"Come to pay their taxes?" Agnes screeched. "They slaughtered her family." Agnes pointed at Catherine. "They defiled her aunt and cousins, and they're coming for my family and me next."

Catherine's temper snapped. Propelled forward with a rage unlike any she'd felt since first learning of the women's death, she drew back her hand. The slap she laid across Agnes's cheek seemed to ring in her ears.

"Be grateful it was ma palm and nae ma fist, ye bitch." Catherine didn't notice her burr, and she wouldn't have cared if she had. "Dinna ever use ma family's loss to make ye the victim. And nay mon is coming within a hair's breadth of ye unless it's to grind yer teeth back like a horse ready to be put out to pasture. Gawp at me like a beached trout all ye want. I've heard enough men say they wouldnae fuck ye even if they were the ones getting paid, so ye can lay yer fears to rest that anyone will molest ye. Ye'd have to gouge their eyes out and fill their ears with dough before they'd even fondle ye. But ye can go fuck yerself."

Catherine stood before Agnes, who'd gone deathly pale. Catherine cocked her eyebrow in a challenge far too many people in her clan would have recognized and warned anyone away.

"But—but—you—you..." Agnes stammered.

"Speak. Ye sound like a bluidy seal barking." Catherine leaned forward until their faces were nearly touching. "Naught to say now? I give ye fair warning, Agnes Buchanan. Use ma family again to make yers sound better, to make someone pity yer worthless arse, and ye will find out that nay mon in ma clan has a temper worse than mine. I will challenge ye, and I will kill ye. Ye are a Highlander, but ye are without honor."

"I didna mean ye any harm." Agnes was so shaken that her own brogue came back. No one had ever heard the woman sound like the Highlander she was. "I meant them, those MacLarens. I—I shouldnae have mentioned yer family. Please dinna kill me."

Catherine thought the woman might pish herself by the time she was through, but Catherine was certain she'd made her point to Agnes and the other women she'd caught whispering about the MacLarens and their attack on her family. In her mind, she defended Rab as much as she did her aunt and cousins' memory, but she could never speak his name aloud. It made her even more cognizant of the divide between the two clans. Her belly ached as she thought about whether there really was any possibility that she and Rab could make a future together. Could she forsake the family she stood before Agnes defending to become part of the family that nearly destroyed hers? Could she live among the enemy, tolerate them, or feel safe with them?

Catherine backed away from Agnes and took her place between Sileas and Catriona once more. She remained silent for the remainder of the walk, relieved the queen hadn't witnessed her vent her spleen. The group was subdued until they returned to the keep.

"Catherine," Catriona whispered. She canted her head toward an alcove. The women held aside the tapestry and entered the small, recessed space. "If you hadn't threatened to run her through, I'd have done it for you. I'm sorry you had to listen to that. I know it's not the first time. I might not have insulted her quite so harshly, but I think—for what it's worth—you did the right thing to take a stand. It won't stop if you don't."

Catherine nodded as she fought against the tears that once more pricked her eyelids. When Catriona's eyes darted to the tapestry and she shifted uncomfortably, Catherine's tears seemed to flee, and trepidation took their place. "That wasn't all you wished to say."

"It's not. Catherine, I found out my uncle sent a missive to Laird MacLaren to suggest Rab and I marry."

Catherine felt as though the world around her warped and nothing was in focus. She knew Catriona and Rab had known one another since they were children. She couldn't deny that the marriage benefited the MacLarens, though she couldn't figure how it helped the Douglases, unless it was to antagonize the Campbells. It felt like a genuine possibility that she was talking to Rab's future wife, and she wasn't talking to herself.

"Catherine, I'll never agree. That mon has loved ye since ye tossed him that apricot. He didna even notice I was with ye." Catriona lapsed into her brogue as she remembered sneaking out of the orchard while Catherine spoke to Rab and Douglan watched. She'd seen the way Rab watched Catherine, a mixture of interest, bewilderment, and physical attraction. It hadn't surprised Catriona to watch the pair become a couple who many thought might marry. "Ye're ma friend, and so is Rab. I'd do aught that I can to help ye. I simply dinna ken what that is."

"Thank ye. I dinna ken that there is aught that can be done. I willna lie and say it doesnae break ma heart. I've loved him for as long as I've kenned him. I canna help but think mayhap the Lord kenned I wasna meant to marry Laird Gunn. Mayhap He intervened, but I also dinna ken if He means for me to be with Rab."

"I've seen how ye look at one another since he arrived. Wheest—" Catriona pulled Catherine into her embrace. "Nay one else has because they dinna ken what to watch for. But I've kenned ye both a long time. I remember how it was, how I think it still should be. But ye must be careful. If anyone realizes ye share feelings for one another, it will obliterate yer reputation. Worse yet, it may get Rab killed. It's exactly the type of excuse, that he's corrupting ye or seducing ye, that someone can use to challenge him. It willna be Óg, I dinna think. But a mon who'll claim he wishes to court ye might."

"I ken." Catherine appreciated Catriona's support, but she didn't dare share her secrets with anyone. She refused to volunteer that she and Rab were courting, and she would never confess that they planned to marry. Despite being shaken by Agnes's comments and mindful of Catriona's cautioning, she found herself even more resolved than ever that they would marry. She returned Catriona's embrace, then they slipped out of the alcove as cautiously as they entered. They returned to the other ladies who milled around the bailey.

Rab stood in the ring of MacLaren men as two of his guards trained against one another. From his position, he watched Catherine and Andrew as they walked together. He'd turned his attention back to his men until Cullen nudged him. He looked toward the gardens in time to watch Catherine stalk forward and swing her arm. He could imagine the force she used since the woman, who he recognized as Agnes Buchanan, swayed and took a half step back before covering her cheek with both hands.

"What do ye think she said?" Cullen whispered.

"Something aboot Aveline, Fia, and Greer. That's the only thing that could make her react like that. I almost pity the foolish woman. She's probably being challenged to single combat as we speak."

Cullen glanced at Rab, then the men they stood among before looking back at the garden. "Ye ken we all wish things had worked out differently back then and now. Most of the clan believes if ye two had married like we all wanted, none of this would've happened. Ye may love one another, but yer marriage is what would've made people happy. It could've brought us peace."

Rab stood in stunned silence. None of his men ever approached the subject of Catherine and him. He hadn't realized anyone in the clan still thought about them as a potential match. He wondered what else people talked about, of which he was unaware.

"I overheard Óg talking earlier to the Keith mon he's been chewing the fat with lately. He's leaving in the morn for home." Cullen turned toward Rab, so his voice didn't carry. "Whatever Agnes said to Catherine isnae what she'll tell Dennis. She will be the victim, and Dennis'll seek his own sort of justice. The kind that involves hurting Catherine."

"I ken. I already deduced as much. I have to speak to Óg."

"Or ye can watch out for Catherine."

"Ye ken I'll do that anyway, but he needs to ken. In case aught happens that I canna prevent, he needs to ken that his men should be with her always."

"When will ye talk to him?" Cullen turned to where the MacFarlanes trained. It was nearly across the lists, but both clans were aware of one another's presence. Rab followed Cullen's gaze and found Andrew looking back at him. He tilted his head toward the keep, then glanced back over his shoulder in Catherine's direction. When he turned back at Andrew, he canted his head toward the keep again. Andrew's chin jerked down before he said something to one of his men.

"I suppose now," Rab answered. "Keep them occupied."

Rab made his way out of the lists, returning his blunted training sword to the armorer. He walked toward the undercroft, hoping Andrew watched him and followed. Once he was in the shadows, he raised both hands like he had the first time he spoke to Catherine's cousin. He didn't want the man suspicious that Rab intended to stab him in the dark.

"What?" Andrew demanded.

"Kitty and Agnes had some kind of disagreement. One bad enough that she slapped Agnes. Hard. Ma mon

Cullen heard talk that ye're leaving for Inveruglas tomorrow. Take Kitty with ye." Rab hated the suggestion, but he hated Dennis Buchanan and the man's perverted sense of justice more.

"Ye think Buchanan will seek her out."

"I dinna doubt it for a moment. At best, he'll trap her into marriage by making it appear that he compromised her. But either way, he will make her pay. Ye and I ken the mon he is. He's just like…" Rab raised his chin and met Andrew's gaze. "I canna do to him what I did to them. But I can ask ye to protect her. Take her home with ye."

"I would if I could. The king and queen are hosting some royal emissary from France. Queen Elizabeth will put her ladies on display, and she will want to present the largest entourage she can. She won't let Catherine miss it." Andrew jaw set and his lips pursed and pressed together. "I can't delay my trip either. I do not loathe your clan any less and have found no more respect for you, but Catherine and ma father are all I have left. I have enough humility and enough sense to know no one will protect her better than you while I'm away. Do not take advantage of this. It isn't an invitation to woo her. Keep her out of harm's way."

"Óg, ye ken I love her. I told ye before, I willna do aught to harm her. What I wish for will never be more important than keeping Kitty safe." Rab shook his head. "I ken ye hate it when I call her that, but I canna help it. It's how I think of her."

"If only you weren't a MacLaren."

"If only she wasna a MacFarlane." When Andrew bristled, Rab chuckled. "Settle, Óg."

"I'm trusting you when everything that's happened says I shouldn't. But I also trust Catherine's judgment. You're who she will turn to if aught happens. Be sure you're there if she does." Andrew moved to step away, but Rab grabbed his arm. Before Andrew could yank it away, Rab released him.

"Always."

The two men stared at one another before they went their separate directions.

⁂

"MacLaren."

Rab was quickly becoming sick of hearing his own name. If every head didn't turn in his direction when people heard it too, he might not mind. But it was impossible to remain inconspicuous within the pit of vipers when people kept announcing his presence.

"Douglas." Rab nodded and tried to continue walking past Maxwell, but the man stepped into Rab's path.

"I've gotten word back from your father."

This gave Rab pause. He hadn't realized Maxwell Douglas was in touch with his father. It boded poorly for Rab. "And?"

"He agrees a match with Catriona is advantageous to both clans."

"Catriona? She'll never have me." Rab attempted to keep the surprise and fear from his voice. He knew his father viewed a chance to ally with the Douglases as a boon, and he already knew why Maxwell took an interest in him and the MacLarens.

"She knows she hasn't a say."

Rab crossed his arms and leaned back on his heels. He knew he didn't intimidate Maxwell since they were still the same size, but he made sure the man knew he wasn't some sapling that bent to Maxwell's will. "She'll have plenty to say at the altar, and it willna be vows and pledges of love."

"She doesn't have a problem with you or your clan.

You've known each other for years. Your mothers are friends."

"Were friends. And that's why she willna have me. She will argue I'm too much like a brother to be a lover. Besides, she willna want to come to such a small clan as ours. She kens her duty here is to find a far more useful match than me."

"Her duty is to do as she is told."

Rab snorted. "When has she ever? As savvy as ye believe ye are, Catriona is a far better politician than any mon here. It will take naught but the right whispered words in her father's ear or yer other brother's to undo what ye're trying to arrange. Save yer time and yer energy. Find her a match she will agree to."

Rab wasn't lying. He'd described Catriona accurately, and he hoped that his childhood friend held true to her past disposition. He didn't wish to find himself walking down the aisle to meet one of Catherine's friends as his bride.

"Don't be so quick to discount what this can do for your clan. One day you will be laird. You won't care who warms your bed if she came with a healthy dowry and a clan willing to fight alongside you."

"Be sure to include that in our wedding toast. I'm certain Catriona will appreciate that sage advice." Rab shook his head and clapped Maxwell on the shoulder. "If she already kens of yer plans, post guards at her door. She'll run home before ye can even saddle yer horse to chase her."

Rab walked past Maxwell, praying he'd been dismissive enough for the man to believe pursuing a match between Rab and Catriona was futile. When he glanced up, he spotted Catherine and Catriona watching him. Catriona's annoyed expression confirmed what Rab warned, but Catherine's stricken one made him want to run to her and assure her that he never intended to marry Catriona. He might have laughed at Maxwell's suggestion, but Rab knew, from a distance, it likely appeared as though he agreed with Maxwell.

Catriona wrapped her arm around Catherine's and nearly dragged her into the keep. The glare she shot Rab spoke louder than if she'd screamed for him to follow them. Catriona steered Catherine toward a flight of stairs while tugging her sleeve before urging her into a music room. Only moments later, Rab appeared, closing the door softly behind him.

"I'm nae marrying him, Catherine. And there isnae a chance that he wishes to marry me." Catriona saw no point in prevaricating. "Ma uncle can suggest all he wants, but he kens ma father and our laird listen to ma counsel as much as they do ma uncle's. I willna agree to accept Rab, so there is naught either ma uncle can do."

Catriona squeezed Catherine's hand before patting Rab on the arm as she walked past. When she reached the door, she paused. "Catherine, I stand with ye against Agnes. But Rab is who can protect ye from Dennis."

Catherine watched as her friend disappeared, then shifted her gaze to Rab. They met halfway, Rab's embrace engulfing Catherine's smaller frame.

"What did Agnes say aboot yer aunt and cousins?"

"How did ye ken?"

"I watched ye slap her from all the way in the lists. I already asked Óg to take ye with him to get ye away from Dennis. He says he canna because of some guest the king and queen are expecting."

"Ye talked to Óg?"

"Aye. He kens things arenae over between us, but he worries more aboot ye than he does trying to keep us apart right now. He kens ye need ma protection, and he kens I willna hesitate to offer it."

"I wasna even thinking aboot Dennis when I lost ma

temper with Agnes. Bluidy hell. I dinna even want to show up for the evening meal."

"Then dinna. Stay in yer chamber and out of sight. Can ye make an excuse?"

Catherine bit her lower lip as she considered her choices before nodding. "I think I can. But, Rab, I'm nae missing ma chance to be with ye tonight." Catherine's earnest expression melted Rab's heart, even if it didn't ease his fears. He pressed a soft kiss to her mouth as she wrapped her arms around his neck.

"I have breeks. I'll wear those and meet ye at the end of yer passageway. Without ma plaid, I willna be so recognizable. Wear something plain, and we might even pass for servants once we're off yer floor."

"Aye." Catherine returned Rab's kiss, but it was over far sooner than either wanted. "We canna linger here. I need to find the Mistress of the Bedchamber and make ma excuses."

"I'll eat in the Great Hall this eve. I'll make sure people notice me enter and leave with ma men."

"Vera well. Be careful, Rab. I catch the rumors. I dinna believe them, but they scare me."

"I ken, *mo piseag*. I will take care. I willna let aught keep me from ye, least of all me being foolish and letting ma guard down."

"Then I will meet ye an hour after everyone retires." Catherine kissed Rab's cheeks and hurried to the door. It took only a moment for her to disappear, and Rab spied no trace of her as he left the music room. He made his way to the passageway leading to the Privy Council chamber, where he took a spot against a wall. He knew the king wouldn't see him that day, but other people would. He figured if he kept just visible enough, no one would link him to Catherine. However, he doubted the wisdom of his thinking when Dennis Buchanan entered the passageway.

CHAPTER 8

*R*ab appeared to gaze straight ahead of him, but he watched Dennis from the corner of his eye. He'd never liked the man and had always avoided him, especially since he persuaded his father to support the MacGregors when they began encroaching upon the MacLarens after the Campbells annexed MacGregor land. The MacLarens and Buchanans were on the cusp of an outright feud, and Rab refused to be the catalyst for bloodshed.

Dennis merely shot Rab a smug glance as he sauntered past, and the chamberlain admitted him to the Privy Council chamber immediately. Rab silently cursed as he continued to wait. He could only imagine the stories Dennis attempted to fill King Robert's head with, and how they were at the MacLarens' expense. His only consolation was Dennis didn't appear upset when he entered the chamber, so Rab assumed he hadn't spoken to Agnes yet. He couldn't say the same for the man's temperament when he left the chamber, storming down the passageway. Whatever the Bruce told him hadn't sat well with Dennis. Rab's belly tightened, knowing that once Dennis spoke to Agnes, his temper would boil over, and he would set his sights on Catherine.

"MacLaren," the chamberlain boomed. Rab pushed away from the wall and straightened his sporran. He approached the smaller man and clasped his hands behind his back. "The king bids you to wait elsewhere until he summons you. He is disinclined to grant you an audience at present. The disturbance your presence creates displeases him. Go sulk elsewhere." The pugnacious little man attempted to peer down his nose at the much larger warrior.

Rab turned on his heel, annoyed at the man, annoyed that his time was wasted, and annoyed that the king summoned him to court only to toy with him. As he left the passageway, he rolled his shoulders back and considered his choices. He could remain in a foul mood, or he could assess the situation as a boon since it wouldn't force him to endure so many people's scrutiny as he stood alone. He returned to his chamber to write a missive to his father, updating the laird on the lack of progress. He also shared the more damning rumors he'd heard, not because there was anything his father or he could do, but more a forewarning of what might happen once their punishment became public.

The first two people he caught sight of when he entered the Great Hall were Dennis and Agnes. It took little to realize Dennis was even more irate than he was when he departed the Privy Council chamber. As Rab drew closer, he watched Agnes point toward the ladies-in-waiting, who were taking seats at their tables. Rab watched what he was certain were crocodile tears stream down Agnes's cheeks as she whined to Dennis.

"Then she slapped me," Agnes wailed. Rab forced himself to keep from interjecting that Agnes deserved it and had she been a man, she'd be in a shroud by now.

"Where is she?" Dennis demanded as he leaned

around Agnes's shoulder. His sister turned back to her peers, her brow furrowing.

"I don't know. She was with us earlier."

"She will pay her penance; worry not, Agnes."

"She humiliated me."

"And you were a right piece of work to start," Catriona interjected. She turned to Dennis. "She's lucky she isn't a mon because you'd be paying for her funeral right now. She said despicable things, cater-wauling that the MacLarens intended to attack her. She shouldn't have mentioned Catherine's family. She crossed a line from which she cannot return."

"I didn't say aught that wasn't true."

"Truth or not, you henwit, you shouldn't have said it. You might find sympathy with your brother, but you won't find any among us." Catriona crossed her arms, challenging the Buchanan siblings. Rab watched from a discreet distance, impressed with Catriona's willing-ness to not only stand up for Catherine but to face Dennis to boot.

"Don't stick your neb in other people's business, Lady Catriona. It's likely to get caught along with the rest of you."

Catriona laughed before pointing to several people. "By all means, threaten me, Dennis. But if I wind up with even one hair out of place, my family and our al-lies will wipe the Buchanans from this earth. You may be from one of the auldest clans in Scotland, but I'm from one of the most powerful. Maxwell may be my only uncle here, but do not forget who my other uncle is. The Black Douglas is quite fond of me." Catriona turned away but paused and looked over her shoulder. "And don't forget, my aunt was a Stewart. Stay away from Lady Catherine. I extend my family's protection to her."

Short of tossing in the name Campbell, Catriona

had just reminded everyone within earshot that she hailed from the families with the closest ties to the crown and helped to defeat the English. She hadn't exaggerated that her family would rally behind her. James "the Black" Douglas was not only her other uncle, he was the laird of her branch, which dominated the entire clan.

"You are in no position to offer her aught but some ribbons and frills," Dennis countered.

"Do you wish to wager on that?" Catriona lifted her chin with an arrogance that could only come from the niece of one of the most powerful men in the realm. "Even breathe in her direction, and we will see who is more respected here at court. And Agnes," Catriona shifted her gaze, "pipe down. You haven't any words or a voice anyone wishes to hear. Lady Catherine didn't exaggerate. You sound like a braying ass and have as much sense. I have been here longer than you, and I will marry before your family can ever sell you off. Do not doubt that whomever I marry will come from a clan worth allying with the Douglases, and I have a long memory."

Rab continued to observe, pondering whether he should draw Catriona away before she got herself killed, but far too intrigued by what she might say next to move. A man approaching the trio caught Rab's attention. Andrew came to stand beside Catriona, who offered him a warm smile. It gave Rab pause as he watched his childhood friend and his nemesis. There was something between them he'd never noticed before. He wondered if it was what Catriona and Andrew both witnessed between Catherine and him.

"Buchanan." Andrew nodded and quipped, "Never a pleasure. Keep your sister away from my cousin." Andrew wrapped Catriona's arm around his and escorted her to a table, where he bowed as she sat. He didn't linger but cast a brief glance at Rab. Their eyes locked, and Andrew offered a terse smile. Both men knew Dennis could do nothing to Catherine now, but neither man put it past Dennis to arrange for Catherine to have some accident or for some tragedy to befall her. He prayed for Catherine's sake that he cooled his heels and licked his wounds but did nothing more. He prayed for Catriona's sake that Dennis misstepped. He didn't doubt Catriona spoke the truth, and Maxwell and the Black Douglas, along with the young woman's father, would hold no compunction about retaliating. It would solve one of Rab's neighborly problems.

"Catriona stopped at ma chamber before she retired," Catherine said in her relaxed burr as she pulled the plug from a flask containing summer ale Andrew brought back from his last trip to Inveruglas. "She mentioned she exchanged words with Dennis and Agnes. She warned I was the safest woman in Scotland or the one most in danger. I assume she was as plain-spoken as ever."

"Ye could say that. She made it clear that ye arenae to be touched lest yer attacker wishes for the House of Douglas and the House of Stewart to rain down hell-fire." Rab accepted the mug Catherine poured as they whispered in the hayloft. "Óg was there toward the end. He kens I heard it all. From the look he gave me, we agree Dennis will nae muddy his hands now. But neither Óg nor I put it past Dennis to dupe someone else, or even pay someone else, to get revenge."

"I wish I could take back slapping her. Nae because I repent but because I've made ma life far harder than need be. If Dennis werenae here, I'd likely go back for a second round with Agnes, mayhap even drag her out for single combat like I threatened."

"Dinna underestimate Agnes, Kitty. She's still a Highlander. She kens how to wield a dirk to protect herself. I'm certain Dennis and her father made sure of that before she came to Stirling."

"I'll gladly keep ma distance." Catherine reclined against Rab's shoulder as he wrapped his arm around her waist. They sat in the hay pile like they had the night before. They'd shared a brief and heated kiss when they stepped into the loft, but both desired time to talk and merely be together as much as they desired physical intimacy.

Catherine shifted to rest more on her side, so she could see Rab's face more easily. She'd considered whether it was wise to ask the burning question she had. She concluded it wasn't, but she did it, anyway.

"Rab, what didna ye want me to ken that first day in the stables? What did ye do to them?"

"Kitty, please dinna make me answer. I never want ye to ken what I'm truly capable of. I dinna wish for ye to ken the monster I can be."

Catherine sat up. "Ye believe I would stop loving ye for it."

"I fear it will scare ye enough for exactly that to happen. If nae scare ye, then disgust ye enough. I didna want anyone but ma father and the handful of men who went with me to ken. It's bad enough that the Bruce and Óg ken. I have nay guilt for what I did, but I feel guilty that anyone else shares those memories."

"Whatever extreme ye went to, why? Why nae simply hang them or behead them and be done?"

Rab set his mug aside and laced his fingers with Catherine's, bringing her hand to his chest. "Because ye could have been there. They could have done those vile things to ye. They would have. They would have done it to destroy me as much as to destroy yer family. It's never been a secret how I feel aboot ye, even when people ken I've been with Katherine for two years. I didna ken until this morn that people still wish we'd been able to marry. Cullen shared that."

Rab used his other hand to tuck hair behind Catherine's ear. His touch was so gentle that it might have been a butterfly's wing. He gazed into Catherine's blue eyes, his heart burning as she returned his gaze with such patience and openness.

"They never accepted it was by chance that I was born to the aulder brother, and I will inherit the lairdship. They acted as though I'd done it to spite them since they were all aulder than me. Their father pitted them against one another as soon as they were all auld enough to enter the lists. He encouraged their rivalry and taunted them when I bested any of them. He fueled their resentment because he resented ma father being the aulder brother. I've long suspected ma uncle was Cain, and ma father was Abel. It was only the clan's steadfast loyalty to ma father since he was a wean that kept ma uncle from killing him. He kenned if he did, he would be the next mon buried, never having the chance to be laird. I may wish a flood washes away every MacGregor who has stepped on our land, but I'm grateful one of them killed ma uncle. He likely would have been our ruination."

"Rab, do ye think yer uncle had aught to do with why the feud broke out? Do ye think he instigated it against ma clan?"

"I thought that for a long time, but nae anymore. At least, I dinna think it was him personally. He was a sickly mon shortly before his death. I think he rode into battle to die with what he thought was the last of his honor, or mayhap hoping to find some honor. It was only three moons after the gathering, and the trouble persisted well past that."

"Yer cousins?"

"That seems more likely, probably at ma uncle's behest. But, at the same time, I canna picture them razing our fields or killing our own people merely to blame it on yer clan. They had an endless list of sins, and I dinna put such vile ideas past them. However, they kenned it was too easy for ma father and me to learn if they were involved. Nay one would have kept that secret for them. So I really just dinna ken."

"What made them decide to raid?" Catherine's voice rasped as she asked what had practically burned a hole in her mind.

"I dinna ken that either. Mayhap it was merely because they learned Mòr and Óg were on the mainland hunting. I dinna think they did it for the clan. I think they did it for their own perverse enjoyment. They enjoyed hurting animals when we were weans, and ma father punished them more than once—taking a lash to them himself—when they were too rough with women at the alehouse. They had nay concept of right and wrong, only to fight to get what they wanted at any cost. I witnessed it with ma own eyes. The more brutal they were in battle, the more attention ma uncle paid them. Even after ma uncle died, they used brutality to compete."

"That's why they did what they did."

"Aye, Kitty. And that's why I did what I did."

"Please, Rab. Tell me. I dinna want this secret between us for the rest of our lives. I worry ye think ye canna tell me everything, and I dinna wish to wonder what ye're hiding. Whatever ye did, ye did it as much for me as ye did in the name of justice. Ye've practically said as much."

"All the more reason nae to tell ye. I dinna want ye

ever to feel responsible for ma choices." Rab hung his head and shook it. "Please dinna ask me."

Catherine stroked back hair that hung over Rab's face before cupping his jaw. She shifted to straddle him as she had the night before. Her kiss was a balm to Rab's soul. It was loving and patient, supportive and tender.

"I willna press ye on this because I see how it pains ye. I dinna wish to cause more. But we've never kept secrets. Nae when we were younger, and certainly nae now. We both confessed things the first chance we talked. I ken I feel better for it, and I think ye do too."

"Aye. I will do all that I can to never keep aught else from ye, Kitty. I trust ye with all that I have and all that I am."

"I ken. I feel the same. Rab, I never felt this way toward ye, but I had so much rage inside me. I hated everyone who bears the MacLaren name, even yer mother. Nessa has never had aught but a kind word for me. But I loathed her because, somehow, she hadnae stopped them. I blamed everyone in yer clan for letting yer cousins ride out. I blamed yer father for nae having more control, and I thought him a weak mon and worthless leader. I couldnae stop thinking that if ye'd been laird, it never would have happened. I wished ill things upon Caelan, certain that if ye became laird, the feud could end. I felt so raw and brittle. I wanted to go home, but Queen Elizabeth refused. I believe she thought she offered me mercy, so I wouldnae have to see where it happened. But it only made the pain worse. I've never seen their graves. I've never said goodbye, and I never got a last chance to tell them I loved them as though Aveline was ma mother, and Fia and Greer were ma sisters. Mòr and Aveline raised me. I lost ma mother twice over."

"I understand. What they took from ye is yet another thing I couldnae forgive."

"Mòr is hardly a sentimental mon. He was always loving toward Fia and Greer, but he wasna affectionate like ma father was. I suppose that comes from Mòr being laird while ma father was free of constant scrutiny. I kenned he was fond of Aveline, but I hadnae realized how deeply he loved her until she died. We didna ken if he'd survive the loss. He shut himself in his chamber for a sennight. Óg told me he only accepted three trays in that entire time. Óg feared he might find himself an orphan before that sennight ended. From what he told me, it took several moons before Mòr could say Aveline's name without having to excuse himself. Óg says nay one ever sees Mòr cry, but his eyes are permanently bloodshot."

Rab rested his hands on Catherine's thighs, giving her time to share her grief. He doubted she'd talked to anyone about her feelings, not even Andrew after he bore the horrible news.

"I think Óg still sees it. I think he still sees riding into the bailey and finding Fia half bare and bleeding in the bailey. She was already dead. Mòr fought to get to Aveline while Óg searched for Greer. He heard her screaming near the postern gate. He saw—he saw yer cousin—raping her. He—he tried to get to Greer, but he was too far away before Albert slit her throat." Catherine sobbed, having spoken one of the assailant's names for the first time since the attack. "Mòr watched Alfred stab Aveline in the heart before he—he pulled away. He grinned at Mòr as he lowered his plaid. Benedict was already in the boat and putting the oars in the water. Albert and Alfred made it out with a few of their men. They never looked back at the ones they left behind."

"Those men who returned with ma cousins died for

their sins, locked away in a forgotten cell in our dungeon. Their last meal was the one they ate before they left Edinample."

"Rab, I dinna think Mòr will ever recover. Óg says he appears to age a year by the day. Hatred for yer people is all that keeps him going. Óg says he thinks his father would already have joined his mother and sisters if it werenae for his need for retribution." Catherine fell forward against Rab's chest, and his arms enclosed around her. "I love Óg. He was a tether when I felt like I would blow away. I regret I wasna there to comfort him, and I dinna think I ever have been much comfort. But as much as Óg helped me, having ye hold me finally makes me feel like I can live through this. I have felt so lost and alone until now."

"Kitty, *mo ghaol*, I wish I could lift yer grief from yer shoulders and yer heart. I wish I could bring yer family back. I canna do any of those things, but I can always be by yer side." Rab kissed the top of Catherine's head as he called her his love. "I will tell ye what I did."

"Ye will?" Catherine sat up.

"I dinna ken if hearing the details will console ye at all, but I need ye to ken yer family didna die without consequences. Yer loss weighed heavily on me, and I couldnae—still canna—forgive Albert, Alfred, and Benedict for what they did. Ma father sentenced them all to banishment; however, he gave me his dirk. But I alone chose how. Each mon who rode out on that raid is burning in hell. It was ma father's blade that was ma tool. I want to claim what I did was in the name of justice, but it wasna. It was revenge. I tortured them until their last breath, Kitty. I—I—"

Rab swallowed, bile rising in the back of his throat. He doubted whether he could go through with telling the truth. He drew a ragged breath before continuing.

"I had them bound and gagged, then dragged behind

horses for five miles. I made sure nay one from the keep found us. I made them strip off their clothes. They knew there was nay where to run, so they did naught. The men I brought encircled them. I—I—had a broomstick. I used that to do to them what they did to those women, to yer kin. I listened to their howls of agony and spat on them. I took any dignity they might have clung to and stripped it from them. I beat them for falling to their knees and laughed at their pleas for mercy. I gelded them and made them hold their own bollocks. I unmanned them before ma father's dirk cut them open to tear out their innards. They were still alive when the horse ripped away their limbs. I left their entrails to lure the predators that ate them. I went back three days later, and there was little left of their carcasses."

Rab waited for Catherine to scream as he described the most heinous deeds he'd ever committed. He expected her to push away from him and run. He held his breath as he awaited the tirade of disgust and loathing. But nothing came.

"Good." The single word unleashed a torrent of emotions for Rab. He pulled Catherine back against him, and she wrapped her arms around his waist as his body trembled. He'd held that secret and planned to take it to his grave. He'd been unable to release his anger that still gnawed at him night and day. It had terrified him to tell Catherine lest she reject him once they finally found one another. He shuddered as he finally felt the last of his burden float away.

"Ye dinna think me wicked and despicable?"

"Rab, I understand why ye didna want to tell me. I never imagined ye doing such, but I also ken ye to be a mon who believes in honor and justice. I ken ye to be a mon who is loyal and devoted to yer clan. I ken ye were nae only protecting me but any and every woman.

They wouldnae have stopped with only ma kinswomen. I doubt that was the first time they had overpowered women and took what wasna offered. Mayhap I wouldnae have done exactly what ye did, but I canna deny part of me is happy to ken they suffered. Does that make me wicked and despicable? I ken it's nae for me to pass judgment on any mon's actions or his soul, but I also hope they burn in damnation until the end of time."

"Ye can still look me in the eye?" Rab's throat still felt tight and raw, and his heart pounded against his ribs. Catherine cupped his jaw and lifted his chin.

"Nae only can I look ye in the eye, but I plan to look into them for the rest of our lives."

"Kitty, I love ye. There is naught I wouldnae do to protect ye, and regardless of whether Mòr or Óg want it, that extends to those who ye love too."

"I ken, *mo chridhe*. Ye dinna ever have to speak of this to me again. But I am glad ye did. I think ye needed to unburden yerself, and I think it was a secret too heavy for ye to bear alone. Ye said the other day that ye wish for me to be at yer side as yer partner. That's what I'm doing now."

"Kitty, will ye marry me?" Rab held his breath, praying he hadn't chosen the wrong moment to press Catherine for a decision.

"Aye. I dinna ken if the mon I once kenned would have done something like that, but the mon I ken now is still the mon I love."

Their kiss was passionate as they clung to one another. Catherine leaned back as Rab shifted to hover over her. His hand kneaded her breast as hers glided down his back to his chiseled buttocks. She hummed as she felt the muscles shift when he pushed his sporran out of the way before settling some of his weight onto her. Her body pinned her skirts around her, but she widened her legs enough for him to fit. His rod pressed against her mound. Their feverish kisses threatened to consume them as Rab pushed Catherine's skirts to her knee. Frustrated, she yanked them higher as she wriggled to free them from beneath her. They grinned at one another, sharing in their impatience. But Catherine's eyes drifted closed as Rab's fingers brushed the inside of her thigh.

"Touch me," Catherine whispered as Rab kissed the length of her neck.

"I dinna plan to stop." Rab swept his forefinger along the crease where her thigh met her hip before running it through the dew gathered at her juncture. "This eve, it is ma finger. But once ye're ma wife, it will be far more."

"I want naught more than for that day to come." Catherine murmured against his ear before nipping at his lobe. With a teasing growl, Rab pressed his finger into her entrance while his thumb sought her pearl. Catherine's hips moved in time with Rab's fingers. She bent her leg left, forcing Rab to shift more to his side. Her hand dove under his plaid, where she found what had intrigued her since she was four-and-ten. She'd wondered all those years ago what a man's body was like beneath a plaid. It was soon after that she wondered about a specific man's body.

As her hand wrapped around Rab's length, he groaned, telling himself over and over not to thrust, not to be too eager. But Rab's dreams had comprised this very moment too many times for him not to relish in it. When he'd been with Katherine, he'd always ensured it was dark, and he'd kept his eyes closed. He'd encouraged her to remain quiet, so he could concentrate on imagining he was with Catherine. Now he wanted to hear every sound, every breath Catherine took. He watched her intently as she moved toward her release.

When her back arched and her body tensed, he was certain the blissful expression she wore was the most enticing he'd ever seen. Too wrapped up in the pleasure of watching Catherine, too consumed with the desire to join with her, he felt his own climax wash over him. He thought for a moment that it might embarrass him to spend in Catherine's hand. However, it was something he had fantasized about for years, so he couldn't find a moment of discomfort, only his own bliss to match hers.

Rab rolled over, bringing Catherine with him. They rested together as Rab pulled hay from Catherine's hair. He kissed her crown over and over as her hand stroked his chest. "Kitty, the chamberlain told me the king intends to make me wait several more days for an audience. I hate leaving ye here alone, but I must ride back to Edinample. I canna put off ending things with Katherine. I also need to find a village where we can post the banns. Will ye promise me that ye will stay near Catriona the entire time I'm gone?"

"Aye. And while it likely willna please ye to hear this, Dominic and Emelie are coming to court. King Robert insisted a Campbell attend while the French delegation is here. From what I gather, Brodie can still barely say the Bruce's name without turning scarlet. The mon holds a grudge."

"Nay. I'm nae thrilled aboot that, but Dennis willna do aught if ye're standing with Dom and Emelie. Between the Douglases and the Campbells at court, they're likely better protection than I can ever be."

"Dinna say that. I will never feel safer than I do with ye." Catherine tightened the arm she now draped around Rab's waist. "When will ye leave?"

"Before daybreak. If the weather holds, then we can be at Edinample by the following night. I'll see Katherine, end it, and be back on ma horse within an hour."

"Ye canna be serious that ye will ride that far, dump such news on a woman who likely believes ye really will marry her—or at least continue yer relationship even after ye marry, then ride off easy as ye please."

"I have told her countless times that I will never marry her, and I've told her I will always be faithful to ma wife. In ma heart, I never ceased believing that would be ye. I will never stray from ye, Kitty. I've waited too damn long, wanted ye too damn much, ever to leave ye for another."

"I ken, Rab. But be careful. A scorned woman is more dangerous than any armed warrior."

"I'll heed yer warning. I'd guess ye've seen more than one here at court."

"So many I've lost count. It rarely ends well for the mon involved."

"Will ye lie here with me for a little longer?"

"I'd lie here all night then hop on Bolt's back behind ye if I could."

"Ye'd ride in front." Rab waggled his brow. "That way I can hold ye."

"Then ye owe me a ride." Catherine's suggestive mien told Rab she wasn't thinking about Bolt.

"Soon enough, Kitty." They kissed before settling back into the companionable silence they enjoyed together. Neither dozed that night, both wanting to savor each minute together before Rab rode out the next morn.

CHAPTER 9

*A*fter two days of hard riding, Rab reined in Bolt at the edge of the forest that bordered the outskirts of Edinample's village. He dismounted and handed his reins to David and studied the other men.

"I ken ye wish to visit yer families. If it wouldnae alert ma father, then I'd say make yer visit quick. But we all ken why he canna find out I've been here. I willna be long." Rab nodded before jogging toward a croft set on the far side of the village. When he reached the croft's door, he listened for a moment. When there was no noise, he knocked and entered.

"Rab." Katherine MacLaren brushed strands of chestnut hair from her forehead as she wiped her hands clean of the dough she'd been kneading. "I hadn't expected ye."

Rab walked farther into the cottage but grasped Katherine's forearms before she could wrap them around his neck.

"I'm only here to speak to ye."

"Miss me that much? We dinna usually do much speaking," Katherine purred. The sound irritated Rab in a way it never had. He didn't want a reminder of what they used to do, either.

"Katherine, I came to tell ye that things must change between us."

"What?" Katherine's face dropped, and a hard edge entered her gaze. Rab recalled of what Catherine warned him. The woman in front of him was quickly becoming an angry, spurned former mistress. "Yer father has said naught aboot ye being betrothed."

"Nor would he. Katherine, I just ken it isnae right to continue as we have. It's nae fair to ye when ye're young and should find a mon to settle down with."

"I—I thought—"

"Katherine, I told ye from the start," Rab interrupted. "I can never marry ye."

"I think ye might believe differently now." Katherine placed her hands on her belly, pulling her kirtle taut. The rounded bump that was hidden only a moment ago was now obvious. Rab stared. It took what felt like forever before he looked up at Katherine's beaming face.

"I took care to never sire a bastard, but I also kenned there was always a risk. I dinna want a child with that stigma, but I still canna marry ye." Rab's tongue seemed to stumble as the words flew forth. Part of his mind railed at him for rejecting his child and the woman who carried his bairn. But a larger part of him refused to relinquish his dream of marrying Catherine when they finally felt so close to realizing it. Even if Catherine hadn't reentered his life, he knew duty dictated he marry a woman who wasn't from his village.

"Who is she? Some tart ye met at court?" Katherine's tone had a bite Rab had never heard before.

"Ye've kenned from the beginning that I will marry a woman from another clan. Ma marriage must make an alliance."

"But what of yer child? Things have changed now that I'm having a bairn."

"They have, but nae in the way ye're hoping. I'll provide for ye and for the bairn. Always." Rab's heart pounded as he listened to himself. Something niggled at the back of his mind, which made him continue to refuse Katherine. But a very noisy part of his mind bellowed at him for rejecting Katherine and the bairn.

Am I that selfish that I'm willing to put wanting a life with Catherine ahead of the life of ma bairn? But something isnae right aboot this.

"Katherine, how far along are ye?" Rab watched as Katherine leaned away, as though she might try to move beyond his reach.

"Aboot four moons."

Rab's mind scrambled to recollect what happened four moons ago that made him reckless enough to have gotten Katherine pregnant. Nothing came to mind.

"Katherine, I must go. I swear to ye that I'll provide for our bairn. I'll acknowledge the bairn as mine, and our child will have every opportunity he or she can as the future laird's child."

"Every opportunity that a bastard can have, ye mean." Katherine's eyes filled with tears. But Rab recognized a note of desperation that didn't seem to come from fear for the child's future.

"We'll decide more when I return from court for good."

"What is there to decide, Rab? Ye're abandoning me, and ye're abandoning yer child. Never mind that everyone will brand me a whore for carrying yer bairn, but ye'll ruin his life before he's even here."

Rab paused. "Ye believe the bairn is a lad?"

Katherine shrugged. Rab ran his hand through his hair, doubting whether he could walk away from Katherine as cavalierly as he'd planned only moments ago. He was stuck. He feared disappointing Catherine or ending the chance they had for a future. But having an illegitimate child might do that, regardless. He didn't want Catherine to face a child who was his, but not hers for the rest of her life. He knew the precarious future any illegitimate child had. A daughter would find it difficult to marry, but a son faced harsh treatment among the other warriors. And an illegitimate son would have to watch a younger brother inherit what could have been his.

"Changing yer mind?" Katherine asked as she stepped closer to Rab. In his distraction, he was unprepared for her to press her body against his. He jumped liked a scalded cat.

"I dinna ken. This changes things, and I canna deny that."

"Stay and we can talk."

"I canna do that. I must return to Stirling immediately. Things arenae resolved there." Rab glanced down at Katherine's belly and nearly reached out to touch the protrusion. As the idea of a child—his child—penetrated deeper into his mind, he grew less certain that he could set Katherine aside. He marveled at the idea that he'd helped create a new life, even if it wasn't with the woman he wanted. "I will return as soon as I can."

Rab looked back at Katherine, who watched him as he walked out of the croft. He jogged back toward the forest but stopped short.

Four moons? I was riding the Campbell border for nigh on six sennights. I wasna anywhere near Katherine. That's what I was trying to work out. Even if she were only three moons, it couldnae be mine. I was riding near the Buchanans, then hunting for a fortnight. What the hell?

Rab turned around and sprinted back to Katherine's croft. He burst through the door and nearly pitched forward as he took in the scene before him. He hadn't been away ten minutes, but Katherine hadn't returned to baking after he left.

"Douglan?" Rab stared at his brother as he scrambled to grab his plaid that lay at the foot of Katherine's bed. His younger brother rolled from the mattress as Katherine pulled the covers up to her chin. "Ye're bedding ma leman. Ma own brother."

Rab turned his attention to Katherine as he stalked forward. He crossed his arms as he glared at her. "That's his bairn, isnae it?"

Katherine darted her eyes between the men before nodding.

"Rab—"

"Shut yer gob, Douglan," Rab snapped. "Ye've just seen her bare as the day she was born, so ye kenned long before I did that she's with child. Ye planned to let her pass yer bairn off as mine. Ye planned to let yer bastard be ma heir. Do ye plan to kill me to become laird, then have yer child take the lairdship afterwards? Or were ye merely going to deceive me, Da, Mama, and our entire clan?"

Rab was so stunned that he didn't realize he'd reverted to calling his parents by his childhood names for them. He stared at the couple, but as the seconds ticked by, he realized he was neither hurt nor angry. He was relieved.

"It wasna like that, Rab. We didna want to hurt ye." Douglan stepped around the bed and approached Rab with caution.

"Hurt me? Did ye think I agreed to marry Katherine? Did ye plan to continue the affair once she and I wed?" Rab watched Douglan, knowing his younger brother better than the man knew himself. "Ye did. Well, ye're a right pair. Ye deserve each other. Since ye're the spare, Douglan, there's nay reason ye canna marry Katherine and make yer bairn legitimate."

"Rab—" Katherine spoke up.

"Nay. Dinna speak ma name. Dinna try to convince

me of aught. But I will thank the pair of ye. Ye made breaking things off with Katherine so much easier. I dinna need to feel a moment of guilt for walking away from a pregnant woman. Ye can have each other."

Rab marched through the door without looking back. He was nearly to his horse when Douglan caught him. Douglan grabbed Rab's arm and yanked. Rab whirled around but didn't strike back as Douglan expected. Instead, Rab laughed.

"I came here to break things off with Katherine. Ye both tried to trap me, but ye ken the same as I do, I could and would never marry her. Ye ken I couldnae because she doesnae bring the dowry or connections a laird's wife must have. And ye ken I never would because she isnae the right one."

"I dinna understand how ye're nae angry. I didna set out to betray ye, Rab. But I ken I have."

Rab stood, watching his brother as he tried to sort through his emotions and thoughts. They raced between wanting to launch himself onto Bolt's back and ride away to trying to understand why he didn't want to bash his brother's head in for betraying him. But once more, the only thing he felt was relief.

"Douglan, Katherine is a beautiful and seductive woman. I dinna fault ye for being attracted to her. I suppose I should be livid and feel betrayed, but I also ken ye, little brother. Ye arenae the type to covet what I've had. If ye're involved with the lass, it's because ye care for her enough to choose her over me. I understand that."

"I love her, Rab."

"But does she love ye? She must have been bedding us at the same time."

"Never both of us when ye were here." Douglan glanced away. "Nae that, that makes it any better. We didna want to humiliate ye by having people ken she

114

wanted me over ye. She thought to end it with ye, then we could make it seem as if we got together once she was nay longer yer leman. But then the bairn." He shrugged. "It wasna aboot tricking ye or trying to pass ma bairn off as yers. I ken ye dinna want an illegitimate child any more than I do. But if everyone kenned she carried ma child when she was still yer leman, well, nay one would come out unscathed."

"People must already ken ye're tupping her."

Douglan grasped Rab's leine. "Ye may have tupped her. Ye may have fucked her. But that isnae what's between us. I am going to marry her, so dinna ever speak that way of ma wife again."

Rab swatted Douglan's hand away and adjusted his leine. "At least, ye have some loyalty to one of us."

"I dinna understand why ye arenae furious. Why were ye coming to break things off? Father received a missive from Maxwell Douglas aboot Catriona, but Father hasnae said aught aboot ye marrying. Have ye found someone else at court?"

Rab lifted his chin and set his jaw, challenging his brother to say aloud what Rab was certain Douglan had deduced. Douglan shook his head.

"Nay, Rab. Ye will get both of ye killed."

"Ye love yer Katherine, and I love mine."

"But ye're the heir, like ye said. Ye must marry to make an alliance nae make a feud worse."

"Then wee brother, ye should prepare to be laird one day. If Father disinherits me, then ye'll be in charge. If he doesnae disown me or kill me, then we might actually have a truce with the MacFarlanes. Father doesnae wish to attack them ever again, and he was always fond of Kitty. He willna wage war against her people once she is one of us."

"Mayhap. But Mòr willna think twice aboot wiping us from this earth. And I canna say that I blame him.

The mon canna be expected to lose yet another kinswoman to us."

"Ye make it sound as though I'm going to force maself on Kitty and drag her to the altar at knifepoint."

"That's how he'll see it nay matter what the lass tells her uncle."

"Dinna tell Father I was here, and dinna say a word aboot Kitty and me. But ken that they willna stop me this time."

"What of yer duty to the clan?"

"I'm nae stepping aside. Father will have to put me aside. Marrying Kitty might be the one thing that ends this feud. If Father and Mòr canna come to a truce, the king willna allow it to continue once we're bound by marriage."

"And what has the king had to say so far?"

"Naught. I havenae seen him."

"Bluidy bleeding hell, Rab. Ye left court without even meeting with the king. Are ye trying to ruin us all? We're unlikely to have any land left after he adjudicates against us, and we'll be worse off than the MacGregors if ye marry Kitty with nay one's consent."

"She and I are both of a legal age to marry. If Mòr and Father, and even King Robert, canna accept it, then like I said, ye'll be the next laird. But if they have any sense, they'll realize that rather than fighting one another, we'd do well to fight alongside each other against those who harry us both."

"Buchanans?"

"Aye. And the MacGregors. The MacFarlanes and the Campbells are allies, so they are the MacGregors' rivals too."

"But we arenae on great terms with the Campbells. That'll put Mòr in the middle."

"We havenae been on safe ground with the Campbells because of the MacGregors. If we ally with the

MacFarlanes and, in turn, with the Campbells, then the MacGregors will have to look elsewhere for land. Let them go to the Buchanans."

"Ye seem to have thought of everything."

"I had plenty of time during ma ride here."

"Rab, I'll always stand beside ye and Kitty. Ye two should have married three years ago. Father willna be pleased, and Mother willna be able to show how ecstatic she'll be to have Kitty as her daughter-by-marriage at last. But the clan still wishes ye two could marry."

"Cullen told me that the other day. I had nay idea."

"The only person who doesnae realize why ye took Katherine as yer leman is Katherine herself. Everyone kens ye've been pining for Kitty. It didna surprise anyone when ye chose a woman with the same name and the same dark hair. It's also how I kenned ye could never have serious feelings for Katherine. It's always been Kitty."

"It has, and it always will be."

"Ye should go before someone spots us."

"Does Katherine really nae ken? I assumed she figured it out from the start and accepted it."

"I'm certain she suspects it. But she hasnae accepted it. What woman wants to ken the mon bedding her wishes she were someone else? It's easier nae to."

"It was never ma intention to hurt her, even if I kenned I used her."

"Neither she nor I are saints considering what we just attempted."

"True. But I'm glad she has ye, and I'm glad ye love the lass ye'll marry."

"What will ye do?"

"Douglan, I canna tell ye. If ye ken, Father will only blame ye for nae telling him and stopping me."

"Likely. But dinna come back without Kitty as yer wife. If ye do, ye'll never get another chance with her."

Rab nodded, and the brothers embraced. It was hardly the brief trip home Rab planned. As he joined his men, he watched Douglan make his way back to Katherine's croft. He mounted Bolt and guided the men through the forest to a spot where they could make camp at the edge of MacLaren land.

"What was that aboot?" Cullen asked as they tethered their horses. "We watched Douglan come out of Katherine's croft, and he barely had his plaid wrapped around his waist. How is he still breathing?"

"Dinna concern yerself with what goes on between ma brother and me," Rab warned. Cullen raised his hands and stepped back.

"Ye ken we're loyal to Douglan, but ye will be our laird one day. Our loyalty is to ye before him."

"What happened is our business, and we are both happy with the outcome. That is all ye need to ken. Ma brother and I are as close as we have ever been, and I am happy for him." Rab patted Bolt's neck before placing his bedroll beside the fire. He quickly organized the men into watch shifts and was asleep before the first man posted.

Even more weary and covered in dirt than they were when they arrived at Edinample, Rab and his men tied off their horses in front of the monastery in the village of Dunblane. It took the men a day and a half to ride to Dunblane, but it was only an hour to Stirling. Rab shook his plaid, attempting to knock some of the dust from the wool. He smoothed his hands over his hair and tugged at his leine's neckline.

"Nervous as a virgin," Cullen teased.

"Why are we stopping?" The youngest guard, Herbert, asked.

"I have something to do." Rab's piercing, ice-blue eyes bore into Herbert until the younger man glanced away. "Cullen, with me."

Rab trusted no one in the group more than Cullen. They'd known each other since before either could walk or talk. Their mothers shared stories of their heated hair tugging matches as babies. Rab always teased that he'd clearly won since Cullen started balding in their early twenties. He hadn't explained the purpose for their visit home or to the chapel, but Rab knew Cullen suspected why he'd seen Katherine and why they were now searching for the village priest. He also assumed Cullen had worked out why Rab wasn't angry at his younger brother, despite what they'd all seen.

"What names will ye give?" Cullen whispered.

"I must give our real clan names, or the banns willna be official. But I'm going to use our middle names." Rab and Cullen grew quiet as a young man stepped out of the sacristy. Rab wanted to run. He recognized the young priest, and after the initial shock, he doubted finding success at this chapel.

"Rab MacLaren?"

"Aye, Michael. Pardon me, Father Michael." Rab locked eyes with the former Sutherland warrior. He'd known Michael as long as he'd known Lachlan Sutherland, since the priest was Lachlan's cousin and Laird Hamish Sutherland's nephew. They'd competed against one another as adolescents at gatherings, but he hadn't seen Michael in years. It was clear why not as the tonsured priest approached.

"What brings you to Dunblane Monastery?"

"I need a priest. What brings ye to Dunblane? Ye're far from Sutherland."

"That I am. I was at an abbey for several years, but with my training done at Cambuskenneth and neither Maude nor Blair still at court, I accepted this assignment. Why do you need a priest?" Michael watched Rab, then glanced at Cullen, a deep crease forming between the priest's brows.

"I'd like ye to post the banns for me to marry."

"Here?" Michael blurted before recovering himself. "Why not at Edinample or the lass's home?"

"That's nae possible."

Michael once more glanced at Cullen, who'd taken a discreet spot several pews back from where Rab and Michael stood talking. Michael ran his eyes over Rab, noticing the travel stains and how Rab's tired eyes drooped.

"Who do you wish to marry that no one can ken aboot?" Michael inhaled a sharp breath as soon as he finished speaking. "Have you been at court?"

"Aye."

"Lady Catherine? Yer da and her uncle will skelp yer arse. Laird MacFarlane will geld ye, and yer father will hang ye upside down by yer toes until the blood drains out of yer eyes."

"Ye might live near the Lowlands, but ye still tell a tale like a Highlander," Rab quipped after Michael lapsed back into his brogue. "But ye arenae wrong. That's why I came here."

"To a small village far enough from Edinample or Inveruglas that nay one kens ye're here. But close enough to Stirling for Lady Catherine to appear each Sunday. Do ye wish to wed here too?"

"That was ma thought."

"And she agrees?"

"I didna pick Dunblane until I was only a few miles from here. But, aye, she kens ma plan to find somewhere close to Stirling but far from our clans."

"Things are still that bad?" Michael expression grew regretful as he watched Rab, recognizing the determination in the warrior's stance and gaze. He'd seen the same when he met his cousin Maude's husband, Kieran MacLeod. The man barely knew Maude when Michael met him, but it was clear from the moment Michael watched Maude and Kieran together that the man was determined to marry Maude. Unfortunately, Michael was far from convinced that Rab and Catherine could have the happily ever after his cousin had with Kieran.

"Aye. Politics pulled us apart and has kept us apart for three years. We arenae willing to risking losing the rest of our lives together. Only a marriage in a kirk will work. The king or the pope can overturn a handfasting or marriage by consent. A priest's blessing and an entry in the parish records is what we need."

"Do ye have three sennights to wait?"

"Likely nae, but I will make it so." Rab shifted uneasily but caught himself. He crossed his arms, hoping pretending to be self-assured might make him feel that way.

"Ye ken it's three Masses, nae strictly three sennights. Usually, it's the Sunday Mass when everyone gathers and can hear them. But Sunday isnae the only day I perform Mass. We have All Hallows Eve on a Sunday followed by All Souls and All Saints this sennight."

"Do ye mean ye could them read sooner?" Rab straightened from the end of the pew he leaned against. "I could marry Catherine in less than a moon?"

"I think that's likely advisable if ye wish for nay one to tell yer father and her uncle." Michael swept his eyes around the nave before gesturing for Rab to follow him into the sacristy. The priest drew forth a tome and flipped it open to a half-written page. "What names do ye give?"

"Clyde MacLaren and Eloise MacFarlane."

"Ye ken that I will have to use yer full names in the marriage registry?"

"Aye. Robert Clyde MacLaren and Catherine Eloise MacFarlane."

"I nearly forgot yer name is really Robert," Michael chuckled.

"And I nearly forgot to call ye Father." Rab grinned as he watched Michael dip a quill into an inkpot and wipe the nib on the side. The former warrior cum holy man was quick to record the names.

"I must warn ye that this is irregular, and nae because of how close together I'll post the banns. This isnae either of yer home parishes. The point of the banns is to prevent clandestine marriages, and I'd say this is exactly what they're meant to keep from happening. Yer families and the king could still contest the marriage."

"Catherine has lived in Stirling for three years, and I'm here until King Robert sees me. At the rate I'm going, it might be a decade. Dunblane is within the burgh of Stirling. Couldnae we argue that any parish within the burgh could be our—or at the vera least, Catherine's—home parish?"

"I wouldnae stake ma place in heaven on it, but I could make a sound argument for it. However, nay one from court ever attends Masses here."

"Can we worry aboot that if someone stands against the marriage?"

"I suppose, but I'm giving ye fair warning." Michael paused as he considered an alternative. "Have ye heard of a marriage license?"

"A what?"

"It's nae something the Church speaks of often, but to discourage marriages by consent and recognizing there are myriad reasons that make reading the banns difficult, the Church can issue a marriage license to make the union legal if a couple canna observe the appropriate period of waiting."

"And how much does the Church ask a mon to donate?" Rab cocked an eyebrow, returning Michael's grin as the priest shrugged.

"We need a new roof."

"I think nae, Father." Rab laughed loudly. "I'm nae putting a roof over yer head or this cathedral."

"I suppose I shall have to go back to praying for that. Rab, the bishop willna be happy that I suggested this, nor will he be happy when he learns I issued one for twenty pounds."

"Twenty?" Rab stood gobsmacked.

"Aye. Do ye have any idea how much the ladies at court spend for one gown? Some pay upwards of sixty pounds. Ye are in Stirling now, as ye already pointed out."

Rab stood, aghast. Twenty pounds was nearly a fifth of the money he'd brought to pay his clan's taxes. He already knew it would cost the MacLarens far more than the one hundred and five pounds he'd brought for the levies to pay reparations to the crown and the Mac-Farlanes. He couldn't afford to spend even a portion of it on a marriage license.

"We shall have to wait for the banns to post," Rab conceded as they left the sacristy. He looked at Cullen, who appeared as regretful as Rab felt.

"Could Lady Catherine…?"

"I willna ask her that," Rab objected. He knew Catherine would pay the fee if she could, but he didn't want to begin their marriage by spending whatever allowance she might have saved.

Michael nodded. "Then I will read the banns on Sunday and the two holy days. Ye can still wed in a little over a sennight. But ye must be present, and it's best if Lady Catherine were, too. It helps make this appear as though Dunblane is now yer home parish."

"I pray she can leave court each morning."

"I pray the same." Michael made the sign of the cross before Rab, who dipped his head and followed suit, moving his hand in tandem with Michael's. "Godspeed, Rab."

"Thank ye, Father." Rab genuflected to the cross above the altar before he and Cullen rejoined the men outside. Rab mounted Bolt and led the men back to Stirling, arriving as the bells rang for the evening meal.

CHAPTER 10

*C*atherine watched Rab ride into the bailey as she crossed the castle's expansive square. She walked beside Emelie Campbell and her husband Dominic, who carried their infant son, Nic. It was obvious Emelie was expecting again as she waddled with each step. She and Emelie hadn't been close while the latter was a lady-in-waiting, and she wasn't close with Emelie's younger sister Blythe, but Blythe was always kind to her. Andrew asked Dom to watch over Emelie while he was away since she'd known Dominic, and his brother, Brodie, for most of her life. She felt comfortable with him, and she discovered she enjoyed Emelie's company now that neither viewed the other as a rival.

Catherine noticed how exhausted Rab appeared, his leine an off-shade of beige after traveling for so many days. Dirt covered his boots, and mud splattered his legs. He was still the most handsome man she'd ever seen, and she longed to dash across the bailey to launch herself into his arms. Their eyes met, and Rab dropped his chin. It appeared deferential, but the excitement that entered his gaze told Catherine the trip was a success. She glanced toward the stable's roof, certain Rab followed her gaze. When she glanced back, one side of his mouth twitched. She recognized that expression too. It was one they'd shared many times over the years when they wished to sneak away at gatherings.

"MacLaren," Dominic greeted Rab when it was inevitable that they crossed paths.

"Campbell." Rab dismounted and handed the reins to a stable boy. He bowed to the two women. "Lady Emelie. Lady Catherine."

"It's nice to see you, Rab," Emelie offered despite her husband's deepening scowl.

"The same to ye, Lady Emelie." Rab shifted his attention to Lady Catherine. "Lady Catherine, I hope ye are well."

"I am." Catherine tempered her smile. "I've enjoyed Emelie and Dominic's company while my cousin has been away. They've kept an otherwise uneventful time entertaining." Catherine looked over at the babe, Nic, and waggled her eyebrows. The little boy cooed and gurgled. "I've made a new friend."

"Campbell, might we have a word?" Rab's need to know Catherine was safe outweighed his wariness around the Campbell laird's younger brother. He was certain Dominic knew more about anything Dennis plotted than either of the women. He also knew Dominic was no fool and had already figured out that something still existed between Rab and Catherine. He'd been on the hunting trip when Rab christened Catherine with her pet name. He'd seen Rab give Catherine bouquets of wildflowers after the women's archery tournaments.

"Aye." Dominic agreed, but it was obvious he didn't wish to step away from his wife. He watched the Campbell guards, who surrounded the trio, and the MacLaren men, who arrived with Rab. He handed the babe to Emelie and moved out of the circle with Rab.

"Ye ken, dinna ye?"

"That something is still between ye and Lady Catherine? Aye. Neither of ye can hide yer twitchy smiles. What do ye want?"

Rab ignored Dominic's bluntness, both mildly annoyed and amused that Dominic described their expressions the same way Andrew had. "Andrew must have spoken to ye before he left. Ye ken Buchanan isnae pleased with Kitty. Has he done aught?"

"Nay, he hasnae. Andrew warned me and asked me to keep Lady Catherine with ma wife whenever we could. Lady Catriona has been with us much of the time too, but she's out riding with her brother and uncle."

"Rather late for a ride," Rab mused as people hurried toward the Great Hall for seats since the evening meal began soon. Dominic shrugged, neither caring nor inclined to speak about the Douglases. He liked Catriona well enough since he'd known the lady-in-waiting as long as he'd known Rab. "Do ye think Dennis has let it go, or is he merely biding his time?"

"I'd say the latter. He was a mardy wean, and he's a mardy mon. He shall make all our lives miserable once he's laird. The wind blows in the wrong direction, and he claims someone did it to spite him. He'll do naught but cause more strife." Dominic rolled his eyes and gave a small shake of his head.

"Aye. And that's what I fear now. Ye ken I canna be at Kitty's side, but I'm still concerned."

"And ye still call her Kitty." Dominic arched an eyebrow and kept it raised.

"I always will." Rab's jutting chin dared Dominic to say more, but the man remained quiet. "Thank ye."

That surprised Dominic nearly as much as Rab's apology took Andrew aback.

"Ye're welcome. I ken what happened, and Lady Catriona was right. Had Agnes been a mon, she'd have died in that garden or in the lists. Lady Catherine mayhap wasna prudent in slapping the woman, but she was within her right to respond."

"I ken ye wish to return to yer wife, and I dinna wish to keep anyone from their meal." Rab offered a tight smile before turning toward his men. He and Dominic joined the women, where Rab bowed once more. "I bid ye good eve, Lady Emelie, Lady Catherine."

Catherine watched Rab hurry into the keep. She couldn't guess whether he planned to retire for the evening meal and take a tray in his chamber or if he might change and make his way to the Great Hall. Either way, she was certain about their rendezvous that eve. Giddiness made her want to bounce on the balls of her feet, but she contained her excitement as she walked sedately beside the Campbells until they left her at the ladies'-in-waiting table.

Servants were presenting the second course when Catherine spied Rab entering the Great Hall. She supposed he knew it behooved him to make his presence known to the Bruce. She'd heard the king was displeased that Rab left court without permission, so she understood the necessity for the king to realize Rab had returned after only four days away. She wondered if Rab's unexpected absence might spur King Robert into granting Rab an audience sooner, if for no other reason than to admonish him for his absence.

Despite missing Rab while he was away, she hadn't missed the other ladies' running commentary on what they believed were his shortcomings. They recommenced their litany of complaints as soon as Margaret spotted the MacLarens.

"He's filthy. And we're supposed to believe Highlanders aren't heathens when he looks like he's been rolling around with swine." Margaret sniffed. "I can smell the beast from here."

"Where does Liam Oliphant hail from again?" Catherine asked softly. No one at the table was unaware that the Oliphants' territory was nearly as far north as the Sinclairs, who lived at the northern most tip of Scotland.

Margaret glared at Catherine. She was eager to brag that the betrothal had been set, and the couple planned to marry after Christmastide. But the pretentious lady-in-waiting also avoided acknowledging that marrying Liam meant moving to the wilds of the Highlands.

"I could teach you to wear an arisaid," Catherine offered. "I know you think only barbarians wear their plaids, but it gets mighty chilly that far north."

"I have a sealskin cloak. I have no need of one of those peasant blankets."

Catherine, Catriona, Evina, and Sileas glared at Margaret. All four women were either a daughter, a niece, or a cousin to a laird. None were peasants, and while plaids were often used as bed coverings, they were never the same ones that a laird's family wore as garments.

"Lady Margaret, I'm certain your new clan will enjoy your views on their clothing and habits. Pray, do be sure to share them as soon as you arrive." Sileas spoke the false encouragement with a mocking tone. While normally the quietest of the Highland ladies and most conciliatory to the Hay sisters, she bristled at comments that might disparage her people. She rarely took comments made about her specifically being a Highlander to heart, but she was fiercely loyal to her clan.

"I agree with Lady Margaret. They are beastly and scratchy," Agnes complained. "The gowns we wear here are far superior and far more appropriate to our status."

"Only plaids made from inferior wool and poor

weavers are scratchy. That must be why your clan reives sheep. The ones you raise aren't worth shite." Catriona stared directly at Agnes. "Or do you steal from your neighbors because your land is so worthless you can't feed your own flocks?"

Catherine nudged Catriona under that table. While she knew Rab still worried about Dennis hurting her, and Dominic had been vigilant since Andrew approached him, the tension between Agnes and her had eased. Catherine didn't want Catriona reigniting the now low burning fire.

"You speak to me of stealing? I'm not the one who has kin named "Black" to match his soul," Agnes countered.

Catriona shrugged. "At least it means people remember him. What's your laird's name again?"

"My father—" Agnes didn't have a chance to finish before servants cleared their tables, forcing the women to move aside. They separated into smaller groups as they waited for the dancing to begin.

"Don't antagonize her," Catherine whispered to Catriona.

"But it's just too damn easy." Catriona grinned as a Farquharson delegate approached and extended his hand to Catriona in invitation. Catriona winked at Catherine before taking her place in line.

"Lady Catherine?"

Catherine turned to find a Keith representative behind her. She wanted to groan since she believed the man was the laird's nephew. She didn't want to discuss a potential match between her and the young man's uncle, even if that was part of what sent Andrew home to see his father.

"Aye." Catherine dipped into a curtsy as the man bowed over her hand. They took their places in line not far from Catriona and her partner. As the music began, and the couples moved through the steps, Catherine scanned the crowd for Rab. He stood near the wall much like he had the first night they'd talked. He sipped whisky from a flask, but his attention followed her as she moved from one partner to another before returning to the Keith warrior. His expression remained neutral, but Catherine wondered if watching her dance with another man bothered him.

When the set ended and the next required Catherine to stand closer to her partner and remain with the same man throughout the song, she noticed Rab flinched. She knew Rab understood he had nothing about which to be jealous. It was the same envy she would have felt watching another woman dance with Rab when all either of them wanted was to dance together.

During the country reel with a third partner, Catherine pitched to her right and stumbled several steps. Her dress's hem caught beneath her foot and ripped. "Oh dear." Catherine smiled apologetically at her partner. "I don't think I can finish the dance. I've twisted my ankle and torn my gown. Please excuse me."

Hobbling back to the table where she knew several ladies witnessed her nearly fall, she lowered herself gingerly to the bench.

"Are you hail, Lady Catherine?" Mary Forbes asked. Another Highlander, Mary preferred to only associate with her extended Lowland family, the Scotts. She'd been only too happy to pretend she wasn't from the Highlands. But the Scotts' recent troubles with both the Armstrongs and Elliots made the woman try to ingratiate herself with the few other Highland ladies. None were interested in accepting her after she'd snubbed them upon her arrival.

"I twisted my ankle rather badly." Catherine said as

she lifted the torn hem away from the joint that appeared suspiciously fine.

"Mayhap you should retire rather than try to dance on it," Mary suggested.

"We'll make your excuses," Evina said. The shrewdness in Evina's gaze told Catherine two things: her roommate knew she was pretending, and she knew Catherine intended to sneak away again. Evina hadn't asked her directly, but she knew Catherine began spending most of the night away from their chamber when Rab arrived, then she remained in her bed each night that Rab was gone. Catherine supposed Evina believed she was doing far more with Rab than she was because she'd never been out so late with Edgar. She'd only slipped away for a half an hour at a time when the disgraced laird courted her. Catherine now returned in the wee hours of the morning.

"Thank you." Catherine's appreciation was heartfelt. From the smile Evina offered, Catherine knew Evina understood she meant far more than simply telling others that Catherine injured her ankle. Moving with a slight limp, she wove her way through the crowd until she could walk past Rab. She kept her gaze straight ahead as she passed where he stood, but she didn't doubt he understood she intended to go to the hayloft earlier than usual.

Rab swept his eyes over the crowd, ensuring no one watched Catherine with excessive interest. He waited five minutes before scanning the Great Hall once more. A few people stared at him as they talked. He couldn't be bothered to imagine what they were saying now. He pressed the stopper into his flask and dropped it into his sporran. Like the other nights when he lingered in the Great Hall, his men had already left for the barracks. With a look of mild disgust, he wanted anyone watching him to notice that he made his way to the doors opposite the ones Catherine used. It meant he had to go up a floor and backtrack to come down a different flight of stairs to enter the bailey at the right place, but it should keep anyone from putting them together.

He wasted no time heading to the stables. When a few hay pieces fell from above, he knew Catherine was already in their secret hideaway. He scaled the ladder, skipping rungs. He threw open his arms wide as she launched herself into his embrace. He lifted her from her feet, and her legs wrapped around his waist as their lips fused. The separation hadn't been long, but after three years apart, even four days now felt like an eternity.

Rab tugged at the laces to Catherine's kirtle as she pulled his leine from his belt. She squirmed until she freed the front of his leine and slid her hands over his scorching skin. The late autumn air was brisk, but he radiated heat. Rab groaned as Catherine's movements made his cock ache even more than it had since he first spotted Catherine in the bailey. His tongue caressed the recesses of her mouth as she slanted her head and opened wide. Bracing her with one arm around her waist, Rab tugged the loosened garment down Catherine's shoulders until her breasts were only covered by her chemise. Impatient for their skin to touch, he lowered Catherine to the floor and yanked his leine over his head while she plucked the ribbons at her shoulders and let the chemise fall to her waist, where her gown now rested.

With hands clasped, they lowered themselves to the bed of hay. Rab lifted Catherine to straddle him, but she shook her head.

"I like it when I'm beneath ye. I like the feel of ye, to

watch as yer muscles bunch. It makes ma heart flutter." Catherine ran her hands over his corded shoulders and washboard abdomen.

"And I fear crushing ye against the hard floor. Mayhap on a soft mattress, but I worry aboot hurting ye. The hay isnae that thick tonight."

"It isnae ma back—nor ma ankle, so ye ken—that hurts. I ache for the feel of ye, Rab. I kenned ma mind and ma heart would miss ye, but I couldnae have imagined how ma body would miss yers."

"I ken, Kitty. I didna expect how restless I felt without having ye to hold each night. I missed ye even more than I ever have because I couldnae touch ye."

Catherine laid her body against Rab's as their kiss once more exploded into a raging inferno. Together, they gathered Catherine's skirts above her hips. Guiding them, Rab eased Catherine into a rhythm that rocked her mons against his rod. With a moan, Catherine placed her hands beside Rab's head and pressed her arms straight. Rab massaged the globes that swung before his face until he could wait no longer to taste her. Raising his head as she bent her arms, Rab suckled Catherine.

Moaning again, Catherine increased the speed and pressure as her bare mound moved over Rab's plaid covered cock. He sucked her nipple and tugged until it elongated, and he could press his teeth to it. The short spike of pain registered only as pleasure to Catherine as she threw her head back.

"I want to watch ye, Rab. But I canna keep ma eyes open, canna think straight."

"Dinna fash. I'm watching ye, and I have never seen a more glorious sight." Rab's thumb sought her nub, rubbing circles around the bud as it emerged from its hood. Catherine moved her hands to brace herself against his chest, swooping in for a kiss that stole their breath.

Nearing her release, Catherine leaned back, reaching behind her until she flipped his plaid high on his thighs. She wrapped her hand around his cock and stroked. She only moved her hand thrice before Rab grasped her wrist.

"It'll end far too soon." Rab offered her a guilty, lopsided smile that made her heart flutter. Rab watched as a thought he couldn't guess created a speculative expression on Catherine's face. "What is it, Kitty?"

"I've heard—I ken—a mon and woman can join in a way that isnae exactly coupling. I told ye I havenae used ma mouth, but I ken what I can do." Catherine whispered her suggestion, mortified to say it aloud and regretting it as soon as she did.

"Kitty, we can explore whatever ye want. I already admitted I dinna mind kenning ye have some experience. I dinna ever want to frighten ye with what we can share. I'm nae so keen on kenning how ye came aboot yer knowledge, but I'm nae so prideful that I canna admit that it benefits me. Do ye understand how we can do that?"

"Aye. At least, I ken how it can be done for one of us then the other. Can we both?"

"Aye, Kitty, we can. I would discover if ye even like the feel of ma mouth on ye."

"Ye really think I might nae?" Catherine giggled then nearly shrieked when Rab wrapped his hands around her hips and lifted her over his head. She held her skirts out of the way, stunned as Rab pressed her down, so the juncture of her thighs met his lips. The first swipe of his tongue made her lightheaded. With each pass of his tongue and each draw of his lips around her nub, she felt as though she floated above herself. She swayed as he rocked her hips once again.

Pleasure tightened her core, and she ground her mons against Rab's face, unaware of what she was doing, entirely entranced by the sensations his mouth elicited. As her release erupted deep within her core and spread through her limbs, her legs quivered while bearing her weight. She sagged forward once more, breathless as her hands supported her. Rab shifted her to sprawl across him, but he groaned as she pressed his throbbing cock between them. Catherine glanced up at him. "Now can I? Though I'm nae quite sure how, even though I understand what."

"As long as ye dinna bite me, I dinna think aught ye do will feel bad."

"I willna bite," Catherine teased as she snapped her teeth together. She eased herself backward, but Rab lifted her and twisted her to face his toes. She peered over her shoulder.

"I'm showing ye how we can both enjoy this in more than one way." Rab winked, squeezed her bottom, and offered her a lascivious smile that made her mouth water. But his smile faded as he added, "But if ye dinna like it, dinna do it. I never want ye to feel like ye must do aught ye dinna want or like."

"Let me try it before either of us decides whether I like it or nae." Catherine stared at Rab's length for a moment. The few times she'd touched Edgar had been brief and without looking. The man had never lasted as long as Rab did, so that alone surprised—and pleased—Catherine. Rab's cock didn't intimidate Catherine, but it gave her pause as she considered what she was about to attempt. Rab didn't move, waiting patiently, though his rod pulsed and jumped when Catherine's breath wafted over it.

She considered what Rab had already done that she enjoyed, recalling the feel of his tongue pressing against her entrance as he laved her seam. She lowered her head, drawing her tongue from stem to stern. Rab's fingers bit into her hips as he tugged her back toward him. With the next pass of her tongue, she swirled it around his tip only to be met with Rab's tongue pressing between her netherlips. They moved in alternating sweeps of their tongue until Catherine grew brave enough to ease her mouth down his length. Rab groaned softly as he fought the urge to thrust. He reminded himself that Catherine wasn't an experienced woman like those in his past. He focused on lavishing his attention on her core to keep from growing too eager too fast.

As Catherine grew more confident, she increased the pressure with each glide of her mouth. Rab matched the intensity as he ran his teeth over the sensitive bundle of nerves before sucking. Excitement coursed through Catherine, making her move faster as the desire to give and receive pleasure filled every sense. With the first salty taste of Rab's seed, Catherine pressed her hips back to accept more of Rab's questing tongue as she continued to grip his length with her lips. Their releases swept them away in a current that drew them out to sea and left them clinging to one another.

Practically tumbling from straddling Rab, Catherine felt ungainly as she maneuvered herself to snuggle into the crook of Rab's arm. They remained silent as their chests heaved, and they rested with their eyes closed. Eventually, Rab rolled onto his side, and they shared a tender kiss.

"I love ye," they said in unison.

"Tell me how it went?" Catherine asked.

"None of it was quite as I expected. The traveling was easy, but I couldnae have imagined how visiting Katherine would go." Rab felt Catherine tense, so his hand stroked her hip. "Wheest, *mo piseag*. I doubt ye will like much of this, but ken that I believe it shall work out. When I got to her croft, I discovered she's with child."

"What?" Catherine lurched upright. Tears brimmed in her eyes. "Ye're going to marry her, arenae ye? We just..."

"Nay. The bairn isnae mine, Kitty." Rab watched as Catherine tried to make sense of what he told her. The tears made her eyes glassy, but she eventually nodded, yet she didn't recline against him again. "She planned to pass the bairn off as mine, and while I told her I still wouldnae marry her, it did make me wonder if marrying ye makes me selfish and a poor father. I left without a clear decision, but I only made it halfway back to the men when I realized that I couldnae be the father. She said she was four moons along. I was out patrolling then hunting for nearly two moons straight. I burst back into her croft to find her coupling with Douglan."

"Douglan?" Catherine sat with her mouth hanging open as she tried to keep up with Rab's story. "Is the bairn his? He betrayed ye like that?"

"It certainly feels like a betrayal when I talk aboot it, but the rest of the time, I'm rather grateful. I'm still angry that they both intended to dupe me into claiming his bairn, but kenning Katherine's carrying his child means I dinna have to give a second thought to marrying her. It also means that I've made a clean break from her."

"But it also means she was with both of ye." Catherine couldn't hide her disgust. "They played ye for a fool."

"In a way. I ken I should view it as Douglan cuckholding me, and I didna ask how it started. But they intended for Katherine to break it off with me, then they could make it seems as though their relationship started after she ended mine. But they learned she was with child. They feared humiliating me if people kenned it was Douglan's bairn, nae mine."

"That's a load of tripe." Catherine glared at Rab because she couldn't direct her anger at Katherine and Douglan. "What if ye had felt guilted into marrying her? That meant claiming Douglan's illegitimate child as yer own, possibly yer heir. This wasna aboot saving yer face so much as protecting their arses. Ye'd be halfway to the altar with her if ye hadnae turned back and caught them."

"True. But I did. I choose to be relieved and grateful that there isnae one more thing in the way of us being together. I dinna need to waste ma time or ma feelings on them when ye're the only person in all this who means the world to me. They'll marry for love, and so will we."

"I'm nae so quick to forgive and forget, but I'll accept that ye are." Catherine's mouth turned down, but she nodded. "Ye make it sound as though we can go through with the marriage. Did ye find somewhere to post the banns?"

"Dunblane Monastery. Do ye remember Michael Sutherland, Lachlan's cousin?" Catherine nodded to answer Rab's question. "He's now a priest at Dunblane. It didna take much for him to deduce I still want to marry ye and why I went to Dunblane. It seems everyone kens we still wish to marry." His mouth turned down, his eyebrows rose, and he gave his head a few quick shakes in disbelief and capitulation. "It's hardly a secret among any Highlanders. He agreed to post the banns for us if we both attend the services. It's a stretch to call a church in the burgh of Stirling yer home parish, and even further to call it mine, but he'll do it if we attend and make it look as though it is now our church."

"But it's a monastery."

"True, but from what I can tell, villagers worship there on Sundays and holy days."

"All Hallows Eve, All Souls, and All Saints are in a few days."

"He'll post the banns during each Mass. By the end, we can marry."

"What if someone objects to them being read so close together or that they arenae posted at Edinample and Inveruglas?"

Rab hesitated but wouldn't keep the alternative from Catherine when it was something they might have to consider. "We can get a marriage license."

"What's that?" Catherine's brow furrowed.

"Michael explained that to avoid marriages by consent or in secret, the church can grant a couple permission to wed without posting the banns."

"And how much does that cost?" Catherine asked skeptically.

"Twenty pounds."

"Twenty? Bluidy hell."

"That's why we must pray it works out with the three Masses."

"Rab, I'm sure ye didna bring extra coins for such an expense. And I can already guess ye'll refuse, but I willna listen. I have the twenty pounds squirreled away. I will pay for the license if it means we can marry legally." Catherine paused. "If we marry at a monastery, we probably canna spend the night there. That means an inn. Should we have the village midwife and mayhap even Michael witness a bedding ceremony, so nay one can contest we're actually married?"

"Nay. Absolutely nae. I am nae subjecting ye to that. I trust Michael nae to covet ye, and the midwife is probably auld enough to have delivered us both. But nay one is watching such a private moment. We can ask if we can spend the night at the monastery and show Michael the bedsheet the next morn."

"I'd prefer that, but I'm willing to do aught we have to, so nay one can try to overturn our union."

"I ken. Pray that it doesnae come to the inn, but I ken I canna totally refuse the idea yet."

Catherine once again reclined against Rab. They fell into their usual companionable silence as they both considered the two looming scenarios. Eventually unable to remain quiet any longer, Rab asked Catherine, "Do ye think ye can escape court for the three Masses?"

"We dinna have much choice. I'm going to have to." Catherine frowned and gave a long shrug. "I must find a way. It's best if I could pack the most essential items I need, and we could leave on All Hallows Eve morn and nay return at all. But I doubt that'll work. If I canna be away from court for at least those three days without causing a stir, then I will have to return after each Mass, until we are wed."

They sat in silence again, both lost in thought as they tried to determine how best to execute their plan. Neither wanted to speak aloud the various things that could go wrong.

"Kitty, now that I can think more clearly aboot this, there is nay choice but for ye to return each day. Even if ye could somehow find an excuse to be away, the monastery willna let an unwed woman and an unwed mon traveling together, but arenae related, stay there. I canna take ye to an inn. It costs less than the marriage license, but we'd have to say we're already married. If anyone at the inn hears the banns read, they'll ken we're lying."

"I suppose that answers the question aboot us leaving on All Hallows Eve and nay returning, or at least nay coming back each day. But what do we do after we marry? Where do we go?"

"I dinna have an answer to that yet." Rab gazed through the hayloft window as the stars continued to multiply in the ebony sky. "I dinna think it would be wise to go straight to Edinample, but we canna remain here or roam the countryside without a plan."

"How will we tell yer father and mother? I canna even imagine trying to tell Óg or Mòr what we've done."

"Neither can I, but we both kenned all along the time will come."

"That doesnae make it any easier, does it?" Catherine smiled.

"Nay, it doesnae, but we will figure it out together. Always together."

"Can we sleep on it and make the hard decisions in the morn or sometime tomorrow? We have two days before All Hallows Eve. Let me figure out a way to escape the queen's attention for those three days."

"Vera well. It's better we think this through than do aught that's rash."

"Ye mean, aught that's more rash than eloping?" Catherine nudged Rab with her shoulder.

"It isnae eloping when the banns are posted." Rab grinned, feeling more lighthearted than he had for the past five minutes. "But promise me, ye willna let planning this distract ye from being vigilant aboot Dennis. I'm glad that I sorted things with Katherine and arranged for the banns, but I feel guilty that I left ye here while I dealt with ma past deeds."

"I willna. I dinna think he will do aught while Dom is nearby, and I'm certain he's terrified of Catriona. I watched him push three women aside to put distance between them." Catherine grinned as she recalled watching Dennis stare over his shoulder as he veritably bolted from Catriona as they left Mass the morning before. "I look forward to when I can stand by yer side and ken I'm safe."

"I pray that ye are, Kitty. I pray I'm nae endangering ye more than ye've ever been. Part of me fears I'm being incredibly selfish and foolish for wishing to marry ye, but I have felt so damnably incomplete for the past three years. I finally feel like I can breathe fully and think straight. I finally feel like I have purpose again."

"I feel exactly the same. It scares me to imagine what Mòr will do when he finds out. I pray I'm nae sentencing ye to death, but I finally feel hope for the first time in three years. After Aveline and the girls—I didna want to feel hope. It seemed utterly pointless. I was doing what was expected of me, what I had to, to get by. With ye, I feel like I have a reason to truly live rather than barely exist."

They inched closer until their bodies pressed together once more, their arms draped over each other's waists, and their mouths joined them as one. The kiss drew out, neither in a hurry to end it. When they finally had no choice but to draw breath, their soft smiles matched.

"If I thought it could work, I would handfast with ye right this minute and announce it to all and sundry in the morn. But if we let anyone ken our plans, it means people will try to pull us apart even sooner." Rab ran his hand over Catherine's hip and backside in slow, broad circles. She found the sensation soothing and one she intended to have Rab create every night they laid together in their bed once they were safe at Edinample, or wherever they wound up.

"I thought aboot that, too, while ye were gone. If we canna marry in the church, then that's what we will do. I ken Catriona would stand witness for us if we married by consent. Despite how things are between yer clans, it wouldnae surprise me if Dom and Emelie would bear witness too. With three people nae from either of our clans, it makes it hard to contest such a marriage once we consummate it."

"It's good to ken we have alternatives. We need to get to Dunblane those three morns."

A clap of thunder warned of an impending storm neither expected. They scrambled to their feet, brushing the hay from their clothes and each other's hair. They made it to the keep as the first drops fell.

"Rab, I ken what I can do if the rain holds." Catherine prayed the weather cooperated for once in Scotland. "I can find some reason to get drenched to-morrow. The day after, I'll fall ill and blame it on being soaked and chilled. I'll make sure everyone kens I'm too sick to leave ma chamber. There's a hunt planned on All Hallows Eve, which will take the king and queen from court for most of the day. On All Souls, the queen usually visits several almshouses, and she spends most of All Saints in prayer. I should be able to slip away during the mornings, and nay one will be the wiser. The only people who would ken are Evina and ma maid, and neither will say aught."

"Ye're certain Evina willna tell anyone?"

"She kens I come to spend time with ye. She hasnae admitted it, but I'm certain she figured it out. She hasnae said aught to me or anyone else."

"But ye sneaking out with me for a few hours each night is far different from ye disappearing from court for three mornings in a row."

"She doesnae ask any questions, so I dinna have to tell any lies." Catherine embraced Rab when they reached her floor. "I love ye."

"I love ye too." Rab bussed a quick kiss against her lips before Catherine gathered her skirts and sprinted down the passageway. He watched until she disappeared into her chamber. He wished he'd bathed before attending the evening meal, but there hadn't been time. Despite having no fresh clothes to change into, he'd found enough time to run back to his chamber and run soap and a wash linen over his body. But a soak in a hot tub would have done wonders for his weary muscles.

As Rab returned to his chamber, it tempted him to summon a bath, but the servants would gossip if he requested the tub and hot water in the middle of the night. Instead, he shucked off his clothes and fell onto the bed, exhausted. It was several hours past dawn when he stirred, much later than when he usually awoke, but he felt hopeful once more. It had been so long since he'd awoken looking forward to the day, but the feeling had finally returned now that he was with Catherine.

CHAPTER 11

Catherine listened as rain pounded the stone walls around her chamber's window. As she lay in bed, she considered what excuse she could devise to go outside when anyone with sense would tuck themselves away with a peat fire burning in the hearth. She tried to come up with a reason to visit Timber in the stables, or why she might need to go to the gardens, or even why she needed a desperate trip into town. But she drew a blank on something believable.

As she left morning Mass, one of her guards greeted her in the passageway, soaked but smiling.

"Óg's been spotted. He'll be in the bailey in five minutes, ma lady," the seasoned warrior informed her. Catherine's smile was genuine, but it was from excitement not to see her cousin but for a way to justify going outside. She followed the guard to the door, but he blocked her. "Ye'll get drenched, ma lady."

"I ken, but I must speak to Óg before anyone else can overhear us," Catherine reasoned. Her mulish chin warned the guard who'd known Catherine her entire life that she would be notoriously stubborn. He shook his head but stepped aside as he opened the door.

146

Catherine flew down the steps into the bailey and sloshed her way to where Óg dismounted.

"Catherine, have ye lost that little sense I said God gave ye? Get back inside," Andrew barked. Fatigue and discomfort left him sounding like the disgruntled Highlander he was.

"I'm happy to see you too, Cousin." Catherine grasped Andrew's hand and pulled him toward the gardens. When he balked, she pushed back the hair plastered to her cheek. "It's the only place no one will overhear us. I need to ken."

Andrew's scowl deepened, but he nodded. "Ye ken this can wait, but I can tell ye willna. I want a hot bath, a tot of whisky, and some food. But vera well, have it yer way."

Catherine stretched to kiss her cousin's bristly beard and playfully tugged a few hairs. "It's even longer. I can think of someone who might like you to trim it before you see her."

"Catherine," Andrew warned.

"You tell me to be more discreet. You ought to listen to your own preaching. Now tell."

The cousins entered the garden, and Andrew unpinned the extra length of his plaid before wrapping it around Catherine's shoulders. It was awkward to talk, standing side-by-side, but it allowed him to cover her head too. But it mattered little since she was soaked and already shivering.

"When ye fall ill, I shall tell ye I told ye so."

Catherine secretly prayed that's exactly what he would do when she pretended to have the ague. She nodded and attempted a guilty smile. Andrew narrowed his eyes but answered her demand.

"Father isn't interested in the MacDonald of Keppoch. He'd rather nae get into bed—have ye get into bed—with them. He doesnae trust the mon."

"Good. What aboot the Keith?"

Andrew paused and swallowed. Catherine's eyes widened as she vigorously shook her head.

"He hasnae decided, but he's considering the mon."

"But why? Their land is up near the Sinclairs, close to the North Sea. My dower lands will do them no good, and they will have to march across the width of Scotland to come to our aid. They aren't even that influential in their region, let alone the Highlands or Scotland."

"That's what I said." Andrew held up a hand. "I told ye I had to present the options to Father, and I told ye to prepare yerself for him to accept one of them. But I also told ye I wouldnae recommend either of them. A visit home wouldnae be such a bad thing after all. Ye ken he can barely deny ye aught. Mayhap some cajoling on yer part might convince him to continue looking. Once the dignitaries leave, do ye think ye could travel back to Inveruglas with me?"

Catherine didn't hesitate, even though she knew there was no possibility for what Andrew suggested. "Once they return to France, I don't think the queen will deny that request."

"Then plan for that within the fortnight." Andrew cast Catherine a shrewd look. "Ye've been sneaking around with him. I'm certain he returned already. Have ye at least been careful? Traipsing around for secret rendezvous gives Dennis a chance to accost ye or spread rumors aboot ye."

"Andrew." Her cousin balked and pulled away. She rarely called him by his given name when they talked together. "You can't expect me to stop loving the mon I've wanted since I was barely more than a lass. I ken you and Mòr thought sending me to court would make me forget aboot him. It didn't. How do you think I feel being here and not being able to talk to him because someone might see us?"

"Catherine, I hate telling ye that yer feelings dinna matter because they do to me. But ye ken naught will come of this. Ye must marry, and it will be to someone else."

"So must you. How aboot I send Mòr suggestions for brides? I can come up with a lengthy list he can choose from." Catherine watched as anger settled into Andrew's stormy gray eyes. "Aye. You don't like that much, do you? I know who you want, and I believe she wants you, too. But the MacFarlanes aren't nearly wealthy enough or strong enough for her father and uncles to agree. You know how it feels, yet you still dance with her every chance you can. You talk to her when it's possible. You don't seem to stop your feelings any more easily than I can."

"And it feels wretched. I would spare ye that, Catherine."

"You think ordering me to ignore him spares me?" Catherine scoffed. "Why not take your own advice? Hmm? Because you can't. You can't keep from wanting to be near her any more surely than I can stop wanting him. The only difference is, talking to her isn't likely to get you killed. Lucky." Catherine's last word had a bite, a bitter edge.

"It may vera well get him killed. That alone should be the reason for ye to stay away. If ye love him—"

"Finish that thought, and I'll knee you in the bollocks," Catherine warned. "We're careful."

"Careful nae to have a bairn?" Andrew knew he crossed the line when Catherine stepped around to look him in the eye. The fury in her gaze reminded him of when they were children, and he'd mocked her for being upset when her favorite dog died. She'd knocked him over, kicked dirt in his face, and hadn't spoken to him for a fortnight. Her mother finally convinced her to forgive him. There was no one at court to rally behind him.

"Mayhap that's exactly what I should do. Neither Mòr nor Caelan want a laird's niece carrying an heir's bastard. That would solve it all."

"Ye wouldnae dare."

"I wouldn't risk an uncertain future for any bairn, but don't put aught past me, Óg. Push me to desperation, and you won't like what I choose." Catherine and Andrew stood staring at one another, at an impasse, neither wanting to back down. A clap of thunder and a streak of lightning forced them to walk inside, but neither spoke. They parted ways, going to their respective chambers to change.

Catherine hadn't had to pretend to sneeze when she approached the Mistress of the Bedchamber the day after she met Andrew in the bailey. She'd prayed she hadn't truly made herself ill by standing out in the rain. She sought the woman who oversaw the ladies-in-waiting after pretending to shiver in front of Evina, when her roommate prepared for Terce. Evina offered to make her excuses and suggested Catherine skip morning Mass. Once Catherine was alone in her chamber, she stoked the fire, wrapped herself in her arisaid, and added her sealskin cloak. She was soon perspiring, but it didn't convince Catherine that her skin was warm enough if anyone checked.

When she believed Mass was over, and she nearly convinced herself that she had a raging fever, she made her way toward the Great Hall, pinching the tip of her nose nearly the entire way. She rubbed her eyes until they watered. She was certain she looked nearly on her deathbed by the time she presented herself to the matron. The woman took one look at her and sent her back to her chamber with the command not to appear until she fully healed. The woman hissed that Catherine had better not cause an ague to sweep through the keep and infect the French emissary.

Catherine was only too happy to rush to her bedchamber and lock herself inside. She knew Rab observed her performance because he sucked his lips in between his teeth as he struggled not to laugh as she walked past his table. Their gazes didn't meet, but a charge of excitement thrummed through them both as Catherine made her way out of the Great Hall.

Once in her chamber, Catherine took advantage of the quiet and slumbered most of the day. She'd slept poorly while Rab traveled, and she was already sleep deprived before he left. She foresaw several hours on horseback over the next three days, and likely far more if they fled the castle. She was determined to get as much rest as she could. She squirreled away food from the midday tray her maid brought, nibbling on the leftovers when she turned away the evening tray. She had no way to let Rab know all was well on her end, so she had to pray he knew, and that nothing prevented him from taking her to the monastery in the morning.

It was a few minutes before sunrise when Catherine slipped out of her chamber on All Hallows Eve morning. She wore her plainest kirtle, the one she wore to visit the poor and orphans. The weather had cleared, but it was freezing that morning. She knew she couldn't wear her arisaid, since anyone who knew plaid patterns could recognize her as a MacFarlane. She hesitated before wrapping her finely stitched cloak around her, but she feared she had no other option. It was far too fine to match her gown. As she peered at herself in the looking glass, she shook her head before darting a glance at the sleeping Evina. She removed the cloak, hoping Rab or one of his men might have a spare plaid for her. She figured wearing a MacLaren plaid among the MacLaren men made her far less conspicuous.

She creeped from her chamber, easing the door shut without a sound. She turned toward the end of the passageway and discovered a shadowy figure near the stairs. Like the first night she slipped out of the Great Hall to meet Rab, the hulking figure would have scared her if she hadn't recognized him immediately. She gathered her skirts to keep them from swishing around her legs and dashed to his side.

Rab stood with a MacLaren plaid in his hands and opened it for Catherine. It took her but a minute to have it folded and wrapped around her as an arisaid. She pulled the wool over her head and kept her head down as Rab guided her through the keep.

"The postern gate," Rab whispered. Catherine didn't respond but followed Rab as he led her to the smaller hatch in the bailey wall. When they passed through, Rab explained, "Ma men and I rode out as soon as the gate opened. I left them with the horses and came back through the postern gate in these breeks and doublet. I'm glad ye thought nae to wear yer own plaid or yer cloak."

"I'm grateful that ye thought to bring an extra plaid. I was going to ask for one." Catherine raised her head as they moved through the town, needing to watch where she stepped as people began moving around the streets. They stopped outside a pub called the Wolf and Sheep, making Catherine look askance at Rab.

"It appears normal for a group of men to gather outside a pub with their mounts. It seems like we're aboot to leave, which we are. Let's get ye onto Bolt and be away before anyone considers why a woman has joined us." Rab hoisted Catherine onto the steed's back and leaped into the saddle behind her. He barely had his feet in the stirrups before he spurred his horse forward. The guardsmen fell into a circle around them. Once again, Catherine kept her head down, shielding her face from anyone who might recognize her since she frequented various merchants.

The hourlong ride passed in a blur as Catherine leaned back against Rab's broad chest. He wrapped his left around her waist, loose when they trotted, but much tighter when they cantered. Each time he pulled her closer, she sighed, despite also needing to clutch more of Bolt's mane to brace herself. The men walked their horses into the monastery courtyard as villagers filed in for the Sunday Mass. Catherine thanked God once again that All Hallows Eve fell on a Sunday when a priest would say Mass anyway, and then there were two holy days following it. There weren't many times in the year with two holy days together, let alone a Sunday followed by two holy days. She considered the timing Divine Providence.

Once they stabled their horses, the party took their places toward the back of the cavernous church. It reminded Catherine far more of a cathedral than any monastery she'd ever seen or heard described. They watched as Father Michael took his place to begin the holy liturgy. Catherine recalled squirming in her pew as a child, but it had been years since she wanted to fidget in church. She went through the motions, even apologized to God a few times for not being attentive, but she couldn't concentrate. Her mind raced with all the ways in which the posting of the banns could go wrong.

"Mayhap we should have handfasted first," Catherine whispered. "Then I could claim MacLaren as ma clan name, and it seems like we're clansmen marrying."

153

"I just thought that too. He'll have to pass us to reach the doors. Mayhap we can stop him before he nails aught to the door." Rab glanced around the congregation. "I dinna think anyone here can read, so they wouldnae ken if he changed it."

"Aye."

"Catherine Eloise MacFarlane," Rab began, shooting an intimidating glare at the few people who frowned upon their whispering. He softened his volume further. "I pledge maself to ye for the rest of ma days. Once we depart from this earth, I pledge to seek ye in heaven and remain by yer side until the end of days. To ye, I pledge the clothes on ma back, the meat on ma plate, the coin in ma purse, and all other worldly goods along with ma love eternal. Unto ye I pledge to be yer faithful husband. To thee I plight ma troth."

"Robert Clyde MacLaren, I pledge all that I have and all that I am to be a faithful and loving wife to ye in this life and any to come. Ye are the mon who I will fall asleep beside, and it is in yer arms I shall wake. It will be ye who I turn to in times of joy and sorrow, and nay other. I pledge to love and honor ye until ma last breath and then in eternal life in the Lord's kingdom. To thee I plight ma troth."

Unable to share a kiss, they entwined their fingers and squeezed each other's hands. They knew they likely resembled fools grinning broadly, but neither cared. Catherine shifted so their shoulders pressed together. Hands still clasped, Rab brushed his knuckles against her thigh, hidden by her kirtle's fabric. As the service ended and the congregation rose, Rab inched halfway out of the pew. It wasn't hard to catch Father Michael's attention, since he stared directly at the couple.

"We handfasted," Rab whispered when Michael could hear. "She's a MacLaren."

Father Michael's brow furrowed for a moment as he regarded the sheet of parchment in his hand. He glanced at Catherine, then nodded. "Follow me." Michael made his way to the doors of the church, standing as he often did, to greet his parishioners as they left the church. People milled around talking to one another, making both Catherine and Rab wish the villagers would be on their way, so fewer people listened to Michael's proclamation. Michael stood on the top step and raised one hand. Catching people's attention, the crowd fell quiet.

"I publish the banns of marriage between Clyde MacLaren of the Parish of Dunblane and Eloise MacLaren of this Parish. If any of you know cause or just impediment why these persons should not be joined together in Holy Matrimony, you are to declare it. This is for the first time of the asking."

There were several confused expressions as people stared at Rab and Catherine, but no one stepped forward. The couple breathed a silent sigh as Michael hammered a nail into the church door, posting the banns for the public.

"I'll fix it this eve," Michael murmured as he pulled the door open. "Be sure to be back tomorrow."

The MacLarens, with their newest member, mounted and left the village of Dunblane. Once they were clear of the village, Rab called a halt. He lifted Catherine from the saddle and led her to the side of the road, into taller grass. Their kiss was tender, but jubilant. Their plans were coming to fruition, and they were married at last, at least in their eyes, and those of most Highlanders.

"Husband," Catherine whispered before kissing Rab again.

"Wife," Rab responded between kisses.

The sound of an approaching wagon made them

pull apart. Catherine pretended to straighten her skirts as the farmer drove past, looking like she'd needed a moment of privacy. Before they stepped onto the road, Rab paused.

"What aboot tonight?" Rab asked.

"I—I dinna ken. We've risked a great deal sneaking out. But it will be an utter disaster if anyone finds me after I've sworn to being too ill to leave ma chamber." Catherine's eyes pricked with tears. "But I hardly want to spend ma wedding night alone."

"I dinna want that either, but Kitty, I dinna want yer first time to be in a hay pile above a score of smelly horses."

Catherine grinned. "I hadnae thought of the beasts until now. I was always too interested in ye."

"I still dinna want to make love to ma wife for the first time with hay scratching places it should never touch. It isnae nearly clean enough nor soft enough for ye."

"And I dinna wish to do it half-dressed." Catherine's shoulders drooped. She pressed her lips together as she contemplated. "There are other things we can do, what we've already done. It may nae be consummating the marriage, but it's certainly bluidy enjoyable. I canna stand the idea of being apart from ye tonight. Well, any night really, but definitely nae tonight."

"Do ye dare it?"

"Aye. We're handfasted now. If anyone doubts it, at least five people heard us exchange our vows, even if they tried to pretend like they didna. We have witnesses."

"And we have posted the banns once. By the time anyone finds us and makes their way to Dunblane, Michael will have corrected yer name."

"Then we'll meet tonight."

"Aye, Kitty. I shall hold ma wife in ma arms tonight. At last."

"And I shall nae let go of ma husband. At last."

The couple mounted Bolt once more, and the party cantered back to Stirling Castle.

CHAPTER 12

atherine and Rab sneaked into the hayloft, like they had the other nights that they dared their clandestine interludes. There was little talking the night of their handfast. Neither enjoyed putting a stop to their love play. But as much as they desired making love and being man and wife in more than only name, they both wanted their first time making love to be memorable and unhurried. And as Catherine pointed out, with a sheet that had the evidence of her virginity but didn't smell like a horse.

The same as they had the first time they slipped away from the castle, Rab, Catherine, and the Mac-Laren guards used the postern gate and went to Dunblane the next two mornings. Each time Michael stood at the top of the church's stairs to read the banns, Rab and Catherine held their breath, waiting for someone to charge forth and contest their intended marriage. But nothing went amiss. Which also made them nervous. It all felt too easy.

"What do ye think Evina makes of all this?" Rab asked the burning question that made his belly ache whenever they returned to the castle.

"I dinna ken," Catherine replied as they rested together in the hayloft on All Saints night. "I guess she believes I'm spending the entire night with ye now. Before these trips to Dunblane, I wasna in our chamber when she retired, but I was always there when she woke. Now I'm nae there when she goes to bed or wakes, but I'm usually asleep, or pretending to be, when she returns after Terce. Mayhap she hears me come in when I come back from the hayloft to catch a couple hours' sleep. We're fortunate Father Michael says the Mass so early each day. I pinch ma nose and rub ma eyes before I talk to her, doing it under the covers. I must still look sick because she always offers to fetch me a tray herself." Catherine shrugged. Guilt nipped at her not for the first time, but there was nothing she could do without changing their plans.

"We had better pray she continues to keep quiet," Rab surmised.

"Dare we return here after the ceremony tomorrow?" Catherine asked.

"I dinna think that's wise. Father Michael said he canna marry us until after sunset without drawing too much attention while we exchange vows on the church steps. It means we both miss the evening meal. That'll draw at least Óg's attention. Once he realizes we're both gone, he'll ken what we've done. We canna avoid that. We must put distance between us and Stirling. Even if he doesnae ken we wed at Dunblane, he'll track us."

"Do ye think he'll assume we're going straight to Edinample?"

"Nay. He kens I willna do that. He kens it's too easy for him to catch up to us. But he may go there or Inveruglas rather than take too much time to search for us. Ma guess is straight to yer uncle. I doubt he thinks he'd make it as far as Edinample with only half a dozen guards."

"Would yer people really kill him?"

"Nay," Rab snorted. "They'd have too much fun taking them back to Edinample bound and gagged to turn them over to ma father."

"What would he do?"

"Have the sense to send them all into the Great Hall for some hot food and ale. Then he'd order Óg to his solar, neither wanting to be there. And from there, all holy hell will break loose."

"Sounds pretty much like how Óg will be received at Inveruglas, without the being bound and gagged. Holy hell and then some."

"Kitty, is this really what ye want to go through with? Ye're still a maiden, and nay one need be the wiser aboot the handfast. We can repudiate it here and now without waiting a year and a day."

Catherine logically understood Rab's offer, that he was trying to do what was right and best for her, but it felt wretched. Bile rose in her throat as her belly sucked back toward her spine. She shook her head as tears streamed down her cheeks.

"Dinna set me aside," Catherine whispered.

"I'm nae. I will never. But we are doing what we want, even though we ken the dangers. Neither of us wishes to shirk our duties or leave our families, but that's what may happen."

"I canna think of a better duty than bringing peace to our clans, which is what our marriage will do if the men leading our clans were reasonable." Catherine wiped away her tears. "Ye ken yer father and ma uncle will demand a midwife examine me, nae to ken if I'm still an innocent but to ken if we married because I'm with child."

"I'd thought of that. I dinna want ye forced to be humiliated like that."

Catherine shook her head. "It wouldnae be a bad

thing if I were with child. That binds our clans even more tightly than our marriage alone. And despite how prickly Mòr can be and how ornery Caelen is most of the time, they both love bairns. I've seen them when they've thought nay one notices. And I believe they both wish for each of us to have a family of our own. If there's a bairn, they might nae be so quick to tear us apart."

"Ye ken it could happen the first time we make love, or it could take years."

"I ken, but if we arenae going straight to Edinample, mayhap taking a few extra days and trying often would help." Catherine waggled her brows.

"Are ye trying to take advantage of me, Catherine Eloise MacLaren?"

"It's nae taking advantage when ye strip off yer own clothes like they're on fire."

"Is that what I'll be doing, wife?"

"Aye."

They came together in a kiss while they both smiled, but it was only a heartbeat later that it combusted with a blaze they thought they'd already sated. Rab rolled Catherine onto her back as he pushed her skirts up her thighs. His fingers delved into her entrance as their kisses grew desperate. Catherine sought the hem of Rab's plaid and slipped her hand around his length. The tip of his cock brushed the dew between her thighs. The temptation to thrust had them rocking their hips, bringing the head of Rab's cock past her netherlips. For a moment, they paused, staring at one another. With regret, they both shook their heads. They knew that if it weren't for the need of proof that they'd consummated their marriage and Catherine had been a virgin when they wed, they would make love rather than settling for stroking one another to completion.

"Bluidy duty," Catherine gasped as Rab rolled off to lie beside her. She shifted to press her body's length against his side as he lazily skimmed his thumb over her back.

"Aye. At least we're doing the right thing aboot that."

"Did we decide aught other than we both wish we were making love right now rather than planning when we can?"

"Nay. But mayhap we should spend the night at an inn at Dunblane. Even if Michael offers us accommodations, mayhap we should have people see us together as a married couple. We can leave early the next morn and make our way north rather than going west first."

"Shite!" Catherine sat up. "Ye still havenae seen the king. How could we forget that? Now what?"

Rab shaded his eyes, pressing his thumb and forefinger into his temples before scrubbing his hand over his face. "I canna believe neither of us thought aboot that. I'm ashamed that I'm that self-involved that I nearly forsook ma clan's wellbeing. I must meet with him tomorrow and resolve the matter, or at least learn what the Bruce expects of us."

"How will ye do that?"

"The mon is an early riser. He attends Prime and Lauds. I'll try to cross his path after one of them."

"And ye could be in the dungeon by Terce."

"I could be in the dungeon at any time, and I'm nae convinced I willna still end up there. But I can try."

"Vera well. Just please, please be careful."

"I have a bonnie bride to marry tomorrow. I willna do aught to jeopardize that." Rab helped Catherine to her feet before they righted their clothes and brushed hay from one another. They parted on Catherine's floor with a last kiss.

Rab rubbed sleep from his eyes as he hurried along the passageway to the castle's chapel. He was accustomed to early mornings, but the tension he'd felt since arriving, coupled with nearly no sleep each night he spent with Catherine, challenged him to get out of bed that morning. He eased his way into a pew as the prayer service began. Going through the motions, following the liturgy, helped Rab's mind to clear. He kept his head bowed but peered out from under his brow until King Robert was nearly to his pew. Making the sign of the cross as he rose, but his head still bowed, he pretended not to notice the monarch before he stepped into the aisle.

"Yer Majesty, ma pardon. I wasna looking where I was stepping," Rab stated as he bent in a low bow after nearly stepping on the man's toes. He stood closer than he intended.

"MacLaren, you've got my attention and cornered me. I suppose you're impatient to have your audience." Irritation laced the Bruce's voice as he crossed his arms.

"If ye have the time, Yer Majesty."

"I haven't, but I suppose I should make it. While I'm content to make you stew, your presence continues to rile many of my courtiers. Follow." King Robert didn't wait for Rab to fall in behind him and his guards, assuming Rab did as the king directed until they reached the Privy Council chamber. It was still so early that not even a scribe was present. Rab wasn't certain if that was to his advantage. The guards posted at the doors while Rab waited until the king sat. "Your father was quite detailed in his missive, explaining your cousins' fate. If I had a weaker stomach... For your sake, I pray God is as merciful as we're taught. However, I am not. Your cousins purposely made Laird MacFarlane's family—his women—a target."

Rab sat in silence as King Robert spoke. When the monarch grew quiet, Rab waited. The king hadn't posed a question, so Rab opted not to volunteer anything the Bruce didn't ask him.

"Humph," King Robert grunted. "You and the Mac-Farlanes have been at each other's throats for three years, so it doesn't surprise me that this exploded. But I can't believe anyone in your family thought they could do what those men did. What say you?"

Rab inhaled a deep breath before he spoke. "I dinna have an explanation to what they were thinking because I canna imagine how any of them believed their decision was sound, how they thought to survive the MacFarlanes, ma father, or me."

"I hear the rage in your voice even as you attempt to keep calm. I don't think it comes from the shame they brought or the fear of my decisions." King Robert watched Rab, but the younger Robert didn't move. "Are you that great a protector of women that anger should so consume you that you doled out the execution you did?"

"Nay one at court who has been to the Highlands is unaware of how things were with Lady Catherine. She could have been there. For that, I canna forgive them. For that, they died as they did."

"But she wasn't there. They didn't harm her."

"They intended far worse if she had been. They took from her people she loved, who were her family. Her aunt and cousins can never come back, just as neither can her parents. I made certain at least ma cousins can never take aught from her again."

"You still haven't justified your rage. So you were once fond of the lass." King Robert's mouth turned down in a dismissive frown. Rab shifted his gaze to King Robert's, defiance oozing from him, daring the king to make him speak aloud his feelings for Catherine. "Ah. You are still fond of my wife's lady-in-waiting. That's most inconvenient."

King Robert studied Rab as he steepled his fingers beneath his nose and pressed them against his lips. He wasn't certain what to make of the Highlander sitting before him. He understood the people of northern Scotland held themselves to a different code of honor and justice than those in the Lowlands, and he'd relied upon that and the brutality they often brought to battle. He couldn't fault the young man for being so resolute with anyone who posed a threat to the woman he clearly still loved. Despite that, he couldn't determine how a man who appeared so controlled while he sat across from the Bruce could be brought to such rage. It made him question the soundness of Rab MacLaren one day becoming laird when the clan was already in a precarious position with nearly all their neighbors.

"Yer Majesty, if I might speak freely." Rab suspected he knew what the king contemplated, and he intended to make his position clear. "I will say with nay shame or hesitation that I love ma father, ma mother, and ma brother dearly. I am loyal to ma clan to ma last breath. But as much as I care for them, I admit there is only one person's life who can make me so fiercely protective and so uncontrollably violent. I based ma decisions on how to execute ma cousins on emotion nae wisdom. I confess to that. Ma only regrets and remorse are the memories ma men will carry with them. I'd do the same over again if it meant retribution and protection for her. However, that is nae ma usual disposition. I'm nae a mon set on vengeance for slights and wrongs done to me. I'm nae a mon who will risk every mon, woman, and child in ma clan to continue feuds that have proven futile over and over. I am a mon who sees nay weakness in compromise, if in the end, ma clan benefits from giving a little to get much more. That mon in the meadow that day has only one reason ever to come back. If she isnae in danger, then he will remain tucked away."

"And will you go charging across Scotland when she marries someone else if you learn she's in danger?"

"I pray I never have to make that decision."

"You came on the pretense of paying your taxes, but everyone knows why I summoned you. You have shown patience and savviness while you've been here. That is part of why I made you wait. I wanted to watch how you handled the scrutiny and aspersions. No one has seen you even flinch when you're called uncouth and a savage. You do not seem to take out any hidden anger in the lists. Mayhap your mind is not as calm as you appear, but you are hardly rash."

Rab nodded, once more remaining quiet. He'd explained himself and had nothing more to offer if the Bruce didn't press him to answer a question. King Robert sat back, his elbows on the armrests, his hands folded across his still trim abdomen.

"I've known your father since we were young men. He and Andrew Mòr fought alongside me in many battles, bringing men from your clans to defend our lands and our people. This feud erupted with little warning, and I thought it was slowly burning itself out. Your cousins have likely ruined any chance that Mòr or Óg will forgive your clan. I cannot overlook the harm done to them." Robert paused, and Rab nodded his agreement. "I also do not need a repeat of the Campbells and MacGregors if I strip you of land. The MacGregors already encroach upon you. If I take that land from you and give it to the MacFarlanes, the MacGregors will remain despite that. That will only fuel the Campbells to pursue the MacGregors further."

Rab bit his tongue to keep from reminding the king that the only reason the MacGregors were landless was because King Robert gave their home to Clan Campbell in reward for their loyalty and commitment to fight for Scottish independence. If King Robert hadn't meddled, the MacGregors would still be where they'd been for generations in Glencoe, which was not on MacLaren land. The MacLarens would also be on better terms with the Campbells if they weren't the reason for the unwanted squatters in MacLaren territory.

"I ken," King Robert flapped his hand. "Everyone lays the blame at my feet. What's done is done, and I stand by my decision. Which brings me back to not being able to seize any of your land to give to the MacFarlanes. Neither can I insist you pay reparations with livestock. If I starve your people, you'll just reive them back from the MacFarlanes or go after the sheep the Buchanans stole from you. That'll merely ignite another feud, which is precisely what their idiot laird wants. Bluidy fool thinks I'll side with him, which isn't far off since I can't side with you after this mess. The records show you owe one hundred and five pounds for your taxes. I assume you brought that amount."

"Aye, Yer Majesty."

"That money must go to the crown's coffers. What was your harvest's yield?"

"Enough to store ample grain for the winter and spring with leftovers to sell." Rab and Caelan expected King Robert to order them to either give the grain outright to the MacFarlanes or any profits they made. They'd pinched pennies ever since the day his cousins murdered the MacFarlanes, anticipating losing the much-needed income.

"You will pay seventy-five percent of your profits to the MacFarlanes." The amount was steep, but it was less than Rab and Caelan feared. Rab kept his face impassive. "You will surrender to them the number of sheep and cattle you've stolen from them over the past five years."

"Aye, Yer Majesty. But that isnae a significant number. We pass our sheep back and forth, nae taking more, just the same ones."

"At least you're honest aboot that, but that doesn't create much hardship, which means not much of a punishment. You can give them an extra score."

Rab wished he'd kept his thoughts to himself. But they'd enjoyed a good breeding season with both their sheep and their cows. They could survive the loss, but he pictured a great deal more fish in his future. He loathed most fish. As he watched King Robert, he realized that his interview was ending, and the man expected his agreement.

"Thank ye, Yer Majesty. I will inform ma father posthaste, and we will plan to deliver the coin and the animals."

"You can make those arrangements with Óg before you leave." King Robert gave Rab a dismissive nod but canted his head as he studied Rab. "It's a shame you and Lady Catherine never wed. There'd be no feud, and none of this would have happened. It would have bound your clans as allies rather than bent on killing one another."

Rab took another deep inhale as he struggled to maintain his neutral expression, sensing King Robert tested him. "It shall always be the greatest regret of ma life that I didna seek her hand the year earlier. I waited too long. I should have spoken to Mòr sooner, but I didna ken if Lady Catherine wished to marry so young. More's the fool am I for nae asking her first."

"You believe she might have said yes?"

"I ken so. She'd already said aye when ma father and Mòr argued. We were both on our way to tell our lairds that we agreed we wished to marry."

King Robert's eyes twitched ever so slightly. "A shame you made no promises. You might be married now."

Rab bowed as King Robert turned his attention to parchments on his massive table that he sat behind. Rab hurried from the Privy Council chamber, wondering if the monarch had given a hint. Catherine and Rab had promised to marry one another that summer. He wondered if the Bruce thought they could make an argument that they already pre-contracted to marry and were betrothed because they'd said aloud their intention to marry, even if no one witnessed them. He could think about that while he waited to ride to Dunblane with Catherine for their wedding.

CHAPTER 13

Catherine peered around Dennis's shoulder, regretting that she'd lingered at the end of Terce to wait for Evina, who wished to say an extra prayer for an ailing family member. It was the first time she'd joined the royal court for anything in the past three days, and Evina now stood behind Dennis's left shoulder with eyes so wide Catherine feared they might fall from her face. She shifted her gaze back to Dennis, who loomed in front of her, having stalked her until her back was against a wall.

"Don't bother looking for someone to save you now. She can't do a thing, and everyone else is breaking their fast. How fortuitous that you should be such a good friend to at least one lady. Now here you are." Dennis attempted to use his larger size to intimidate Catherine, who was so frightened she felt her knees trembling. She refused to allow Dennis to realize how he terrified her, so she raised an imperious chin and cast her eyes down the length of her nose. "You haughty bitch."

Catherine caught movement behind Dennis as Evina spun around, looking for someone, anyone. Evina shook her head. When she mouthed "Rab,"

Catherine dipped her chin as though she gave Dennis the haughty appraisal of which he accused her. Then she lifted her head again but kept her eyes on Dennis. Evina didn't wait. She ran from the passageway, leaving Catherine to pray her fellow Highlander found Rab or Óg or anyone quickly. Catherine was certain Evina's presence wouldn't temper Dennis's choices, so it was likely just as well that he would only have one victim now.

"Did you think I'd just forget what you did to my sister?"

Catherine remained silent, keeping her snide response to herself, praying her silence didn't antagonize him as much as her comment might. She slid her hand up her side, hoping to reach one of her dirks, but Dennis grasped her wrist so tightly she feared it snapping. He wrenched her arm away.

"Carry a knife, do you? Not surprising. Would you like to see what I can do with mine?" Dennis drew a wickedly sharp *sgian dubh* from his belt. Catherine continued to keep her eyes locked with his, but she was hyper aware of the blade. She twisted at the same moment as Dennis attempted to press the blade to her belly. "Uh-uh. You're not leaving this passageway the way you came in."

"You'd kill me while Dominic Campbell is at court? More fool are you," Catherine muttered the last four words.

"Fool? Fool? The only fool between the two of us is you. Like I said, did you think you could touch my sister, and naught comes of it?"

"Did your sister think she could toss around my family's murders, and naught comes of it?" Catherine felt her temper rise as her fear abated. She reminded herself that either emotion would likely have Dennis pounce. She needed to stall him long enough for either someone to stumble upon them or for Evina to return with help.

"My sister didn't speak any untruths. Those animals butchered your family, defiling women and leaving their men to bed whores."

"You will not kill me, and even if you beat me, you won't dare leave me for dead. I suggest you tread carefully since Óg and Dominic are still here. And while Brodie and the king are not on good terms, the king will always side with the Campbells, and thus their allies—we MacFarlanes—before he sides with your clan. You've been at court too long, Dennis. Óg is not long from the battlefield. I hold little hope that you can come out victorious, here or elsewhere."

"You think to intimidate me, yet I am the one holding the knife."

"I was thinking to do no such thing, but if that's how the truth makes you feel, then you're wise to leave here. We can pretend you never waylaid me."

"Your family doesn't frighten me any more than you do."

"Mayhap." Catherine shrugged. "With luck, it'll be Catriona who finds us. She scares the shite out of you. The only mon who runs faster from a woman is one trying not to get married."

"Bitch."

"I'm no dog, but I have heard you're a bastard." Catherine reproached herself for not keeping a better hold on her temper and her tongue. Dennis raised the *sgian dubh* to the hollow at the base of Catherine's throat.

"A bitch in heat is what I hear. As though everyone hasn't seen how you and MacLaren pretend not to stare at one another. Word is he was your lover once. No wonder Óg can't find anyone to marry you. How much did he offer Gunn to take you?"

"Nowhere near as much as your father will pay some daft sod to take your sister." Catherine overcame the temptation to bray like a donkey, knowing that might very well ring her death knell. But she couldn't think of any way to distract Dennis other than to antagonize him into talking more. She knew she trod a fine line between making him defend himself and pushing him to the point of stabbing her.

"I may not kill you here and now, but we know accidents happen. Neither Mòr nor Óg will live forever. Neither can Rab. How easy it would be to make it look like a MacLaren murdered a MacFarlane, or a MacFarlane murdered a MacLaren. Mayhap you will be left all alone. Then who will protect you?"

Catherine screamed as Rab launched himself at Dennis, sending them both crashing to the floor. She hadn't seen or heard him approach. He growled, "Me," as his fist landed against Dennis's mouth. Blood trickled from the corner as Dennis stared up, stunned.

"Catherine!" Andrew called as he ran to her, Dominic beside him. He pulled her from where Rab had his hand wrapped around Dennis's throat.

"I have enough trouble without having yer death on ma head. Ye live today, but if we meet outside these castle walls, ken that ye've seen yer last day." Rab drove his fist into Dennis's nose, blood spurting everywhere. Dennis's head lolled to the side. Rab rose to his feet in one fluid motion as Catherine tore away from Andrew's hold. Rab pulled her close as he glared above her head, daring Andrew or Dominic to interfere. When neither stepped forward, Rab kissed the top of Catherine's head and rubbed her back. "Wheest, *mo piseag*. We're here."

"Ye're here," Catherine muttered as she tightened her hold around Rab's waist.

"Catherine, are ye hurt?" Andrew's concern was evident in his tone and his burr. "What did he do?"

"Naught but insult and threaten me."

"I saw the *sgian dubh*, Catherine." Andrew pointed to the small but deadly blade that lay on the floor beside the unconscious Dennis.

"Like I said, he threatened me." Catherine didn't turn to her cousin, her face still buried against Rab's chest. "He said ye, Rab, or Mòr might have an accident, and that he could make it seem like Rab killed ye or Mòr, or like ye or Mòr killed Rab. He wants to create more trouble between our clans. The way he said it." Catherine shook her head as her forehead rested against Rab's chest. "It wasna an empty threat. It felt more like a warning."

"It suits his father and him if there were more strife between your clans," Dominic mused. The three men and one lady stared at the supine body. "Mayhap they've already had a hand in that."

"Do ye think the Buchanans have something to do with the raids?" Andrew asked. Catherine finally focused her gaze on her cousin, who watched her. Her heart ached at the pain she glimpsed in his eyes. She pulled away from Rab with a tap on his chest. She accepted Andrew's embrace until she playfully coughed.

"Ye shall suffocate me, Óg."

"Or mayhap I shall never let ye get farther than arm's reach."

"I'm all right," Catherine whispered as she met her cousin's gaze as she leaned back. "Truly. He scared me, but he didna harm me. I promise."

Andrew nodded, looking only mildly pacified. Catherine kissed his cheek and tugged his beard as she often did. When his hold slackened further, she stepped from his embrace and turned back to Rab. She ignored the guttural sound of disgust Andrew made.

"How did ye all come to be here? I dinna think ye were breaking bread together," Catherine wondered.

"Evina raced into the Great Hall and ran to me," Rab explained. "I could barely understand more than yer name, Dennis's, chapel, and dirk."

"We saw them talking. When Rab bolted toward the doors and burst through them without waiting for the guards to open them, we followed," Andrew elaborated. "There's only one person here who can make Rab react that way."

Catherine and Rab exchanged a look. They knew they thought the same thing: they wished they could tell Andrew, and inevitably Dominic, too, that they already handfasted and were set to marry that night. But they both understood it would be disastrous for their plans.

"Aye, well. Ye already ken I dinna take threats to Kitty well."

"Ye can see she's well. I'll take ma cousin to her chamber," Andrew said as he held out his arm.

"Dinna dismiss him like a servant. And I'm nae interested in going to ma chamber unless it's for several drams of whisky. I was starving during Mass, and I'm even hungrier now." Catherine caught herself before she reached into Rab's sporran. "Do ye have yer flask?"

"Aye." Rab pulled the whisky container from his sporran and pulled out the stopper. The potent fumes threatened to burn Catherine's nose, but she relished it. "Ay-up! Dinna be drinking all of it, lass. I could use a little fortification too."

Rab playfully tugged the flask from Catherine, who pretended not to let go. Another grumble from Andrew made Catherine grin. She handed the flask to Rab, who took a long draw. It was the only hint to how rattled the situation left him. Catherine peered up at Rab and offered a soft smile.

"I'm really all right," Catherine assured him. She lowered her voice, hoping only Rab could hear. "I'd tell ye if I werenae."

Rab nodded before returning the flask to his sporran. "If ye're hungry and up to it, let's go to the Great Hall. Ye might still find some porridge left or at least some bread and cheese."

"I will take ma cousin to the Great Hall." Andrew stood to his full height and thrust forward his hand. He held it there as Rab examined it, then cautiously grasped Andrew's forearm in a warrior handshake. "Thank ye. I ken the restraint it took to only hit him twice."

"Óg—" Catherine shook her head when Andrew extended his arm to her again.

"Kitty, Óg is right. I canna take ye to the Great Hall." Rab shifted his gaze to Dominic, then Andrew. "I spoke to the Bruce this morn. He isnae stripping us of any land only because he kens that'll make the MacGregors yer problem. We're to send seventy-five percent of our wheat profits to ye. If ye prefer it, we can send the equivalent amount of grain sacks. We're also to send a score of livestock to ye."

"Seventy-five percent?" Catherine asked, aghast. "Is he trying to bankrupt ye?"

"Nay. He kens we can manage for this year. If he leaves us to starve, he merely makes more trouble for himself. But it will undoubtedly take us several years to recover. That's his goal." Rab turned his attention back to Andrew. "Ma father doesnae ken of this yet, of course. But it willna surprise him. If yer father can accept the terms, I'll plan with ye today before I leave for Edinample."

"Leave?" Andrew glanced between Rab and Catherine, suspicious of how calmly Rab mentioned departing court and how unmoved Catherine appeared. Sensing

Andrew's scrutiny, Catherine turned a woeful gaze to Andrew. He'd expected her to speak up, but the tears in her eyes made him believe she couldn't find her voice. He didn't know Catherine's sadness was sympathy for the MacLarens not regret that Rab planned to leave soon.

"Aye. With King Robert's decision now made, I have nay reason to remain. I dinna fit with court life to begin with. I'm an outsider at best, but I'm still the villain to most. It's best if I dinna linger." Rab locked eyes with Catherine. "It's best that I be on ma way as soon as I conclude ma business."

"Vera well. Catherine, let's find ye something to eat. Then I'll take ye to the gardens to find the queen and the ladies. Rab, shall we discuss the arrangements when I come back inside?"

"Aye. I shall go to ma chamber," he glanced down and waved his hand in front of his blood splattered leine, "and change. I must draft a missive to ma father. I'll bring parchment and ink with me to the Great Hall. We can meet there, and we can write our agreement and sign."

The four Highlanders made their way to a flight of stairs. Rab took them to the bachelors' quarters while the other three turned left toward the Great Hall. Catherine forced a smile to her face when Andrew continued to whittle. She wanted nothing more than to escape and find Rab, but she accepted they couldn't see one another until they met to ride out to Dunblane. She needed to pack, anyway.

As Andrew prepared to walk out of the gardens, once he and Catherine caught up with the ladies in the garden, Catherine rested her hand on his arm. "Do ye think they really could be behind some of what's kept this feud going?"

"I dinna ken. Mayhap they've stirred up trouble a

few times, but the MacLarens started this and have kept it going."

Catherine stared at her cousin in disbelief. She shook her head and turned around. She left Andrew calling her name. She might agree that the MacLarens started the feud all those years ago, but it was hardly only them who kept it going. She didn't want to fight with Andrew on her last day with him, so she opted to end their conversation before it erupted into an argument. It saddened her that even after Andrew knew Rab defended her twice, chose justice and her over his own family, Andrew still believed Rab was the enemy. Her marriage to Rab would either bring peace to their corner of the Highlands or create a war that would be the demise of both their clans. She prayed for the former.

Rab wanted nothing more than to ride out of Stirling Castle's bailey, with Catherine beside him, and never look back. Instead, he lingered in the Great Hall after the morning meal, a piece of vellum, a square of wax, a quill, and inkpot on the table before him. He opted to draft the missive to his father after he negotiated with Andrew. He watched as Andrew finished speaking with the MacFarlane warriors, who hastened to find Catherine in the gardens. It was clear Andrew ordered them to guard her, which was the only reassuring thing to happen that morning.

"Let's be on with this, MacLaren," Andrew stated as he swung one long leg, then the other over the bench and sat across from Rab. After the incident with Dennis only an hour earlier, neither was feeling magnanimous, but Rab overlooked Andrew's brusque tone. He intended to draft the agreement based on the king's orders, have Andrew sign it, then escape to the lists for a few hours before he packed his meager belongings.

"The king ordered us to pay ye seventy-five percent of our grain profits as reparations. We havenae sold all our grain yet, but we are negotiating with the Stewarts. If ye wish for only the coin, then I will have our seneschal count it. I will deliver it maself." Rab gave no hint to when he might do that since he hadn't a clue. It depended on when he felt it was safe to first return to Edinample, then set foot on MacFarlane land. "The other choice is we give ye what's left of the grain rather than sell it and pay ye the difference."

"Coin." Andrew locked eyes with Rab, and the latter understood Andrew didn't trust the MacLarens not to poison the MacFarlanes or send inferior quality.

"Vera well. I canna give ye an exact amount since we havenae agreed with the Stewarts yet. But I can give ye a fair estimate. We've had a good harvest with three-and-ten bushels for each acre. We farmed eight hundred acres, so at six shillings per bushel per acre," Rab paused to tally the amounts and tried not to sob. His father said he had a head for numbers, and it ached more with each mark he made. "I estimate it'll be seventy-eight shillings per acre, so—bluidy hell. Sixty-four thousand, four hundred shillings."

"Pounds. I want to know pounds," Andrew demanded, his burr gone now that he didn't fear for Catherine.

"Unless ye can do all of this in yer head, ye'll have to let me calculate it. I canna do it in ma head." Rab stared at Andrew, daring him to say anything else. Andrew nodded, and Rab returned to his calculations. With twenty shillings in a pound, he said, "That's three thousand, one hundred and twenty pounds."

Andrew grinned, smug satisfaction clear on his face. He sat back and crossed his arms, knowing that even with only seventy-five percent of that number, the Ma-cLarens would suffer for years.

"Ye can save yer gloating for a moment. That isnae our profit. That's what we should earn if we sold it all. If ye figure we need to keep five hundred acres' worth at three-and-ten bushels, that's... six thousand, five hundred at six shillings each. Thirty-nine thousand shillings... makes one thousand, nine hundred and fifty pounds. Plus our expenses, which were two hundred and eight pounds. I remember that tally from our ledgers. We keep two thousand, one hundred and fifty-eight pounds." It was Rab's turn to gloat. "That leaves nine hundred and sixty-two pounds, and ye get seventy-five percent of that. That's seven hundred and twenty-one pounds and ten shillings."

Andrew's grin dropped when he realized his original excitement was for naught. He wished Rab had calculated the reparations in silence, so he wouldn't have gotten his hopes up. But only a few minutes later he recalled that what the MacLarens kept must last them a year. It would be a struggle for them to pay any laborers for work done at the keep, to pay their servants their meager wages, and to buy anything they needed for the next year's crops.

What Rab didn't volunteer was how his father bartered with the laborers, giving them free range to hunt throughout summer and autumn, and to keep everything they caught. He also raised the price on their aging whisky, which he traded as far as Ireland. It was a steep loss, for which Caelan and Rab had prepared. They'd estimated the Bruce ordering them to forsake ninety percent of their yield's profits. He kept his head bowed as he wrote the agreement and made clear it was only an estimate with a final amount tallied once the MacLarens sold the last of their wheat. He included his offer to send bushels that didn't sell, but he counted on the MacFarlanes refusing them. He prayed the Stewarts didn't purchase as much as his father had offered in the spring. If the MacFarlanes refused the goods, it kept the MacLarens' debt lower and gave them more food for their people.

When he finished, adding on the livestock they owed the MacFarlanes, and read over his offer once more, he spun the parchment around to Andrew and handed him the quill. He watched Andrew's eyes move over the document, reading it twice. But at last, Andrew signed. Then Rab did the same. Rab retrieved a nearby candle and heated the wax. Using his signet ring, he pressed the MacLaren crest onto the parchment beside his name. He offered the candle and remaining wax to Andrew, who mirrored Rab's actions.

"Óg," Rab said as Andrew stood. "I have too many regrets to list when it comes to yer kin and what mine did. I dinna ken if it might have brought ye any satisfaction or peace, but I regret nay sending ye their heads on pikes. I dinna ken if ye cared that they suffered, but they did. I havenae aught else I can offer ye besides ma words and what the king ordered. One day, it willna be our fathers who feud. When that time comes, I dinna choose to carry this on. If it means paying more recompense, then I will. But I dinna need this to haunt the next generation. I dinna want our children to inherit this feud. If ye need us to shoulder the blame, then I will fully. This needs to end."

Andrew stood silently as he assessed Rab. Had they not come from rival clans, he might have liked Rab. He'd always respected him as a peer until the last raid. He struggled to overcome the anger and grief that haunted him with every breath, but he recognized the wisdom in what Rab offered. He supposed his emotions would dull over the coming years, even if the memories didn't. He didn't want to raise sons, already knowing they would go into battle against the Mac-Larens. While the MacFarlanes had the mighty Campbells on their side, it benefited both the MacFarlanes and the MacLarens to find peace. The MacGregors and Buchanans were intent upon causing trouble for their neighbors. Uniting the MacFarlanes and MacLarens would deter the other two clans and create a force that would stop either clan from causing a full-scale battle.

Andrew thrust out his arm, which Rab considered for a moment before wrapping his hand around his forearm. Standing as Highlander to Highlander, Andrew dropped his courtly veneer and allowed his burr back into his speech. "I dinna ken how long the wait will be. Yer father is as fit as a goat, and mine is the same. I dinna like thinking how many more years this will carry on, but I agree. I dinna want ma children to inherit this. I dinna want their lives in danger because of this."

"If the Campbells continue pushing the MacGregors off their land, the clan willna survive. They struggle now. They are both our enemy, since they squat on ma land, and ye're allied with the Campbells. I prefer we fight them together than fight each other. The Buchanans arenae done stirring trouble. They will only grow bolder once our fathers die. They will test both of us as new lairds. I'd rather nae fight them and ye. I dinna want ma clan spread that thin, and I dinna think ye want that either."

"Then we wait," Andrew said with finality. Rab nodded, praying the time wouldn't be long once he and Catherine married before the church. The feud would either erupt or finally be laid to rest. Or they would both be disinherited and clanless. Only one option appealed to Rab. With his wedding only hours away, he figured they would all learn the outcome soon enough.

"Aye. In the meantime, I dinna think there is a one

in ma clan who will consider causing trouble with ye. Nay one but the men who rode with me ken exactly what happened, but I returned soaked in their blood. The others were splattered and nearly as bad as me. Everyone at Edinample, and most who have come to our market, ken ma cousins died a violent death. I didna clean maself up or change, and I ordered ma men nae to, because I wanted ma clan to witness the outcome of ma cousins' choices."

"I will keep that in mind."

Rab realized his last comments did little to reassure Andrew that he meant to create and keep peace. "Ye ken why I did what I did. If it were someone else, anyone else, I wouldnae have reacted that way. But they took people she loves, and for that alone, I willna forgive."

"Aye, aye. Ye've said as much before. I believe ye, even if I still dinna completely trust ye."

"Fair enough." Rab shifted his gaze to the Great Hall's doors, then turned back to Andrew. "I dinna suppose we can walk to the lists together." He flashed a toothy grin, but even after his expression grew serious, his eyes held a hint of mischief.

"Nay. I suppose we canna. I must draft ma own missive to ma father, so I shall do that first." Andrew paused. "I wish things could have been different for ye both. Ye're good for each other and would have been good for our clans."

"Thank ye."

"But dinna think that's me giving ye permission for aught. Stay away, Rab. Ye're going to break her heart all over again when ye ride out."

"I ken. Thinking of leaving her breaks ma heart." Rab gathered the now-dry parchment and his supplies. Both men set off for their chambers, each writing missives to their fathers and dispatching them with haste.

Their timing was not so impeccable when they arrived at the lists at the same moment. A brief nod was all the salutation they offered one another before finding their men. Rab spent the next several hours swinging his sword and training, glad to have something to distract him as he waited for the hour to come when he and Catherine could make their escape.

atherine checked the satchel she'd packed. She'd only put the most essential items, hoping she could launder her stockings and spare chemise along a riverbank or a loch's shore. She packed one other gown, but she suspected they would both be beyond salvage when they reached wherever they settled. But she cared not. She wouldn't miss the trappings of court life, especially the weight of the gowns she wore. She was eager to return to the proper Highlands and wearing more practical kirtles. And more than anything, she was excited for Rab to present her with one of his plaids for her to keep. Circumstance forced her to hand back the one she borrowed each time they returned from Dunblane. She felt twinges of guilt that she longed to wear the MacLarens' colors, but it was wearing something of Rab's that she craved. She was proud of her husband, despite all that stood between their clans.

She hurried to shove it under her bed when someone rattled the door handle. She sat on the edge of her bed, pretending to put on her slippers as Evina entered. They had spoken little since Rab arrived. Their silence was companionable, but it was borne of a need to avoid either asking or saying something neither wished to have spoken aloud. However, Catherine knew inevitably, Evina would discover she ran away. She was likely to be the first person to realize Catherine hadn't sneaked away somewhere within the castle grounds.

"Catherine, I am so sorry aboot this morning," Evina apologized in a hushed voice.

"That wasn't your fault. I acted badly toward Agnes, and I knew Dennis was waiting for an opportunity to pounce. But I stayed with you. I appreciated the few extra minutes of prayer. I'm grateful you went for Rab."

"Catherine..."

"Aye?"

"I will keep your secret, even after..." Evina nudged her chin to where the strap of Catherine's satchel stuck out from beneath the bed.

"I don't mean to put you in the middle of this. You know Óg and the Bruce will question you."

"And as long as you tell me naught, then there is naught for me to tell." Evina leveled Catherine an even gaze with the practicality of a Highlander, despite sounding like a courtly Lowlander.

"Thank you."

"You're welcome. Be careful. I hope you find happiness however that may come." Evina offered Catherine a loose embrace, neither having shared any signs of affection before. "I think I left something somewhere. I best go before it's time for the evening meal."

Evina didn't wait for Catherine to say anything before she slipped out of the chamber. Catherine hurried to pull the satchel from beneath her bed and changed into her riding boots. She already wore the same plain kirtle she'd been wearing each time they rode to Dunblane. She quickly folded and squeezed her sealskin cloak and her MacFarlane plaid into her satchel. She couldn't leave the cloak behind because it was far too valuable, and she couldn't leave her plaid because she was still a MacFarlane, even now that she'd become a MacLaren. The thought of finally sharing a name and a clan with Rab sent a warm rush through her chest and tugged a smile at her lips she saw no reason to hide.

Looking in both directions and waiting with her breath held, Catherine slipped from her chamber and crept to the servants' stairs. She wound her way through the castle, avoiding anyone who might demand an explanation for her satchel. She left the castle and rushed to the stables through the undercroft. She thanked all the saints that a wagon was pulling away, allowing her to remain hidden until she was at the stable doors. She slipped inside and found Rab and his men waiting. He'd retrieved the basket she'd left in the hayloft the night before. She handed her satchel to Rab in exchange for the basket.

Cullen wore breeks and a plain leine. He would pretend to be Catherine's guard, allowing her to leave on Timber before Rab and the others. They all knew it was odd for him to dress as a Lowlander since none of Catherine's guards ever did, but it was all they could think of. Rab hurried to saddle Timber, and Catherine shoved hay beneath the cloth in the basket, making it appear as though she were taking something into the town. When all the horses were ready, Catherine moved toward Timber but stopped.

"I ken ye'll probably hate this idea." Catherine relished abandoning her courtly speech. She faced Cullen and winced before continuing. "But ye should wear ma plaid. Nay one will question ye if ye wear MacFarlane colors. If ye look away from the guards as though ye're looking for something in the lists, then they may nae recognize ye."

Cullen stared at Catherine, then shifted his gaze to

Rab. With pursed lips and a scowl, he nodded. They all knew that was far better than their original plan. He accepted Catherine's plaid and ducked into an empty stall. It was only moments later that he returned with a pleated and properly donned, albeit short, *breacan feile*. "Better than bluidy breeks. Room for the necessary bits to breathe."

Catherine chuckled while it was Rab's turn to scowl. "Help me up, please." Catherine tapped Rab's chest, and he lifted her into the saddle. Cullen mounted and led the pair out of the stables. Both Cullen and Catherine breathed a sigh of relief when they realized the wagon Catherine used to shield her was leaving at the same time. If Catherine rode between the wagon and Cullen, and he turned toward the lists, it was unlikely anyone would recognize him. They made their way through the gates without incident. As soon as they were clear of the town gates, they spurred their horses. They had a rendezvous place fifteen minutes outside of town; they would wait for Rab and the others there.

Rab watched as Catherine and Cullen rode through the gate without incident. He trusted all his guards with his life, but Cullen was one of the few he trusted without reservation with Catherine's. He knew his lifelong friend would do everything within his might to protect Catherine. Rab had told Cullen about his feelings for Catherine before he did his brother, Douglan. Cullen had been the one, just as often as Douglan, to make excuses when he slipped away for walks with Catherine at any event where the couple both attended. It was Cullen who'd suggested Rab seek Katherine as his leman, knowing how much Rab pined for the Catherine he always loved.

He gave the order for the men to mount, but rather than leave through the main gate, they slipped through the postern one. They rode toward a meadow but circled around the edge of town once they were well out of sight of the guards on the castle's battlements. Once clear of Stirling, they raced to catch up with Catherine and Cullen.

Little was said while the party rode to Dunblane, all contemplative but alert. Catherine patted Timber's neck, relieved that sneaking away hadn't forced her to abandon her steed. She'd raised the mare since she was a filly, one of the last things her parents gave her before they were both dead. She glanced at Rab, who watched their surroundings in every direction. Even though he tasked David with riding at the rear and watching the road behind them, Rab looked back several times. Despite his wariness, the ride passed quickly and without incident. They rode into the monastery as a few villagers milled around for the evening prayer service. There were far fewer than during the Sunday and holy day Masses, which suited everyone well. Catherine didn't doubt news of a wedding would spread, and a few more people might trickle in before they were through. She didn't notice Cullen had ducked into the stables until he handed her back the MacFarlane plaid, looking far more at ease in his MacLaren one.

"Are ye ready, *mo piseag*?" Rab lifted his arm, palm up. Without hesitation, Catherine placed her hand in his, and they walked to the church's steps. Father Michael emerged as they reached the top.

"Any trouble getting here?" Michael asked.

"Nay. So far, it doesnae seem like anyone is after us," Rab answered.

"We have until the middle of the evening meal before anyone comments that I'm nae there. We have until after the meal ends before Óg organizes men to ride out." Catherine glanced back at the gate as though she might peer all the way to Stirling and see what her cousin was doing.

"Do you think he will know to come to Dunblane?" Michael asked, wary to have trouble at his doorstep, even if he agreed to perform the clandestine marriage.

"Nay. I think we have until morning before there's a chance that he could stumble upon us. He doesnae ken aboot the banns being read. Of that I'm certain because I'm standing here in one piece." Rab smiled. "He'll likely assume we handfasted or married by consent, so he'll probably head west rather than north."

"Father Michael," Catherine spoke up again. "Might we stay at the hostellary?"

"Aye. It's safer and more discreet for you than the inn. We need to get this underway, or we will delay Vespers." Michael accepted the length of MacLaren plaid Rab unpinned from his shoulder. He wrapped it around the couple's wrists as he recited the ancient pledges.

Rab and Catherine stood with their hands bound, their attention solely on one another. The world slipped away, a haze far from them. They spoke their promises made from the depths of their hearts. After years of waiting, the vow exchange seemed too short in comparison. They lingered, gazing at one another before either realized Michael finished speaking. Catherine glanced down at the sapphire ring Rab slipped on her finger during the service. He wrapped his arm around Catherine's waist and lifted her off her feet. Her free arm wound around his neck before their lips fused in a kiss that was poignant. It shared the love that blossomed between them as adolescents and spoke to the passion they shared as adults. It was a melding of two souls who'd spoken the words to bind them, but the kiss sealed their commitment.

A few more people had gathered by the end of their wedding, curious about the unexpected event. They followed the couple and Michael into the cathedral for the evening prayer service. Catherine and Rab sat in the back where few people could stare. The MacLaren guards took seats on each side of the couple and in the pew across from them, prepared to defend their tánaiste and his wife.

Catherine nearly stopped Rab from unwrapping the plaid from their hands, and she might have had it not been part of what he wore. After they dined with the other monks in the refectory, they made their way to the place for guests, surprised when an aged monk showed them to a room with a bed wide enough for them both. They'd expected a cot, and Rab had been prepared to sleep on the floor—after he made love to his bride. When the door closed behind them, Catherine and Rab collided. The kiss after their wedding had been sweet with a hint of passion, but this kiss left neither in doubt about the desire that crackled between them. They tugged at one another's clothes, leaving a trail from the door to the bed.

Rab feasted upon the sight of Catherine's naked body, and she did nothing to hide her appreciation for Rab's muscular form. They ran their hands over every inch they could reach while standing before slipping onto the bed. Their lips roamed over each other's neck, cheeks, shoulders, and chest before returning to one another's mouths. Rab pressed Catherine's berry-tipped breasts together as he alternated suckling each one, eliciting moans Catherine barely stifled. Her nails scored along his back when his fingers eased into her passage. He fought his eagerness to surge into her when he discovered her arousal, intent upon increasing it to a fevered pitch before joining their bodies.

Catherine nipped at Rab's ear, having discovered

that it made him shiver in the most delightful way. Her hands grasped his chiseled backside, enjoying each time the muscles flexed beneath her hands. Now that she could see her husband as well as touch him, she wondered how they would ever leave any bed in which they found themselves.

"Kitty, I didna ken I could be this happy. I kenned I wanted naught more than to marry ye, and I kenned it would make me happy. But I never imagined how full ma heart would feel. I want to cherish ye every day for the rest of our lives. I dinna ever want a life without ye ever again."

"I feel the same, Rab. God, how it hurt every damn day believing that I would never see ye again. Those first few moments in the stables that day ye arrived, they were agony since I didna ken if ye still felt for me what I'll never stop feeling for ye. But then ye embraced me. I kenned I was home. Wherever we wind up, I dinna care, truth be told. I just want to be with ye."

Their feelings shared with words, demonstrated with action. Rab aligned the tip of his cock with Catherine's entrance, allowing her to get used to the sensation while her dew coated him. He rocked slightly, praying he didn't cause her too much pain. He slipped his arms beneath her shoulders and wrapped his hands over the top.

"I'm ready, Rab. I want us to be married in every way. I ken it may hurt, but I trust ye. Always and in everything." Catherine drew his head down for a kiss as Rab thrust forward. He felt the barrier, but it seemed to give way with little effort. He'd never been with a virgin, so he didn't know what to make of it. He froze, waiting for Catherine to shift in pain or try to move away, but she deepened their kiss.

"I thought it would hurt," Catherine admitted.

"I thought it might be harder for me to enter ye. It's

always sounded like it when I've heard other—" Rab snapped his mouth shut.

"I'd guess that like every mon's cock is different, so is every woman's quim. I dinna ken. Mayhap spending so much time riding astride did something to me." Catherine grasped Rab's upper arms as she pulled her chin back. "Ye do believe I was a virgin, dinna ye?"

"Of course, I did. I felt it." Rab pulled back and peered down between them. Catherine followed his gaze, spying the evidence of her maidenhead on his cock. When they locked gazes once more, Rab offered a tender smile. "Kitty, I didna care that I wasna the first mon ye touched, and I'd have married ye even if ye werenae a virgin. I love ye, nae yer maidenhead. I want ma life with ye, nae with something that doesnae last."

"I dinna ken any other mon who would say that," Catherine mused.

"Then ye have never met a mon who loves his woman as much as I love ye." Rab rubbed his nose against the tip of Catherine's. They settled into another tender kiss, but as they moved together, their need consumed them. Rab lifted Catherine's left thigh and hooked it over his waist, circling his hips between thrusts. She tilted her hips to receive each surge as their pelvises ground together. Catherine strained for the hint of release to explode into a full climax, yet her mind suggested she slow down and enjoy the moment. Her mind and body at war with one another; she closed her eyes and tilted her head back. Her thoughts went blank as the pleasure only Rab had brought her swallowed her whole.

"Rab," Catherine moaned as her belly clenched with her climax.

"I ken, *mo ghaol*." Rab continued to withdraw and thrust as he watched Catherine's blissful expression, but it was only a heartbeat later that she was moving with him again.

"I love ye, Rab. I love all of ye," Catherine declared as he pushed her over the precipice again, and her core tightened around his cock.

"By God, Catherine, I love ye more than aught."

Catherine smiled, surprised that Rab called her by her full name. It was so rare and had been for most of the time they'd known one another that she understood how significant and raw his declaration was. Rab gathered her in his arms and rolled over. She sprawled across him, her hair draped over his shoulder and pillow. He wrapped a finger in a lock.

"Every night since I was nine-and-ten, I've pictured ye lying in bed with me just as ye are. The feel of ye pressed against me, yer hair sliding along ma arm. Ye have beautiful hair, but it was picturing it down that made for plenty of vivid dreams. As a married woman, I ken ye'll wear yer hair up and under a kertch. It was kenning I'd be one of the few people to see it down that was special to me."

Catherine leaned upon her forearm and smiled as her fingers brushed the stubble on Rab's chin. "And I always imagined shaving ye every morning after we rose from our bed." She pulled her lips in to hide her grin but failed miserably. "It might have involved us sitting on a chair together—to be sure I could reach."

Rab grasped her backside in both hands. His cock, having rested for a few minutes, was eager to make love to Catherine again. "And how might that have made it easier for ye?"

"Mayhap it's easier if I show ye." Catherine shifted, straddling Rab's hips and guiding his once again steely length into her core after he sat up. She leaned forward, her breast hovering near his mouth as her hand ran over his cheek and down his neck before moving back to cup his skull in her palm. Rab feasted on her breasts, his cock swelling as he enjoyed suckling breasts he'd always suspected were perfection. Catherine wasn't a generously endowed woman on top, but Rab preferred it. He enjoyed being able to wrap his lips and hands around her pert breasts, feeling like he missed nothing, enjoying it all.

As their bodies tautened in mutual pleasure, they gazed at one another in awe. Neither had known making love could have such a cataclysmic effect on them. That they could experience such all-encompassing emotions. As Catherine shifted to settle against Rab's side, both still panting, he pulled the covers over them.

"I'd love naught more than to keep making love to ye all night, Kitty. But I fear ye'll be in pain tomorrow. And we both need the sleep since I dinna ken where we shall lay our heads next."

"Rab, canna we just go to Edinample? I want to go to our home. We must face yer parents, eventually. Either we will be welcome and start our life together there, or we willna and we'll ken to search elsewhere."

"We could, but that doesnae settle things with yer family. We've already sneaked away and gotten married. To nay see yer family and only go to mine feels wrong."

"But ma uncle is more likely to kill ye than yer father is to kill me. I'm nay ready to be a widow."

"Do ye really wish to tell him in a missive?"

"Nay. But we need to before anyone else does. Óg may do what he can to shield me, but if Mòr learns from someone else, he's likely to raise MacFarlane's Lantern."

"That's the last thing we need. Ye're entire clan rallying. There'll be a full moon next sennight. They'll reive aught we have that isnae already being given as restitution."

"Aye, well, we MacFarlanes have been reivers for generations, so dinna take it personally." Catherine tried to lighten their darkening mood. "Do ye think we could lead Óg to Edinample? We go to yer parents, talk to them, then we ride to Inveruglas with Óg and his men."

"If that's what we do, we need to either catch Óg or let him find us. If he gets to Mòr first…" Neither Rab nor Catherine wanted to repeat the obvious.

"Do ye think he would set off so close to dark tonight? Or will he set off in the morn?" Catherine worried about Andrew riding in anger in the dark.

"Likely in the morn, which will only make him more furious. For the faults I might find in the mon, I canna deny he loves ye, Kitty. I ken ye look at him as a brother, but it's just as obvious that he sees ye as his sister. I dinna ken how he will take fearing he's lost another."

Catherine offered a toothy grin and waggled her eyebrows. "Stay close to me. I'll protect ye."

"And who is going to protect ye from me?" Rab growled as he rolled over and entered Catherine once more. Their movements weren't as impatient, as frenzied, this coupling. They clung to one another as they tipped over into euphoria. They fell asleep in one another's arms.

CHAPTER 15

"*I* havenae seen ye this at ease in three years," Cullen commented while the men saddled the horses. Catherine stood with Father Michael expressing their gratitude and goodbyes.

"I havenae felt this at ease in three years. Granted it will disappear the moment we ride through those gates, and guarding Catherine is all I can think aboot."

"Catherine?" Cullen's brow furrowed.

"Aye. I need to remind maself that I canna use ma pet name for her with everyone. They willna respect her as a married woman or as the future Lady Mac-Laren. I owe it to her to be sure I always treat her with the respect and dignity she deserves."

"We'll see how long that lasts," Cullen smirked.

"Arselick."

"Ah, a name ye will never tire of using in public." Cullen grinned and clapped Rab on the back before Rab went to stand beside Catherine.

"It isnae much, but there are some bannocks and dried fruit in the sack." Michael explained as Catherine held up the bag.

"It's more than enough, Father. Ye've been generous to us since we showed up on yer doorstep." Rab extended his arm, which Michael accepted. The man had been a priest for several years, but his brawny forearm was a testimony to his life before the monastery. The former Sutherland warrior shook Rab's arm then offered the group a blessing before they rode out.

They'd only ridden a half hour before Rab began to worry about Catherine being too uncomfortable. He glanced at her so many times that she finally canted her head and cocked an eyebrow. His gaze dropped to her mound before looking up. At her confused expression, he frowned and looked down again then to Timber's head. Catherine's eyes widened, but she offered him a warm smile and a nod.

"How far do ye think we can go today?" Catherine kept her tone low, but she knew the men could hear. She suspected they wondered the same thing. She knew Rab had only shared the basics of their plan with Cullen. The guards would go where Rab told them, and they would do so without argument. But that didn't mean they weren't curious.

"I dinna ken. We're headed west now. Eventually, we'll have to turn north again if we're headed to Edinample."

"And further west if we're to go to Inveruglas," Catherine whispered. Rab nodded. They'd agreed that morning before they left the hostellary that they aimed for Edinample but were prepared to change course if they needed. They still intended to search for Andrew along the way.

The party continued along the road, stopping for their midday meal. Twinges of guilt nipped at Rab for keeping his men from their families, but he couldn't send them home and keep Catherine safe. He mulled over their choices as they ate the bannocks and fruit. Catherine's gentle smile told him she understood his concerns and suspected what he was thinking. They were on horseback once more when the horses had rested. Rab prayed the day would be uneventful.

"Bluidy bleeding fucking hell!" Andrew hurled his half-empty mug across his chamber, crashing it against the wall. One of his guards, Darren, stood not far from where Andrew's anger left a trickle of whisky down the door. "Where the hell is Lady Evina? Lady Catriona?"

Andrew didn't wait for Darren to answer, storming across the chamber and throwing open the door. He raced through the passageways until he reached a door to the bailey. He flung it open and jumped down the last four steps before running toward the gardens. It took but a minute to find the ladies-in-waiting strolling through the autumn foliage, with the queen and her matrons leading the group. Andrew found Evina and Catriona walking together in the middle of the group. He stepped in front of the two women, whose eyes opened wide as they desperately looked around.

"Where the devil did she go?" Andrew snarled. Evina shied away, but Catriona crossed her arms.

"Dinna think ye can snap and hiss at me, Andrew." Catriona leveled her gaze at him, mutiny in her gaze.

"Ye already ken she's gone, and I just learned of it from ma guard. Where did she go?"

"We dinna ken," Catriona confessed as her arms dropped.

"Ye sound like ye might actually be worried, yet ye didna say aught to anyone."

"Because she's safe with him," Evina spoke up.

"Safe? Safe!" Andrew fisted his hands to keep from wrapping them around the lady's neck. He turned his focus back to Catriona. "Did ye ken? Did ye keep this from me?"

"I dinna owe ye aught, MacFarlane." Catriona crossed her arms once more and raised her chin, her nostrils flaring. "Mayhap I might have one day, but ye're too busy sticking yer neb in yer cousin's business."

"Cat," Andrew whispered, shooting a warning glare at Evina. "I'm worried for her, nae just angry. I dinna fear her with him. It's her being on the road and where he's likely to take her. I'm nae so convinced she's safe among them. I need to find her."

Catriona exchanged a glance with Evina before they both nodded. They led Andrew away from the group to a corner hedge. "We dinna ken where they went. Honestly. She hasnae said aught to either of us, but we ken she's been slipping away with Rab." Catriona paused but placed her hand on his forearm, an intimacy they'd never shared in public before. "She was gone Sunday morning and the last two mornings."

Catriona and Evina waited for Andrew to piece together what Catriona meant without saying it aloud. But Andrew shook his head, bewildered by Catriona's evasive hint. Evina swallowed before explaining.

"We've just had All Souls and All Saints. Two holy days following a Sunday. That's three Masses read in a row."

"Ye think they've been slipping away to have the banns read?" Andrew twisted away, pushing his hair back from his forehead before turning back to the women. "Then they could already be married."

"We suspect that's why they left last night," Catriona stated.

"Last night?" Andrew turned a murderous mien toward Evina. It was so menacing that Catriona stepped between them.

"She doesnae ken any more than I do, Óg. Catherine

didna confide in either of us, which bluidy well hurts. Evina thought she'd merely slipped out to meet him again last night. It didna surprise Evina when Catherine wasna in her bed when she woke. But Catherine's always been back and usually sleeping by the time we finish Terce and break our fast. She didna come back this morning."

"Leave," Andrew barked at Evina as he leaned around Catriona. The lady-in-waiting was only too happy to follow the command.

"Dinna speak to her like that. Ye're angry, but she isnae a servant or a dog."

"Angry? That's what ye think I feel? Aye. That's part of it, but I'm fucking terrified she'll be dead before I can get to her."

"What if she doesnae want ye to 'get to her?' Mayhap that was the entire point of them sneaking around."

"I didna trust him before, and I will kill him now. Just yesterday morning he spoke of us making peace once we're lairds. All the while he was planning to abscond with Catherine and marry her without ma father's consent."

"She doesnae need Laird MacFarlane's consent or anyone else's. She's well past being of age."

"I can think of someone else who doesnae need consent but refuses to consider marriage without it."

Catriona's eyes watered as she shook her head. "That isnae fair," she whispered. "Ye ken what I want, and ye ken the position they put me in. I'm bluidy jealous of Catherine. She did what I've been too scared to suggest. And ye havenae exactly presented the idea either. Ye havenae even asked them."

"We arenae talking aboot us." Andrew sighed as he looked around. He guided them further through the garden and into the orchard, where they were alone.

"Cat, I'd handfast with ye right now if I didna fear how yer father and uncles treat ye. It's the same fear I have for Catherine. I dinna think ma father would lay a hand on her, but he would break her heart. I dinna trust yer uncles nae to beat ye, even if yer father wouldnae. I couldnae live with maself if I were the reason they turned ye out after abusing ye."

"They are likely married and on their way to Edinample, like we could be and on our way to Inveruglas."

"With most of Clan Douglas on our heels. What I want canna ever come before what's best for ma clan. Having yers wipe us from the earth isnae what's best."

"Then we're where we've always been. And I canna help ye with Catherine because I dinna ken aught more. I would tell ye, Óg. I ken ye love her. But I think she did the right thing. If ye, yer father, and Laird Mac-Laren could stop to see reason, ye'd realize that nae only can there be peace between ye, ye could be happy for them. Like it or nae, they are married—the longer we talk the more certain I am—and they will have bairns one day, God willing. Will ye turn away from yer own blood because ye dinna like their name or the keep in which they live? Ye arenae that kind of mon, Óg. I'm certain of that too."

Andrew took Catriona's hand and placed it over his heart. "I'm jealous of them too. I want with ye what they share, and I think we can have it. But I dinna agree with Rab's choices as the heir to his clan. I dinna condone ma cousin's decision because she is going to hurt ma father deeply. It's nae that I'm unsympathetic to them; I just dinna think they did the right thing."

"Aye. If it were up to ye, they would never be together. Ye canna—willna—consider compromise or that a solution can be had even if ye arenae the one to come up with it." Catriona pulled her hand away and shook her head. "That's why we willna be together. It's nae all ma family's fault. Ye dinna want us as much as Rab and Catherine want them." Catriona kissed Andrew's cheek as she wiped away a tear. She walked away, leaving Andrew adrift. Anger, hurt, fear, and desperation swirled within him as he watched Catriona leave him while he prayed he could find Catherine.

When Andrew was certain Catriona was with the other ladies, he hurried to the barracks to gather his men. They were already outside waiting for him, Darren having warned them that Andrew was irate. The men mounted and raced through the gates and town until they were on the road west.

Catherine watched Rab as their first day's travel ended, and the group made camp. She sensed Rab's anxiety was higher than when they set out despite having an uneventful day. She rested her hand on Rab's upper arm and handed him a skewered rabbit leg.

"What's amiss?"

"Naught. But we are on the edge of Buchanan territory. I ken their patrol has seen us. For now, I'm nay too worried since we are keeping to ourselves, and there is nay way Dennis could have let anyone in his clan ken aboot yer—incident—with Agnes."

"Incident," Catherine snorted. "Dennis was an incident. Agnes was merely a difference in opinion."

"Kitty." Rab shook his head with exasperation, but he couldn't repress his smile as he kissed her forehead. "Just be alert, please."

"I will. I dinna wish to cause ye extra worry." Catherine returned Rab's kiss by pressing her lips to his cheek. "I ken ye already worry more because I'm with ye. I dinna want to add to that."

"Thank ye, wife."

"Ye're welcome, husband. When will ye stand yer turn at watch?"

"First. I dinna need ye unprotected in the middle of the night."

"Unprotected? With seven of ye? And isnae the whole point of having a watch to keep us protected?"

"It's to alert us to danger. I canna protect ye if I'm nae near ye. I trust ma men with ma life and yers, but I will never believe anyone will fight harder than me to protect ye. I dinna fault them for that. I couldnae fight as hard as them when they protect their wives because it isnae the same as when ye're guarding the woman ye love."

"And who will protect ye?" Catherine turned to angle her body so the men couldn't see her hand as it ran along Rab's abdomen and over his thigh before it pressed between his plaid and sporran. "I may be the one to attack."

"I wouldnae resist. But in truth, Kitty, how do ye feel? I'll take ye down to the loch's shore a wee ways if ye wish to bathe."

"Will ye scrub ma back?"

"That and some other favorite parts of ye. But I thought mayhap the cool water might feel good. Are ye sore?"

"A little tender, but it's other parts of me that are sore. I didna realize I had those muscles, but they were put to good use."

"Ye will have to tell me what hurts, and I will rub away the ache." Rab offered her a wolfish grin.

"There is only one thing I'd like ye to rub, and it already aches." Catherine ran the tip of her tongue over her top teeth before turning away with a coquettish shoulder raise. She made to take a step away, but Rab's arm wrapped around her. "Ra—"

"Shh." Rab drew his sword as his men did the same.

He scanned their surroundings, keeping his arm around Catherine's waist, prepared to push her behind him or to lift her and carry her away. He couldn't determine the danger, but his men had sensed it too.

"Rab, we ride." Cullen dashed back into the camp. Without a word, the MacLarens scrambled to saddle their horses. No one had laid out their bedrolls yet. Rab nudged Catherine away from Timber after he saddled Bolt. She ran to kick dirt over the cookfire. She swept her eyes over their camp, ensuring they left nothing behind. The eight riders were mounted in five minutes.

"Buchanans?" Rab asked as they spurred their horses.

"Aye," Cullen panted, still out of breath from running from his lookout point back to camp then hurrying to saddle his horse. "At least a score of them. They were searching for someone, and since we ken their patrol spotted us, ma guess is us."

Rab led the group to the loch's edge where they turned west. They rode along the shore, the water wiping away their tracks as they attempted to put distance between them and the Buchanans. The moonlight reflecting on the water helped light their way, making it possible for them to ride well past sundown. Catherine estimated it had been an hour and a half when they slowed their horses to a walk.

"Is that a village?" Catherine asked as she pointed to inky smudges in the distance.

"I believe so." Rab glanced at Catherine, catching the exhaustion she pretended to hide. He knew she hadn't eaten—the rabbit leg she brought him long forgotten--and neither had the rest of the group. But she also was unaccustomed to so many hours in the saddle or the anxious anticipation of battle. "We will see if there's a tavern."

"Nae on ma account," Catherine argued.

"We need to disappear rather than set up a camp for them to find. Everyone needs to eat. If we dinna draw too much attention to ourselves, since they likely have few visitors, we might find a roof over our heads."

Catherine nodded, too tired to argue and finding the merit to Rab's idea. Her chest ached from how hard her heart pounded while they tried to put more distance between the Buchanans and them. She was content to let Rab decide.

"We keep to the dark until I can find out if there's a chamber for Lady Catherine and space in the stables for ye. Nay one can sleep in the tavern's main room. We dinna need anyone taking note of our plaids." Rab guided them around the outskirts of the village until they found the tavern and its stables. The establishment sounded quiet, but Rab assumed nothing until he assessed the patrons. Catherine waited with the men and horses while Rab slipped inside. It was only a few minutes later that he returned to escort Catherine to a chamber. The men tended their mounts and bedded down.

The room the tavernkeeper showed Catherine and Rab was cold and dank. It felt as though it hadn't been aired out in years, but there was wood and peat near the hearth. After he ordered food for them and his men, Rab lifted his scabbard off his back and laid his sword on the table. He found Catherine already building a cheery fire. She smiled over her shoulder at him as he slipped his arms around her waist.

"How do ye feel?" Rab asked.

"Tired. A little sore. But mostly anxious."

"Kitty, we're still on Buchanan land. I dinna want ye to be frightened because that will exhaust ye even faster. But I need ye to be alert. If aught happens while we're riding, ken the men will protect ye first."

"I ken. I'll stay in the circle." Catherine unpinned the

brooch from Rab's shoulder and dropped it in his sporran. She caught the extra length of plaid as it slid from his shoulder, wrapping it around hers, bringing their bodies closer. She rested her head against Rab's chest. "I could stay like this forever."

"Nay, ye couldnae. Ye look ready to drop." Rab kissed her forehead before he scooped her into his arms. He carried her to the bed and helped unlace her kirtle. Since they were still waiting for their food, Catherine kept her chemise on. Rab removed his belt, placing three dirks on the table beside the bed and one under his pillow. He shrugged when he caught Catherine's wide-eyed stare. He folded his plaid in half before wrapping it around Catherine. Despite being half its usual length, it still drowned Catherine. She cared not. She was warm, and she was far too fascinated with how the muscles in Rab's legs bunched and corded once he toed off his boots and only wore his mid-thigh length leine.

When the food arrived, they shared their meal on the bed. As Catherine spread out the dishes, Rab double-checked the door's lock then peered out the narrow window. He eyed the drop from the window ledge to the ground. He was certain it wasn't deadly, but likely to injure them. He knew Catherine fit through the embrasure, but he foresaw himself getting wedged into the tight space. With a frown he gathered his sword from the table and leaned it against the bedside table.

"Where are we? Have ye passed through here before?" Catherine asked as she handed Rab a piece of roast chicken.

"I dinna ken. I havenae been here before, but I think we're nearly on Graham territory. We'll be safe there. They're allied with the Stewarts and dinna care for the Campbells or the MacGregors. They may nae invite us to break bread, but if we can make it onto their land, we should be safe."

"Which way will we ride in the morning?"

"North. If the men Cullen spotted pursued us, they probably turned north thinking we're racing back to Edinample. We're farther west than I planned."

"Closer to Loch Lomond than Loch Earn." Catherine watched Rab as he nodded. "Do we change our plans?"

"If we continue north from here, I expect us to wind up on MacGregor land that's now the Campbells'. That puts us between Inveruglas and Edinample."

"What aboot Andrew? Do ye think he's tracked us at all?"

"I dinna ken. But we're more likely to come across him now than we ever were since we'll be closer to Inveruglas than we intended." Rab moved the tray aside and pulled back the covers. He followed Catherine under them after they both tossed aside their last garments and the tray rested on the floor. They lay looking at one another, an arm tucked under their head. "I still dinna ken what's best. It's nae as though we refuse to tell our families or that we're trying to hide."

"Nor do we want to make it worse. But I genuinely believe that after Mòr's and Caelan's tempers settle, they will accept this is best for both clans. Mayhap it'll never be the strong alliance we wish for, but it will at least end the raiding and fighting." Catherine's subconscious niggled, telling her she was naïve and a fool for believing anything could be so simple.

"I ken. We must weather the hellish storm first. If we can find Óg, and he sees ye're well and married by yer choice, then he can tell Mòr while we tell ma family."

"I'll say the rosary a dozen times tomorrow if it can

be that simple." Catherine inched closer. "Are we horribly selfish and immature for what we've done?"

"I wonder the same. We arenae horribly." Rab stroked Catherine's cheek. "But we are selfish, and I canna deny that without kenning it's a lie. But immature? Nay. It's as though we're the only ones who want to end the feud with Óg once he and I are both lairds. And regardless of whether I married ye or someone else, I dinna wish for ma children to inherit a feud with yer clan. We seem to be the only two people trying to end this rather than perpetuate it."

"That's how I feel. But will anyone else see it that way?"

"I dinna ken aboot yer clan, but I think they will in mine."

"Mine? Yer? Arenae they the same now?" Catherine pressed up on her elbow, not appreciating the distance Rab's words put between them. Rab took her hand and tugged until she laid down with her head against his shoulder.

"Ye are a MacLaren, Kitty. Ye've been meant to be one for seven years. But ye're also a MacFarlane. I will never try to take that from ye. I will never ask ye to repudiate the clan of yer birth. I dinna ken what it must be like for a woman. The clan of ma birth is the only clan I will ever have. But for a woman, ye have two— the clan of yer birth, and the clan of yer marriage. I canna imagine being caught between the two. I dinna envy ye that. Ye made a choice when ye married me, but I dinna want ye to feel like ye must abandon them for me. I never want that."

"Ye make it sound as though yer clan will accept me without hesitation. Yet there's clearly hatred on yer side, nae just mine."

Rab shook his head. "Ma men talk more than auld women. It seems there's a lot that's happened that I was none the wiser to. That irritates me to nay end." Rab scowled as he thought about how blind he'd been to things going on around him at Edinample. It made him questions his soundness to lead. "It turns out it's more than people wish we could marry because they ken how we've always felt. They still hope we'd marry because they believe it could end the feud. They dinna want to fight yer people, especially once ye're a Mac-Laren. They're tired of raiding and being raided. From what the men told me, the families that ken ye have grieved what was taken from ye. Mayhap they dinna have much sympathy for Mòr and Óg, but they do for ye."

"I canna say what ma clansmen gossip aboot because I havenae been home in so long. But I ken people wished we married before I left for court. When I've visited Inveruglas since becoming a lady-in-waiting, people ask me aboot ye. They ask if I wish to marry. A few even seemed sad when they learned I was to marry Edgar. I dinna think ma clansmen and women dislike ye—or even Caelan and Nessa—but it's pride and grief that makes them unable to move past the hostility."

"Aye. Mòr and Óg willna find a warm bed to lie in among ma people, but ma clan would give ye the clothes off their back. I believe they will welcome ye for ye, but they'll also welcome ye if it'll end the violence."

"Let's pray that we're right." Catherine stroked her fingertips over Rab's chest, enjoying the feel of the soft, curly hairs scattered across it.

"Kitty, I told ye before. If we canna make our home at Edinample, and we arenae welcome at Inveruglas either, then I will hire out ma sword arm. There are plenty of clans that want a mon with ma training and experience, even if only as a guardsman."

"I ken. Let's hope it doesnae come to that."

Catherine and Rab gazed at one another, feeling unified and prepared to face the future as partners. They moved together, bringing their lips within a hair's breadth of each other.

"I love ye," they whispered in unison. Their kiss was languid as they relaxed against one another. The strain of the day and of their conversation falling away from them as they found comfort and reassurance in their embrace. Rab rolled Catherine onto her back as his hand trailed over her breast and belly to her waist and down her hip. She clasped her hands behind his neck as she watched him move, fascinated by the obvious strength. A warmth radiated from her chest as she enjoyed his gentleness while knowing he possessed such barely contained force.

Rab dipped his head to suckle Catherine's breast, likely his second most favorite thing to do while alone with his wife. He squeezed the supple flesh as he nipped and licked the tip. Catherine's hand slipped between them, encircling his sword and guiding it toward her sheath. She stroked him as she arched her back in offering. Rab pressed his hips forward while Catherine guided him past her entrance. They thrust together but clung to one another, savoring the moment.

Rab sat back on his heels, bringing Catherine with him. They adjusted so Rab sat with Catherine straddling his lap. The closeness of their embrace amplified the eroticism of the moment as Catherine rode Rab's length. Their kisses and touches drew out their passion, both enjoying the feeling of Catherine's breasts caught between them, the firmness of Rab's back, and the softness of Catherine's buttocks. They moved together over and over, bringing one another to the cliff's edge before inching back. Catherine tunneled her fingers into Rab's hair as her body's demand for release pushed her into a frenzy. Rab helped rock her hips until her inner muscles contracted around his cock. She threw back her head, her eyes squeezed shut.

"Yes." Catherine moaned as Rab intensified the pleasure by catching her nipple between his teeth. "More."

Catherine's arousal wasn't nearly satisfied, and it only heightened Rab's. He laid her back against the pillows, pistoning his hips over and over. Sweat beaded his forehead and between his shoulder blades. He watched as Catherine's skin shimmered with her perspiration. She met him thrust for thrust, her silent pleas making Rab grow wild, inhibitions thrown to the wind.

"By the saints," Catherine panted. "I like this too."

"Like?" Rab struggled to speak. He pushed himself to move faster, to plunge deeper, to place pressure on her nub in a way he knew she craved. He'd learned a great deal about his wife's body in only one day. He intended to use that knowledge to make her as addicted to him as he was certain he was to her.

Catherine watched Rab's expression as their lovemaking moved from sensual to demanding. She reveled in the desire she spied in his gaze, the way his body seemed to hunger for hers. She'd harbored no small fear that Rab might hold back because of her inexperience or might be frustrated that she didn't know what to do. But making love to her husband felt as natural as drawing her next breath. She didn't want to admit that she feared him comparing her with women—*a woman*—from his past.

"Catherine," Rab groaned. "It's only ever been ye. I am nae thinking of anyone other than ye."

Catherine froze for a moment, shocked that he intuited her moment of trepidation. She drew his head down and claimed a savage kiss. Her mind jumped to the comments the other ladies-in-waiting made about Rab being a barbarian, a heathen. As her husband moved above her, pushing her toward another wave of ecstasy, she was grateful for who he was. A Highlander. A man she could put her entire faith in. A man who placed her and anyone else he'd sworn to protect ahead of himself. A man who could face the wilds of Scotland and come back the victor.

He reminded her of the colossal mountain ranges throughout the northern half of the country. They stood as guardians to the Highlands, a place of vast ruggedness and beauty. Just as the rocky formations were unmovable, so too was Rab's resolve. Despite their time apart, he'd been a constant in her life since she was three-and-ten. She could count on him to stand tall and unwavering in his commitment to her and to his clan, just as the mountains steadfastly shielded the Highlands. Catherine recognized that her chest ached from how hard her heart pounded from their vigorous lovemaking. But she preferred to think it came from it swelling with love. With one last thrust and rise, euphoria swept them away like a rushing tide. They collapsed beside one another, just enough energy left to share a brief, last kiss before they were both asleep.

CHAPTER 16

$\mathcal{W}$ith a strategy in place—albeit constantly changing—Catherine and the men set off from the inn as the earliest rays peeked over the horizon. Once they'd fallen asleep, neither Catherine nor Rab moved. They awakened in the same position as they'd been when exhausted bliss claimed them. Unlike the night before, when they'd woken to make love in the middle of the night, the fatigued couple didn't stir.

Catherine burrowed into the plaid Rab gave her as a wedding present the previous morning. It smelled of him: pine, soap, fresh air, and leather. It was a comfort to her senses, which felt on high alert after their mad dash the day before. As the sun rose higher in the sky, and the brisk early morning air grew comfortable, Catherine pushed the plaid back from her hair and looked around. Nothing but them seemed to stir among the rolling hills. She rested her eyes on Rab, who rode at the front of the group that morning. She watched, admiring his profile, when he turned to speak to Cullen. The guard said something to make Rab laugh, and Catherine appreciated the view of the deep grooves Rab's smile cut into his cheeks. She could see the lines crinkle around his eyes.

Watching Rab good naturedly laughing with one of his men helped Catherine to relax. She eased her grip on Timber's reins, not realizing how she clutched them. Her horse had, because the mare knickered and shook her head, as though enjoying the freedom. No one was prepared for the responding whinny that came from the group's right.

"Catherine, remain in the circle," Rab ordered as they all leaned over their horse's withers. "Buchanans."

A band of fifteen men galloped toward them, several with bows in their hands. When an arrow embedded in the ground a second before Bolt's hoof landed, Rab snagged his own bow and arrow that was attached to his saddle. Catherine watched as the men shifted their formation without notice, continuing to keep her in the center of their circle but placing Rab on the outside. He slowed Bolt before he released one arrow after another, felling three men. He swung Bolt around and charged after the other MacLarens. Catherine alternated between watching where her horse headed and looking back to ensure Rab was still with them.

A loud whistle rent the air in the opposite direction from the Buchanans. Catherine twisted in her saddle and released her own bird call whistle. "It's Óg!"

"Where?" Rab asked as he fell in alongside Catherine. She pointed to another group of riders cresting a hill ahead of them. The MacFarlanes barreled toward the MacLarens, and within moments the number of warriors surrounding Catherine doubled. Within moments arrows flew from both the MacLaren and MacFarlane bows, knocking one Buchanan after another from his horse. When the attackers dwindled from fifteen to four, the Buchanans retreated.

"I'm going to murder ye," Andrew snarled as he drew his sword.

"And I will murder ye," Catherine bellowed. "Dinna touch a one of them, any of ye." She swept her glowering expression over Andrew and the MacFarlane warriors.

"Have ma bowels on a skewer after we get Catherine away from here," Rab retorted. The group of temporary allies stared at one another with distrust, but Andrew nodded. They rode in silence for ten minutes.

"That's far enough," Andrew announced. "Catherine, how could ye?"

Catherine glared at her cousin, but her shoulders drooped. She recognized the hurt masked by anger. She dismounted from Timber's back as she looked at Rab. He took Timber's reins as she gestured for Andrew to follow her.

"Óg, I warned ye that ye wouldnae like ma choice if I felt too desperate. Ye refuse aught but what ye believe must be right. Ye and Mòr canna consider that compromise isnae weakness in this case." Catherine looked back at Rab before meeting her cousin's gaze. "I have never put ma wants or ma happiness ahead of our clan. I went to court because it was good for us. I would have married Edgar because it seemed helpful. I would have accepted whomever Mòr decided and done it because that was what he asked of me. Nay, nae asked. Told. But ye have kenned for years how I feel. It's Mòr, Caelan, and ye who keep this alive. Rab and I want it to end. We want our clans to be at peace. What more does he have to do to show ye that he wants a truce between us? He executed his cousins for what they did to us. He didna balk at the punishment King Robert ordered. He offered to come onto our land himself to deliver the coins. He hasnae run from ye or attacked ye. His father may well disinherit him for marrying me, but we both hope our marriage will end this bad blood."

"It's nae yer place to decide clan politics, Catherine."

"Dinna be a hypocrite all over again, Óg. Just because ye have something swinging between yer legs doesnae make ye God's gift to politics. Ye had plenty to learn when ye nearly had the Rosses and Campbells after us."

"We arenae talking aboot me, Catherine." Andrew closed his eyes and turned his head away to compose himself.

"But ma point is, neither ye nor I nor Rab can decide what our clans do. That's yer father's and his father's roles. However, we can be a voice. The voice that reminds our lairds of what we risk losing if we continue this. And we can have the marriage that forms an alliance, which is what ye intended with any clan ye married me off to."

"But—"

"But what, Óg? His clan killed members of ours? Of our family? We ken. We all bluidy well ken. But we've killed members of his clan, his family during raids and battle. Truly, what more do ye want of him? What more does he have to do to prove that he's nae evil and that he has purged the evil from his clan?"

"I dinna ken, Catherine!" Andrew took a step back. "Ye didna see them. I did. I saw ma mother and ma sisters. I watched what those beasts did to them. I canna get past that, and neither can Da. Why would ye ask us to?"

"Because it's what's good for the clan. We canna keep this going. We've already lost too much." Catherine wrapped her arms around her cousin's waist, but his arms hung to his sides. She refused to let go and rested her head against his chest. "I love Rab, and he loves me. We want a life together for our own reasons, and we ken that's selfish. But neither of our clans can endure much more before it rips us apart from the inside. The MacLarens dinna want to continue the feud."

"They had a fine way of showing it," Andrew snarled as he pushed Catherine away, turning from her.

"And those fucking bastards died for what they did. I ken, Óg. I ken what happened to them."

Andrew whirled around, staring over Catherine's head at Rab. He shifted his gaze to Catherine as Rab approached.

"I didna want to tell her," Rab confessed. "But I dinna keep secrets from ma wife. From Kitty. Ye ken why I didna want her to find out, to learn what I'm capable of. One day, Kitty will be Lady MacLaren. She canna serve her new clan if she doesnae ken what's happened."

"Lady MacLaren," Andrew snorted. Catherine shifted to block Rab and Andrew from lunging at one another.

"Enough, Óg," Catherine snapped. "Go home. Tell Mòr whatever ye must."

"Ye think I'm leaving ye with them?" Andrew's disgust dripped from each word, the vehemence taking everyone aback. The MacLaren guards continued to eye the MacFarlanes, but hands inched closer to dirk handles.

"Pride goeth before the fall, Óg." Catherine reminded Andrew of the Bible verse he least liked since she'd taunted him with it since they were children. "This hasnae been aboot ma safety or ma happiness. This is aboot yer pride. Ye dinna want to tell Mòr that ye've failed him again. Ye dinna want people to ken that ye couldnae control me. Ye dinna want to admit that mayhap ye, Mòr, and Caelan have all been wrong to keep this going. I'm fed up to ma eyeteeth of saying that. It's all aboot what ye dinna want. Ye ken as well as anyone who has ever seen Rab with me, he will *never* let anyone hurt me. Anyone who tries doesnae live to tell the tale. We are going in circles, and I'm through. Ride with us if ye wish. Go to Inveruglas if ye wish. Go back to court. Go wherever, but I'm going to ma new home."

Catherine left Rab and Andrew staring at one another. Neither expected, though it surprised neither, when Catherine mounted Timber and spurred her into a gallop. The men from both clans scrambled to mount and gave chase, ignoring the Buchanans who were left for dead. Catherine knew Timber could never outpace the men's warhorses, so she didn't try. She settled into a canter once Rab rode to her right and Andrew rode to her left. She looked at neither of them.

In tacit agreement that the MacFarlanes now escorted Catherine to Edinample, the day passed with barely a word from anyone. The MacFarlanes and MacLarens were all trained warriors and guards, knowing how to ride in formation to always keep Catherine protected. When they made camp for the night, each clan hunted for themselves and picked sides of the fire. They set up their own watches, as though they weren't traveling as one group. Catherine leaned heavily against Rab while they ate the roasted rabbit he caught.

"This canna go on," Catherine whispered.

"I ken. I'll speak to ma men in the morning. We'll be to our border within an hour of setting off. I recognize the land we passed through today. The Grahams spied us but left us alone."

"How do ye always ken whether or nae a clan's patrol has seen us?"

"Because I see them." Rab shrugged. "Often they're merely specks in the distance that I can tell are mon and horse. Other times, I notice markings on trees and rocks that tell me when we've crossed territories or patrol camps. Men riding the borders keep those places in sight. If they dinna approach us, then they dinna have a problem with us being there."

"I ken ye canna be at ma side at all times and ye canna control other people, but ye ken that I never exaggerate how safe I feel with ye, dinna ye?"

"I do. I canna fault Óg for how he feels. If the situation were reversed, I'd feel the same. Time. That's all that we can pray we have. Time for them to see reason."

"What do ye think yer mother will do?"

"After she nearly squeezes the life from ye and nearly drowns ye in kisses? Order ye more food than ye can eat in a month and all the hot water a tub can hold." Rab grinned as he brushed a quick kiss to Catherine's lips. "Ma father listens to ma mother. Hopefully, she can discuss this with him before he sees Mòr, or anyone has aught to say."

"I shall accept yer mother's welcome, especially if it includes that hot bath." Catherine twisted to whisper in Rab's ear. "But only if ye're the one scrubbing ma back."

"Ye shall discover I will make a fine lady's maid, *mo chridhe.*" Rab playfully hooked his fingers beneath her kirtle's laces and tugged. When Catherine failed to stifle another yawn, he urged her to lean against him as he covered them with his spare plaid. It wasn't long before Catherine's eyes drooped, and her breathing deepened. Rab slipped from beside her. He and Andrew stepped away from the circle. "Have at it, then."

Andrew didn't hesitate. He plowed his fist into Rab's cheek with such force that Rab stumbled back four steps. Men stepped forward, but Andrew and Rab waved them away. Rab only blocked blows that would break his nose and jaw, or swell his eyes shut. He accepted punches to his belly and ribs. Andrew landed one on his right temple that made his head ring and bright pinpricks of light danced before his closed eyes. Rab knew allowing Andrew to vent his sorrow and anger could never make up for losing his family members, missing Catherine's wedding, or her marrying Rab. But he could let the man have his chance to defend his family's honor, and Rab preferred Andrew unleash his emotions on him than Catherine.

"Fight, damn it," Andrew growled.

"I'm nae going to strike ye, Óg. Ye havenae done aught to deserve it."

Andrew drew back, his eyes narrowed. "What kind of mon lets another attack him without fighting him off?"

"Ye arenae attacking me. Ye wish for justice for yer family. Ye and I both ken coin and sheep arenae justice. Ye canna unleash upon those men because they're dead. But I am here. I represent ma clan in all things, this included, and I'm the mon who married yer cousin without yer father's blessing. I ken what's coming is ma due."

"Must ye be so bluidy reasonable aboot everything?"

"Ma time for being unreasonable came and went, but I am nae the one grieving." Rab rubbed his jaw where Andrew clipped it with the last jab. "I didna lie when I said I dinna wish to continue this once ye and I are lairds. Ye and yer clan are the injured party. I dinna have a right to pretend to be indignant or aggrieved. I willna do aught to perpetuate it."

"That's a heap of shite. Ye married ma cousin against her laird's wishes."

"And for that, among other things, I'm taking yer fists to ma face and ribs. I think ye may have cracked one."

"Good."

"Aye," Rab quipped with a quick eye roll and shake of his head. "I said it before, but apparently it bears repeating. Again. One day, ye and I will rule our clans. Do ye intend to wage war on Kitty and her children? Do ye think I would attack Kitty's cousins once removed? Ye arenae that kind of mon, and neither am I. Neither are Mòr nor ma father. This will end."

"Ye are a fool or merely naïve. This isnae over. Nae even nearly. Ye've only made it worse."

"For the faults I find with ye and Mòr, I ken ye arenae fools nor naïve. I ken ye willna attack a keep where Kitty is inside. Ye willna ravage fields that might feed her. What men do that? Nae ones yer neighbors and other allies respect."

"Ye assume Catherine isnae returning to Inveruglas as a widow."

Rab grinned. "God help the mon who winds up killing me. He will follow me to hell in the next breath. She's a wee protective."

"Jest all ye want, MacLaren. I'm nae." Andrew crossed his arms as he glanced to where Catherine slept beside the fire. Rab stepped up to Andrew, their boot tips touching.

"Then let me make something clear that ye dinna seem to get," Rab whispered. "Kitty forgave ma father and yers for keeping us apart. She did what she believed was right for her clan. She would have married whoever Mòr ordered her to. But she married me first. She will nae forgive ye if ye pursue me. And I'm nae making ma wife loathe me by trying to kill ye. She's made her choice, and it canna be taken back. Accept it or accept losing Kitty for good."

"Ye would keep her from us?"

"Nay. Ye would do that to yerselves. I'm fighting to keep that from happening. I want her to have the best of both. Peace will do that. Our marriage can do that." Rab followed Andrew's gaze toward Catherine, who now sat up and turned around. "I'm going to ma wife's side, where I belong. I'd say give it a good long, hard thought why ye need to keep this feud going. What's being gained? We already ken what's been lost."

Andrew watched as Rab returned to the fireside. He flinched at the venomous expression Catherine shot him. He couldn't miss it despite the dark. He watched Rab shake his head and draw her attention back to him. Andrew could only imagine what Rab said, but he suspected Rab took the blame. He couldn't understand how the man continued to accept responsibility for things he was only tangentially responsible for. In another man, it seemed like weakness—cowardice—not to stand up for himself. But with Rab, Andrew realized, it showed a strength of character everyone seemed to underestimate. As Andrew watched the couple, Rab reminded him of Atlas with the weight of the world on his shoulders.

Andrew hadn't gone easy on Rab, growing angrier when Rab didn't fight back. But now that they were through, Andrew realized he felt better for venting his grief and directing it at someone connected to its source. Had Rab fought back, it would have only fueled his hatred toward the MacLarens. He realized Rab was wiser than he. It gave him pause to wonder why anyone wanted to continue the feud. It seemed so pointless now, rather than a matter of honor and pride. Neither side had gained anything but heartbreak. It was his own pride that didn't want to admit Catherine had forced his father's and his hands.

Neither would Andrew attack Catherine's home or endanger her. While his father, and eventually, he would light MacFarlane's Lantern and continue to reive, it wouldn't be against the people among whom Catherine made her home, her family. Rab hadn't stolen her, taken her against her will. She'd gone willingly, so there was no damsel in distress to rescue. Andrew's head dropped as he accepted what Rab said was true: Catherine had already chosen.

Now Andrew had his own choices to make. He returned to the campfire and stood beside where Catherine and Rab sat. He held out his hands to Catherine, who slowly took them and rose.

"Felicitations on yer marriage, cousin. I wish ye many happy years with a mon I ken will cherish ye till his last breath." He kissed each of Catherine's cheeks, then wobbled when she launched herself into his embrace. "I will ride to Edinample with ye. Nae to protect ye from yer new clan. I've kenned all along that it was a ridiculous notion, but I clung to it to be right. I'll go so that I dinna have to say goodbye yet."

"Óg," Catherine croaked. "I love ye."

"I love ye, too. Catherine, I'll do aught I can on ma end to make sure this hostility ends. Ye mean too much to me, and to our clan. I dinna think anyone would accept attacking ye. And truth be told, everyone wishes ye could have married Rab years ago. This may surprise people, but it'll make them happy. They want ye to be happy."

"I am. Finally." Catherine squeezed Andrew's waist before he extended his arm to Rab. When they grasped forearms, Andrew pulled Rab forward, extending his embrace and capturing Catherine in the center. "I shall suffocate!"

The camp settled for the night. The guardsmen weren't as quick to trust as the three nobles, but the tension noticeably eased.

CHAPTER 17

"*R*ab!"
The combined MacLaren and MacFarlane contingent reined in as five MacLaren patrolmen raced toward them. At the sight of the MacFarlanes accompanying their tánaiste, the men's brows furrowed. But once they noticed Catherine in the center of the pack, wide grins broke out.

"Lady Catherine?" Johnny, the man who'd initially caught their intention, asked. His eyes caught a sparkle as Catherine adjusted the reins in her left hand. He turned an elated expression to Rab. "Ye finally married the lass?"

"Aye." Rab answered, not bothering to contain his joy. "How'd ye ken?"

"The ring." Johnny pointed to the sapphire resting on Catherine's finger. "Ma mama was a wee lass when yer grandparents married. She remembers the wedding. She thought yer grandmama had a piece of the sky on her finger because of how the stone sparkled. I remember her pointing it out to me when I was a lad. I recognize it."

"This was yer grandmother's?" Catherine whispered, cherishing the ring even more knowing whence the heirloom came.

"Aye. I used to think much the same when I was a child. She left it to me. I'm certain she kenned I meant it for ye before even I did. I've carried it with me for years." Rab admitted the last part only for Catherine's ears. Even though she'd never worn the sapphire ring before their wedding day, it, and the ribbons he'd long ago purchased for her, helped him feel connected to her during their separation.

"Did ye nae pass the king's messenger on the way here?" Peter, a senior guardsman, asked.

"Messenger?" Rab, Andrew, and Catherine asked.

The MacLaren patrol stared at them. Peter responded, "Aye. We didna expect ye since a messenger rode through yesterday. He spent the night. He went north to Edinample while another rode further west to —" Peter looked at Andrew and Catherine. "They met back together this morning, right here."

"Fuck," Catherine muttered. More than a dozen stunned faces turned toward her. "I didna mean to say it out loud. But I'm nae the first lady to think it."

"I take it ye didna say aught to the Bruce before ye tore after us," Rab said as he looked at Andrew.

"Nay more than ye did before ye ran away." Andrew glowered.

But Rab merely nodded as he faced northwest. "*Creag an Tuirc*." The Boar's Rock. The MacLarens' rally point.

"Aye. Ma father will ken that's where yer father will go," Andrew explained. "He willna let the fight be on our land again."

"We ride for there." Rab turned to Catherine. "Do ye wish to ride with me? We'll be riding harder than we have so far."

"I dinna want to slow Bolt with ma weight, but I ken

Timber canna keep up." Catherine patted her mare's neck.

"Lady Catherine?" Peter spoke up. "Do ye still ride as ye did when ye beat Maude Sutherland that year?"

"Aye," Andrew answered for her with a half-hearted scowl, his tone softening compared to a moment ago. The pride was audible.

"Then take ma horse, and I'll take yers," Peter offered. He dismounted before helping Catherine from Timber's back. The warhorse dwarfed Catherine, and Peter looked like he sat on a child's toy. But neither horse balked at their new riders.

Catherine struggled to hold on as the massive beast beneath her ate up the ground, remaining neck and neck with Bolt and Andrew's horse, Hercules. She prayed she didn't slide off, but her need to reach the place where both clans inevitably headed outweighed her fear. The dozen riders charged over hill and dale.

"There," Catherine called over the wind. "MacFarlanes."

They could all hear sword hilts banging against targes, the sound intimidating even to a trained warrior's ear. The MacFarlanes were racing across the meadow, swords drawn and blue woad covering their faces.

"Aye, and over the brow of that rise is ma father," Rab responded as the first wave of MacLarens streamed down the hillside. Their swords and targes echoed the sounds coming from the MacFarlane army. The MacLarens had come for battle just as the MacFarlanes had; woad covered their faces and their arms. Gazes darted back and forth as Andrew Mòr and Caelan became discernible from the larger forces.

The mixture of MacLarens and MacFarlanes urged their horses on as the first men clashed in the expanse ahead of them. Catherine kept her eyes on where her horse headed, trying not to witness the battle's beginning. Rab and Andrew both released earsplitting whistles, their conflicting sounds discordant. They continued their clan calls to cease as they drew closer to the opponents. Rab turned to Catherine.

"Dinna come closer. Cullen, stay with Lady Catherine. I dinna trust that we can stop this." Rab squeezed Bolt's flanks as he left Catherine with his most trusted guard. He and Andrew watched as the battling clans noticed their approach, many turning toward them rather than carrying on the fight. Rab's stomach settled back near his hips rather than choking him. The fighting might have stopped; however, the animosity was nearly palpable. Anger made the air cloying.

"I can only imagine what the king wrote in his missive," Andrew Óg mumbled.

"Whatever it was, caused them to both ride here rather than to court. And they didna come to parley." Rab watched his father break away from the front of the army and make his way forward, his fist held in the air by his shoulder to keep the MacLarens from recommencing the fight.

"Óg!" Andrew Mòr bellowed.

"Aye, Father."

"What the bluidy hell has been going on? I trusted ye!"

"Uncle—" Catherine called as she and Cullen followed at a safer pace now that the fighting had ceased, even if it might only be temporarily. She'd slapped Cullen's hand away when he attempted to take hold of her horse's bridle to keep her from approaching.

"Nay, lass. I dinna wish to hear even a peep from ye." Mòr glared at Rab and practically hissed. "Dinna look at me like that, lad. I'm nae going to touch her, but I canna say the same for ye."

"Threaten ma son, and I will finally wrap ma paws around yer throat—" Caelan shouted.

"Ye have to catch me first. Ye havenae done that yet," Mòr boasted.

"Enough." Rab's voice rang with an authority he'd never used toward two lairds, certainly not one who was his father. He waited for Catherine to rein in her horse alongside him. "Put yer bluidy swords away, so the men will too. We need to talk, nae run each other through. We dinna ken what King Robert put in his missives, but we ken he sent them. Ye two may want to put each other in the grave, but I dinna feel that way aboot any MacFarlane, and I ken Kitty doesnae feel that way aboot any MacLaren."

"And shockingly, I dinna think that way aboot any MacLaren either. Ye and Laird MacLaren may wish to continue feuding, Father, but none of us do." Andrew Óg sheathed his sword and stared at his father until he returned his sword to his scabbard, but he drew a dirk in its place. Andrew Óg figured it was a compromise they must live with. Caelan mirrored his nemesis's actions.

"And ye think it's for ye to decide, lad?" Snideness oozed from Mòr's words as he stared at his son. He vacillated between being proud of the young man and confident that he could hand the lairdship over to his son any day to fearing he could never die lest Óg run the clan into the ground.

"I think I'll be deciding one day whether it's now or in a score of years. I think we'd all do better to end it now. Do ye intend to attack Kitty, send men who might have to choose to kill her to follow yer orders?" Óg leaned forward in his saddle. "Because that's what'll happen. They're married, Father. I'm certain it isnae something that can be undone."

"And I'm certain it can be," Andrew Mòr barked.

"Nay, Uncle. Rab and I married at Dunblane Monastery. A priest red the banns and married us. It's recorded in the parish registry. It canna be undone, and I willna let it."

"Let it?" Mòr stammered.

"Cease yer blathering, Mòr," Caelan barked before he smiled at Catherine. "I welcome ye to Clan Mac-Laren, lass. If yer uncle hadnae stood in the way all these years, I'd have called ye daughter much sooner."

"I stood in the way? Ye bluidy butchering bastard." Mòr drew his sword, making every MacFarlane but Óg draw his.

"Nay!" Catherine called out. "Mòr, this must stop. There is plenty ye need to hear. Mayhap kenning it will put some of yer anger to bed, even if it canna ease yer grief. I'm nay coming back to Inveruglas with ye. But I'd like for ye to visit me at Edinample."

"Then ye should have thought aboot who ye were marrying."

"Thought aboot it?" Catherine exploded. The Mac-Farlanes shifted in their saddles as the MacLarens watched with fascination. "What the hell do ye think I have spent ma time thinking aboot since I was three-and-ten. I've spent seven years thinking aboot marrying Rab. I've spent three years fearing and dreading whomever ye planned to marry me to. I have thought aboot the hell ma life has been because ye have caught me in the middle of this fucking feud. I've thought aboot the misery I'd live in being married to someone who isnae Rab. Ye sent me to court to forget aboot him, but it didna work. It only left me with more time to re-gret yer—" Catherine pointed to Mòr, then to Caelan, "—and yer choices. Fight each other in single combat if winning the feud means more to ye than keeping yer clan safe. Let more people die. That's yer plan. I am nae having it. I married Rab because I love him, but I also

230

married him because I canna bear losing ye and Óg when I've already lost every other person I have ever loved. Ye would really take the last two people from me?"

Catherine was veritably screaming by the time she finished. Her face was flushed, and sweat trickled along her temples. Anger and resentment she'd kept bottled away for years erupted like a geyser. She took deep breaths, trying to calm herself, but she felt out of control, adrift. She turned to Rab, who wrapped his hands around her waist and pulled her onto Bolt's back in front of him. She buried her face in his chest and took a deep breath, before pulling away far enough to speak clearly.

"If I keep looking at ye, Uncle, I shall say things I canna ever take back. That's what got us into this vendetta. Things said that canna be taken back."

"What got us into this feud was them razing our villages during a time when all clans were supposed to be in a truce," Mòr argued.

"Nay. Ye got us into this just as Catherine said— with yer words. Ye accused me of something I didna do and questioned ma honor," Caelan stated. "Ye lied."

"I did nay such thing," Mòr hurled back at Caelan. "I—"

"Catriona?" Óg interrupted his father as a woman with flowing red hair charged toward them at a pace no experienced rider should take. "Catriona!"

Andrew Óg spurred his horse toward a woman he would recognize even with the worst vision. She drew him to her as though she were the last drop of water a parched man could find. He cared not that his father called after him. He barreled forward until he reached her and grabbed her horse's bridle. She lurched forward as she threw herself toward Andrew. He wrapped his arms around her waist as she rested her head on his shoulder. But the moment of comfort was brief before she pulled away.

"It's nae their fault," Catriona blurted.

"Cat? What're ye doing—"

"It was ma uncle. All of it, Óg. From the start, it was Maxwell. And they're coming."

"Who? Ye're nae making sense. How did ye get this far from court alone?"

"They're coming, Óg. Please. I have to tell the lairds."

Andrew watched Catriona as her gaze darted between the gathering ahead of them and the woods she'd ridden from. He'd never witnessed such terror on someone's face who wasn't in the heat of battle. She trembled, and her knuckles were white from gripping the reins too tightly. Her horse sidled away, not liking the tension on the bit.

"Ride with me, Cat." Andrew pried the reins from her hands and tied them to his saddle. He lifted Catriona from her mount's back and placed her in front of him. She curled against him the same as he'd watched Catherine do with Rab. "What happened? Tell me, *mo ghaol.*" My love. He'd finally said it, and he wasn't certain she caught it. But when her lips pressed to his throat, and she inhaled a calming breath, he no longer doubted it.

"Catriona?" Catherine called as Andrew and Catriona approached.

"Aye." Catriona pushed her wild and fiery hair from her face. She looked at Andrew Mòr and Caelan, anger burbling up from her core. "It's all ma uncle's fault. All of it."

"What're ye talking aboot?" Caelan asked.

"I ken ye agreed to me marrying Rab," Catriona said, offering a sad smile to Catherine. "Ma brothers and Uncle Maxwell took me home. I overhead ma uncles and father arguing. It was all Maxwell. I knew he suggested an alliance by me wedding Rab while he was at court, but I hadnae kenned he wrote to ye aboot it."

"It seemed an excellent offer. I've kenned ye yer entire life. Ye're a kindhearted woman and more than capable of being chatelaine. Allying with the Douglases is a boon," Caelan explained. He held no regrets for his decision since he hadn't known Catherine was a consideration.

"Nay one kenned this until yesterday—nae even the Black—but Maxwell has been manipulating both yer clans. Laird MacLaren, who was it who came to the gathering all those years ago to tell ye that the MacFarlanes raided ye?"

"Ma brother, Marcas," Caelan answered without hesitation.

"Aye. For years, Uncle Maxwell paid to cause trouble and make it look like the MacFarlanes did it. He stole MacLaren plaids and MacFarlane ones, then had Douglases wear them when they razed the first few fields. He told Marcas he had to get word to ye at the Gathering. He kenned Laird MacFarlane would learn of it from his clan at the same time. Marcas kenned it was never the MacFarlanes."

"What? Why?" Mòr demanded. Caelan and he stared at one another as they tried to make sense of what Catriona announced. A sickening feeling swept over them both as they wondered if the past three years of destruction and death were for naught. Caelan opened his mouth to speak, but Catriona continued her story.

"He thought the MacLarens would accept our offers of help sooner. He thought ye would welcome the larger clan's support since ye," Catriona peered at the MacFarlanes behind Andrew Mòr, "have the Campbells on yer side. He doesnae like how the Campbells' influence and alliances have grown. He wanted to ally with the MacLarens, so he could maneuver the Campbells into the fight without making it seem like the Douglases started aught. He kens the Black canna stand Brodie. After Marcas died, he paid his sons."

"But why did Marcas do it to begin with?" Caelan asked no one and everyone. His gaze met Rab's. After a long pause, he deduced, "He wanted ye and me dead."

"Cain and Abel." Rab muttered.

"What?" Caelan asked.

"I always thought he was Cain, and ye were Abel. I have believed since I was a lad that he would have killed ye to be laird if the clan werenae so loyal to ye. They never wanted him to be laird. It would have been a disaster."

"I bet that's exactly what Maxwell counted on," Catherine mused.

"It is. If Laird MacLaren died in battle, then Marcas would be laird. Uncle Maxwell assumed he'd have a puppet leading the MacLarens."

"Cat, how do ye ken all this? And what are ye doing riding on yer own? Where are yer guards?" Andrew Óg asked, his arms still wrapped around Catriona's waist.

"I listened to their conversation. I canna say where and how. I willna share that clan secret." Catriona met Andrew's gaze. "I rode out early this morning before anyone but the shepherds were up. This is Maxwell's horse." Catriona's grin was infectious, and Andrew smiled until he recalled Catriona was likely to wind up dead for interfering and taking the man's prized horseflesh.

"Lairds," Catriona turned away from Andrew. "They're riding here. The Black and ma father are hopping mad at Maxwell, but with a marriage agreement supposedly accepted, they are coming to support the MacLarens."

"And the Campbells are on their way," Andrew Mòr

said, as he scrubbed his hand over his face. "Just what he wanted."

"Aye." Catriona nodded as she surveyed at the assembled group. "I am so sorry. I wish I'd learned all of this so much sooner. I'm so ashamed."

"Wheest, Cat," Andrew Óg whispered against her ear. "Ye arenae responsible for their choices."

"But ye dinna understand, Óg. I suspected something wasna right ages ago, but I didna do aught. I didna try to learn more. If I had, mayhap yer—"

"Nay. That wasna yer fault, Cat. Dinna think that for a moment. Those men made their own choices." Andrew looked over Catriona's head to Rab. "And they paid for them just as they should."

"But—"

"Cat," Andrew grasped her shoulders lightly and pushing her back, dipping his chin to gaze into her eyes. "Have ye felt like their deaths were yer fault because ye've suspected something wasna right since before the attack? That because I lost ma mother and sisters that we couldnae be together?"

"Aye. But then ye also never approached ma father or uncles. I thought ye didna want me."

"Cat, I never believed yer family might consider me. Ye've kept the weight of this to yerself?"

"Who could I tell? Whether I was right or wrong, it wasna something to discuss with just anyone. The one person I wished to talk to, I couldnae." Tears welled in Catriona's eyes as her lip trembled. She shifted her gaze to Catherine. "I couldnae tell ma best friend that I could have kept her aunt and cousins from dying if I'd just spoken ma suspicions when I first had them. I felt like such a failure."

"Yer family is going to ken, if they havenae figured it out already, that ye rode to warn us. What will they do to ye?" Andrew asked as he lifted the hair from Catriona's neck then stroked her back.

"The Black and ma father willna do aught but let me languish at court. Maxwell—" Catriona shook her head. "Ma brothers will protect me."

"Da," Andrew Óg looked at the older version of his face and build. Andrew Mòr nodded, stunned into silence as he watched his son. He'd never suspected Óg held any soft sentiments for a woman, but it was clear he loved the woman sitting before him. He shifted his focus to Rab and Catherine, who sat similarly. He looked at Caelan, who watched him.

"Lady Catriona, I'd like ye to come back to Inveruglas with us," Andrew Mòr offered.

"I canna—" The rumble of hundreds of pounding horse hooves cut off Catriona. Everyone swung their attention to where Campbells rode over the same hill the MacFarlanes had not more than an hour earlier. Dominic Campbell walked his horse forward, taking in the scene before him. Two couples sharing horseback and two exhausted looking lairds who seemed to have aged since he'd last seen either of them. He crossed his wrists over his saddle's pummel and waited.

"I dinna even ken where to start," Andrew Mòr sighed. "These two—" he pointed to Rab and Catherine, "—already married. These two," pointing to Catriona and Andrew Óg, "are likely halfway to handfasted. Despite that, he," pointing to Caelan, "agreed to marry Rab to Catriona because none of us kenned half of what we've just learned. Turns out that dung heap Maxwell is who has really been behind it all. He stirred up trouble to draw ye and Brodie out. Used the MacLarens and me like bluidy bait."

"What's the Black's role in all this?" Dominic asked Catriona.

"Naught until last eve. He's livid that Maxwell kept

all this from him. He's surely humiliated that he never learned aboot any of it. Because he agreed with Maxwell's suggestion that Rab and I marry, he feels honor bound to ride out and help the MacLarens."

"Wait," Catherine interjected. "If they all think ye and Rab are marrying, then why do they think they need to ride to the MacLarens' aid? What do they think brought the MacFarlanes and MacLarens back to battle? They canna ken aboot Rab and me."

"Ye dinna ken?" Catriona's face blanched. "I thought ye already kenned."

"Kenned what?" Caelan and Andrew Mòr demanded, shooting disgusted looks at one another.

"There were fields set ablaze last night where yer lands meet. Two villages on either side of the border were raided and burned down. Maxwell paid some clansmen to do it and make it look like ye attacked one another. I thought that's why ye were already here."

"Nay. King Robert sent missives saying Rab and I ran away to marry." Catherine held up her hand.

"Bluidy damn time," Catriona said, a smile wanting to tug at her mouth, but the moment was too somber. She turned to Rab. "Dinna fash, I wouldnae have married ye, anyway."

"I kenned and told Maxwell as much." Rab met Andrew Óg's gaze. "I wouldnae have accepted."

"How far behind ye do ye think they are, Lady Catriona?" Andrew Mòr asked.

"Mayhap another hour if we're lucky."

"Rab, take Catherine and Catriona up *Creag an Tuirc*. Get them hidden. Douglan is there with two score more warriors. Send him down."

"Douglan?" Rab asked in surprise. He watched his father clench his jaw, and Rab realized his father waited for Rab to react. He understood Caelan must have found out about Douglan and Katherine. "It worked out for the best. They love each other, and I love Kitty."

Caelan nodded. "Ye dinna hold aught against him?"

"Nay. I dinna like or agree with what he did, but frankly, I dinna care that much. I have Kitty as ma wife. That's all that has mattered for years. If Katherine can forgive me for using her, and Kitty can accept what I've already told her, then I'm in nay position to pass judgment on anyone."

Caelan nodded and eyed Andrew Mòr, a hint of humor in his tone. "Bluidy complicated, this lot. It was much easier when we were their age and meeting our wives."

Andrew Mòr's expression softened. "Aye. There was never a reason to sneak anywhere with ma Aveline."

No one spoke. Everyone watched Andrew Mòr, shocked to hear him say his dead wife's name, let alone share a memory. He hadn't been able to talk about her since her death. He nodded as he looked at Catherine. "She wanted ye two to marry. I'll never ken if she had time to forgive me before she went. That will always be a regret that haunts me."

"I'm certain she has, Uncle. She only ever wanted what was best for each of us. She understood yer duty to our clan, and she admired how ye always put everyone ahead of what ye might have wanted for yerself."

Andrew Mòr's eyes widened. "I wanted ye to marry Rab. I just didna want ye to marry a MacLaren. Since one couldnae come without the other, that's why I refused to consider it." He shifted his attention to Caelan. "Even if we didna learn aboot the Douglases today, the weans are right. We canna carry on."

"Nay. We canna," Caelan agreed. "Nessa will never forgive me if I did aught to hurt Catherine and fighting ye does that. I willna choose to lose ma son either. It all seems so wretchedly pointless now."

"Aye." Andrew Mòr nodded.

"Mòr," Caelan cleared his throat. "I am sorry for what we took from ye. I wished I could have said that to ye moons ago. I admired Lady MacFarlane and yer lasses, and I ken ma Nessa was fond of them. She's grieved in private for yer loss, but it has taken its toll on her. On all of us."

"Thank ye," Andrew Mòr rasped.

"Óg, ride with me," Rab suggested, allowing both lairds a moment to gather themselves as emotions became too raw. Both lairds stared at their sons, proud of the men they found at that moment. They'd accomplished a truce that Andrew Mòr and Caelan had been too stubborn and prideful to negotiate. Andrew Óg and Rab smiled at their fathers, relieved that the bitterness slipped from both leaders. The two younger men escorted the women into the crags, where Douglan hesitated to step forward. Rab nodded to his younger brother, rapidly explaining the complicated and nearly unbelievable events that unfolded.

With a score of men waiting with the women, both to guard them and as a second wave of warriors, Rab, Douglan, and Andrew Óg returned to the base of the hills to await the Douglases with the MacLaren, MacFarlane, and Campbell armies at the ready. Both Andrews, Rab, Caelan, and Dominic faced their horses toward the woods from which Catriona had emerged. Douglan and a senior MacFarlane warrior maneuvered their horses to stand behind the front line. Nearly a hundred warriors fanned out behind the nobles. Their wait wasn't long.

CHAPTER 18

Rab glanced toward the women's hiding place from the corner of his eye. He could tell Andrew Óg, who sat atop his horse beside him, did the same. Keeping his voice low, he spoke only for Andrew's ears.

"She's been ma friend since we were weans. Ye couldnae find a better woman unless ye wanted Kitty. Her father would take her back, but the Black willna be able to. Nae after she chose our clans over hers. He's fond of Catriona, but he must save face after this blows up, which it will."

"Dinna fash, Rab. I'm marrying her."

"Good."

The two men looked at one another, and Rab smiled. "I hope we can feast together and celebrate both marriages. We didna ken what else to do, but neither of us likes how we didna have our families with us at our wedding."

"We dinna like it, but I ken ma father understands as well as I do why ye did it. Things would be sitting quite differently right now if ye hadnae. I will always be protective of Catherine. I canna change that, and I dinna wish to. But I have never doubted how much ye love her and that she's happiest with ye. I can admit when I've been wrong, and I've erred more times than I like to say aloud. I misjudged ye both on more than one account. For that, I'm sorry."

Rab nodded, his appreciation silent but heartfelt.

"There," Caelan said as he pointed toward the woods far to the left. Barely visible through the low hanging limbs, the MacLarens, MacFarlanes, and Dominic could make out movement. "A bluidy surprise they're in for."

The combined forces watched as leaves rustled before a wave of Douglases emerged, prepared to race forward, only to rein to a halt. Caelan chuckled as he nudged his horse forward. The animal plodded as Andrew Mòr's steed matched pace.

"Do ye spy Maxwell?" Andrew chuckled. "Dare I ride close enough to discover if he piddled in his plaid?"

"Ye'll be able to smell him before ye see it," Caelan remarked. He and Andrew stopped halfway across the expanse. "Do ye recall the year we were likely seven-and-ten and Maxwell was twenty? Ye and I tied in the foot race. We were so determined to beat one another that I tripped him by accident, and ye stepped on him."

Andrew hooted with laughter, making many behind the two lairds wonder what could have taken two men who'd been mortal enemies that morning to being old chums. "I do. He protested and said we'd cheated. We'd helped each other to beat him."

"Helped each other," Caelan scoffed. "I didna dislike ye back then, auld mon. But I wasna interested in helping ye win. I was hopping mad that we tied."

"I didna dislike ye either. I ken our clans have always debated our boundaries, and I understand how our alliance with the Campbells made things harder for ye once the MacGregors started encroaching on ye. But until the last raid, I respected ye."

"And I ken why ye dinna now. I dinna fault ye for that."

"The Bruce's missive did more than tell me that Catherine and Rab likely ran away to marry. It detailed what Rab did."

Caelan glanced back over his shoulder as he nudged his horse a few steps forward as three Douglas representatives walked their horses toward them. "He's nae proud of that. But he doesnae lose sleep over it, and neither do I."

"The Bruce believes he did it for Catherine's sake, something aboot him making sure the three of them could never get to her."

"That and because he kens what they took from yer family. Our clan will always be important to Rab, and he will always put them first, but the mon believes family is everything. That's why he's protective of Catherine and why he couldnae allow members of his own to draw breath while members of yers didna."

Andrew nodded and turned his attention to the approaching force. His eyes narrowed as they locked on Maxwell Douglas. Caelan watched James "the Black" Douglas and his other brother, who was Catriona's father, ignore Maxwell. Nigel Douglas had passed his fiery curls to his daughter while his two brothers shared ebony heads of hair. But their faces announced their familial connection louder than any greeting.

"Go home," Caelan announced. "Turns out we dinna need yer help. Turns out ye dinna offer help."

"MacLaren," the Black started.

"Nay." Caelan held up his hand. "We already ken. Turn around and go home or turn him over to us."

"Ye ken I'm nae doing that," the Black responded, even as he scowled at his brother Maxwell.

"Do ye intend to fight the clan ye came to save?" Andrew Mòr asked. "Like MacLaren said, we ken. We all ken." Andrew pointed over his shoulder. "And soon Brodie will ken too. We've made our peace and have formed our own alliance."

"What?" Maxwell spluttered. He searched beyond Andrew and Caelan. "Where is that little tart?"

"Maxwell," Nigel growled. "Ye have never been ma favorite brother. I've never seen why I needed two. She's ma daughter."

"And she betrayed us," Maxwell argued.

"Enough," the Black snapped. "So ye learned of our role in yer feud. What now?"

"Ye're letting us decide?" Caelan pretended to perk up. "If that's the case, hand him over after all."

"So yer butcher of a son can do to me what he did to yer own nephews? Och, aye. I heard aboot that," Maxwell snarled.

"So did I," Andrew cut in. "And auld rivalries die hard. I'm certain ma Andrew can do far worse than his Rab ever did." The cold steel lacing the older Andrew's voice didn't leave any man in doubt that the younger Andrew could be ruthless too.

"Tempting," the Black said sardonically. "There's still a marriage agreement that we signed."

"Aboot that," Caelan grinned. "Ma son's already married."

"What?" Maxwell demanded, interjecting once more despite the hatred filling the surrounding air.

"Aye, to ma niece." Andrew matched Caelan's grin.

"For how long?" the Black asked.

"Nae longer than that agreement's been signed," Maxwell insisted. "That made Rab pre-contracted. The marriage isnae valid. It's a handfast most likely."

"Nay. Apparently, ma son and daughter-by-marriage are quite resourceful. They had the banns read at Dunblane and wed there."

"Neither of them is a parishioner there. That means the banns were worthless," the Black noted.

"Dunblane is a Stirling parish, where ma niece has lived for three years." Andrew shrugged. "Rab was in Stirling and attended Mass there. Sounds like it was both of their parishes to me."

"That is a ludicrous stretch, and ye both ken it," complained Maxwell.

"Apparently," Caelan reached into his sporran and retrieved a folded piece of vellum, "according to the king, if anyone was already pre-contracted, it was Rab and Lady Catherine."

"He said that to ye, too?" Andrew asked, as he withdrew his own missive with a royal seal. "Seems Rab said something aboot they'd agreed to marry and were on their way to tell each of us when our argument exploded."

"Aye. I remember him trying to tell me some such and mentioning Lady Catherine," Caelan recalled, his brow furrowing. He stared at Maxwell. "Ye kenned that, didna ye? Ye kenned they must have talked aboot marrying, and that's why ye acted when ye did. Ye wanted to keep them apart."

"If this is really aboot the Campbells more than it is us, I'm certain Dominic will be happy to weigh in." Before anyone could disagree, Andrew turned back and called out to the Campbell tánaiste, waving him forward. Dominic moved out of the line, leaving Andrew Óg and Rab shoulder to shoulder, a most unexpected sight. One that was as jarring as watching Andrew Mòr and Caelan smiling at one another as they taunted the Douglases.

"Douglas," Dominic said to the Black, not sparing Nigel or Maxwell a glance.

"Seems ma brother took it upon himself to play chief diplomat for ma clan," the Black stated.

"So I gather. He thought pitting the MacLarens against the MacFarlanes could make them dependent on ye. Either he is far more patient than I imagined because it's been three years since he started this, or he's the greatest fool in the Highlands. I lean toward the latter." Dominic smirked at Maxwell. "Ye think far more of yerself than anyone else does. Brodie isnae interested in proving aught to ye. He doesnae need to. The Bruce respects ye," Dominic nodded at the Black, "and ma brother. Brodie is fine with that."

"Upstart," Maxwell hissed, to which Dominic boomed a laugh.

"If ye say so," Dominic said. "Black, either ye're leading yer clan or ye're nae. If ye are, then decide now: do ye wish to fight us or nae?"

"Dinna test me by trying to shame me, Dom," the Black warned. "I rode out to see if we can put an end to this. I dinna care what Maxwell thought. I'm nae interested in starting a war with ye or anyone else. There's still too much trouble with the English for us to waste our time and our men killing one another in the Highlands."

"To that, I think we can all agree," Dominic nodded. "But yer brother canna just return home with nay consequences."

"Believe ye me, I ken that, and so does he."

"Seems like ye made a long ride for naught," Caelan mused. "Ye could put an end to it by nae coming back and being sure to muzzle yer wee brother."

"We rode out to be sure Catriona is safe," Nigel interjected. "We dinna ken what she told ye, and we didna ken how ye would receive it."

"The little—"

"Finish that thought, and I will call ma son over to

hear ye repeat it," Andrew warned. "Turns out he's fond of the lass. I dinna think he'd take well to hearing a disparaging word aboot her."

"Aye, well." Nigel's mouth turned down. "She told me that more than once. We didna see allying ourselves with ye as useful. Ye ken what we thought. I assume it's ye who thinks we're nae a desirable ally."

"I've never thought ye were," Andrew snarked. "But that's nae the lass's fault."

"Send her out," Nigel responded.

"Nay." Andrew shook his head. "I dinna believe she's safe with ye. And even if she is, I dinna think I can convince ma son to agree. Keep her dowry, and we keep her."

"MacFarlane!" The Black thundered. "Ye go too far."

"Do I? Yer brother got ma wife and daughters raped and murdered. Just how far do ye think I might go?" Andrew drew a dirk from his waist and stared at the tip, as though the sun striking the blade fascinated him. "The lass had naught to do with that, so I willna hold her family against her. But the three of ye? Do ye ken why ye're still breathing? Because ma niece and ma soon-to-be daughter-by-marriage can see us, even if ye canna see them. But this is hardly over. Go home, Douglases. There's nay battle today. But gird yer loins because one way or another, one is coming. As much as I hunger to kill ye, Maxwell, it might satisfy me to tell ma tale of woe to the king's ear directly."

The Black exchanged a look with Nigel, who nodded. The eldest Douglas brother, the leader of the main branch of their clan and friend to the king, cast his stare at Maxwell. He flicked his hand, and four Douglas warriors came forward. Before Maxwell realized they encircled him, they stripped him of his weapons and pulled him from his horse.

"Consider this ma niece's dowry," the Black said before whirling his horse around. Maxwell spun around in confusion, then horror, as the Douglases rode away and left him with no weapons and no horse to faces three angry clans.

"Óg!" Andrew Mòr called to his son. "Bring rope!"

The younger Andrew met his father, confusion clear on his face until he looked at Maxwell. A malevolent gleam entered Óg's eyes as he dismounted. He drove his fist into Maxwell's nose, blood geysering from it. He bound the man's wrists, then his ankles before binding them together.

"The only reason I'm nae going to drag ye all the way to Inveruglas then watch ye trail behind ma boat while ye try to stay afloat is because Cat is here. Thank God for small mercies. But once I have ye in our dungeon, far from where Cat can hear or see ye, I will make ye pay. I will make ye pay for what happened to ma mother, to ma sisters. I will make ye pay for every time ye tried to intimidate Cat, tried to manipulate her. Och, ye underestimated her far too many times. We spent far more time together than ye ken. I ken far more than ye can imagine. Dinna think Rab is the only mon who has a taste of the devil inside him for torture. Ye shall have yer turn." Grasping a handful of Maxwell's hair in one hand and leading his horse in the other, Andrew dragged Maxwell across the field before ordering two MacFarlanes to heave him over the back of a pack horse and tie him to it. He mounted Hercules, then raced along the rocky hillside with Rab. The kiss he shared with Catriona rivaled the one Rab and Catherine shared.

CHAPTER 19

"*R*ab," Catherine exhaled as they drew apart.

"It's over, Kitty." Rab kissed her temple, inhaling her floral scent. "WHat could ye see?"

"All of it, even if we couldnae hear," Catherine said as she looked at her friend and her cousin.

"Catherine, I am so sorry," Catriona croaked as fresh tears tumbled down her cheeks. Andrew drew her back against his chest. She sobbed, "Óg."

"Wheest, Cat. We ken ye had naught to do with it," Andrew whispered. "Ye warned us once ye kenned."

"How could I nae?" Catriona choked. "Ye're ma friend, Catherine. And, Óg, ye're…"

"I'm yer betrothed, Cat. Assuming ye will have me, I am marrying ye, lass."

"But ma uncle? The Black expects me to marry…"

"Nay, he doesnae," Andrew countered. "He already kenned how we feel. He may have to save face and make it appear as though he's turned his back on ye, but he wouldnae leave ye to me if he didna trust that I'll love ye and care for ye always. Yer father certainly wouldnae."

Catriona pushed hair from her face as she swiped at

her tears. "I was so scared. Nae of riding here. But that even if I chose ye, ye wouldnae choose me."

"Cat, I would have been a fool a hundred times over to let ye go. But I would never have abandoned ye. It wasna even a choice. I'm always going to do whatever it takes to protect ye and make ye happy."

"Does that mean ye'll marry me?"

"Are ye the one doing the asking?" Andrew grinned. "Can ye nae be patient even for a moment?"

"Doubtful." Catriona's sparkling eyes alluded to what else might make her impatient.

"Aye, Catriona. I'll marry ye. I already told ye I'm yer betrothed."

"And I'll marry ye," Catriona echoed.

"Ye realize that with us here to witness, ye are married," Catherine pointed out, her grin matching her cousin's. Andrew and Catriona's kiss drew out, leaving Catherine and Rab to look at the guards who'd accompanied the women into the rocks.

"Yer father is still likely to geld me," Rab mused as Andrew and Catriona pulled apart. "I'd like to have done with this, so I can take ma wife home for a proper meal."

"Ye and me both," Andrew agreed as he pressed a kiss behind Catriona's ear.

The two couples and the guards made their way back into the meadow. Catherine caught sight of Maxwell draped over a horse's back, rage swelling in her chest. Her pulse pounded in her ears as she looked at the man responsible for taking so much from her family, the man who'd kept her from Rab for years. As the fury thrummed through her, she had a sudden understanding of how Rab could be so cruel to his cousins because it didn't feel like cruelty. It felt like justice.

Catherine dismounted and walked to Maxwell. She

grabbed a handful of hair and yanked his head up. Despite the awkward angle, his gaze met hers. "I pray the king leaves us to mete out yer punishment. Better yet, I pray ma uncle and cousin are as impatient as me. I pray they take a lesson from ma husband. Och, aye. I ken just like ye do. If Mòr and Óg canna come up with a fitting way for ye to die, I have plenty of suggestions." Catherine leaned in, so only Maxwell could hear. "The first is being buggered with yer own cock. I'll let them figure out the how, but mayhap I willna wait to see what they devise as yer torture. Mayhap I'll suggest it anyhow."

"Whore," Maxwell swore.

The tip of Catherine's dirk poked against the corner of Maxwell's left eye before anyone realized what was happening. "If the sight of me troubles ye, then I'll pluck out yer eyes. If the sound of ma voice troubles ye, then I will hack off yer ears." She slipped the tip of the blade between his lips until it tapped a tooth. "Either way, I'll cut out yer tongue and make ye wipe yer arse with it. Then none of us will have to listen to ye spew lies and filth."

"Catherine," Andrew Mòr stepped beside his niece. "I dinna want his blood on yer hands, and I dinna think yer husband or father-by-marriage want that either. If ye wish for his head on a pike to greet ye each sunrise, then ye shall have it. But I'll do it."

"I'd never take that right from ye, Uncle. Nae after all *he* took from ye."

"Good lass." Andrew pressed Catherine's hand away from Maxwell's face until she drew away on her own accord. She returned her knife to its sheath. "Go with yer husband, Catherine."

Catherine stared at Andrew for a long breath before she nodded. She stepped back to the horse she'd borrowed as Rab slipped his arm around her waist. They watched as the two Andrews spoke, the younger nodding several times. Caelan came to stand beside the couple as they wondered what the MacFarlanes intended to do since they were on MacLaren land.

"Mòr, I extend ma hospitality to ye and yers." Caelan reached out his arm. "For better or for worse, we are family now. I, for one, wish to celebrate ma son's bride. I'm nae so thrilled with him, but I already love ma daughter-by-marriage."

Andrew Mòr studied Caelan's outstretched arm before accepting it. The two lairds shook, their rivalry not over as they both squeezed, waiting to see who relented first. When neither flinched nor eased their grip, they both yanked their arms back.

"I feel the same aboot yer son and ma niece," Andrew grinned. "The least ye could do is feed me a decent meal."

"I've seen ye eat, mon. A decent meal to ye is a feast to anyone else. Do ye intend to eat me out of house and home?"

"Good thing yer wife is a skilled chatelaine. She can manage."

"Och, aye. But just so ye ken, the feast ye'll get is for Catherine. I promise ye Nessa will barely spare the rest of us a glance once she sees our daughter-by-marriage." Caelan returned Andrew's jovial expression.

"Is it really that easy?" Catherine whispered.

"Nay," Rab responded in a low voice. "But with our warriors here watching and listening, it must look that way. The past will be left where it belongs, but it will take time for everyone to heal. The first step is the lairds getting along for all to see. We are bound together as family, but we also now have a mutual enemy. While Maxwell isnae long for this world, our shared anger unites us."

"I ken they're talking aboot our wedding feast, but

would it bother ye if we shared it with Óg and Catriona?" Catherine bit the bottom corner of her lip.

"I already assumed we were," Rab answered. "They're *our* family."

"Thank ye." Catherine beamed as she kissed Rab. She turned toward Caelan and stepped toward him. "I'm sorry ye and Lady MacLaren werenae at our wedding." She glanced at both Andrews. "I'm sorry ma family wasna there either. But I look forward to sharing our happiness with our entire family."

"Lady Catherine. Lass." Caelan engulfed her in a hug. "The part of me who is laird isnae pleased with ma tánaiste for the deception and taking matters into his own hands. But the larger part of me who is a da is elated that ma son finally wed the only woman he'll ever love. The laird and da in me is thrilled that ma son married a woman who will be a formidable defender of our clan and our people but who also has a heart as big as the Highlands. Welcome, daughter."

"Thank ye—Father." Catherine wasn't sure how she felt addressing another man by the title, but as the word slipped forth, she realized it felt right. But a moment of regret flashed through her, almost feeling as though she betrayed Andrew Mòr, since he'd been a father to her for nearly half her life. She twisted to look at Andrew, relieved to see happiness in the man's eyes. She watched as Andrew hesitantly, at first, embraced Rab, clapping him hard on the back.

"Óg, Lady Catriona, feast with us and celebrate yer marriage alongside ma son and his bride," Caelan announced. "We ken ye will have yer own feast among yer people, but I ken ye are both vera important to ma son and daughter. We open our doors and share our hearth with ye and yers."

"I make one request," Andrew Mòr spoke up. "Ma son and I have agreed to how we will handle him." Andrew jerked a thumb over his shoulder at Maxwell. "I dinna usually send out invitations to an execution, but then again, I havenae ended a feud lately either. He will die where ma people can see, so they ken the mon who stole so much from us has breathed his last. But he has caused the MacLarens great heartache too. I want yer people to ken that we have put our differences to rest now that we ken the real cause. He is to die by stoning. The MacLarens, if ye wish, should be among those who cast their rocks."

Catherine and Catriona exchanged a glance, neither eager to watch such a death when they would rather celebrate their marriages, but both women couldn't deny their desire to watch Maxwell Douglas die for his crimes. Catriona had never confessed to Catherine how uncomfortable she felt around Maxwell, but Catherine sensed Maxwell had tried to do more than just intimidate his niece. From Andrew Óg's expression when he looked at Catriona, Catherine suspected her friend confessed things to Andrew that she hadn't shared with Catherine.

"We ride for Inveruglas then Edinample," Caelan stated. The two clans had a full day's ride ahead of them to reach Inveruglas. The MacLarens and MacFarlanes mounted their horses and wheeled them around to face southwest. When darkness forced them to stop for the night, the clans shared a campsite. Each warrior understood they were all safer traveling together and sharing a camp. It made it easier for them to eat together, but more than one man slept with one eye open. When dawn came, they were all back in the saddle.

"There is much to tell," Andrew Mòr boomed as he and the rest of the MacFarlane-MacLaren party led their horses into Inveruglas's bailey. Men had stood stunned on the battlements as Andrew ordered more boats to ferry the MacLarens across to the tiny isle. He didn't hesitate to march to the keep's top step, raising his hand to silence the whispers. "Ma niece, our Lady Catherine, has finally married Rab MacLaren. I ken that must cause ye shock, concern, but hopefully also happiness. It's nay great secret that we've all wished she could marry Rab in the same breath we've wished he werenae a MacLaren. Be they impetuous or wise, they forced our clans to consider why we started feuding and why we've carried it on. What we once believed to be the truth, on each side, we've discovered isnae so. Ma son's bride—aye, that's right. Óg's gone and married too. Lady Catriona was a Douglas yesterday morning, but she arrives here a much-loved MacFarlane daughter. It was she who informed Laird MacLaren and me that neither of us was to blame for how this feud started. The blame lies with Maxwell Douglas."

Andrew motioned for guards to bring Maxwell to stand before Andrew at the bottom of the steps. He'd been awkward that morning when it was time to set off, so he sported a severely bruised faced. When he'd spewed oaths at Catriona, Andrew Óg's boot landed against his ribs several times.

"Maxwell Douglas's ambition for himself and for his clan led him to instigate the feud and perpetuate it. His wish to rival the Campbells led to many deaths for us and for the MacLarens. But we all ken how we've suffered for his last act of malice and manipulation." Andrew Mòr looked down at Maxwell. "For organizing the raid that killed ma wife and daughters and that harmed so many of ma clanswomen, I sentence ye to death by stoning."

"The king will have yer stones for this," Maxwell spat.

"And who do ye think will tell the king what happened?" Caelan demanded as he came to stand beside Andrew Mòr. "Yer own brother handed ye over to us. Do ye think he will cry on the Bruce's shoulder? Do ye think a MacLaren will complain aboot ye dying as ye should? I canna imagine a MacFarlane would. Do ye think the Campbells might take up yer cause?"

Dominic Campbell and his men had parted ways with the MacLarens and MacFarlanes that morning. They were making their way to Kilchurn and not one Campbell had looked back as they rode north. Caelan and Andrew Mòr stared at Maxwell, silently taunting him. When the former delegate to the royal court said nothing, Andrew cast his gaze over his gathered clan members.

"I willna make anyone cast a stone who doesnae wish to. But if ye do, ye'd do well to gather them now. The mon will be dead before the hour changes."

Catherine and Catriona stood together, their husbands at their backs. They looked at one another, neither sure what to do. Catherine spoke first. "I wish to cast one stone. Just to ken that I did to reassure maself that I didna turn ma back on ma aunt and ma cousins."

"I'm the same. I have been angry with that mon for most of ma life. I think I would feel better for it, but I dinna need to watch that kind of slow death."

"Neither of ye have to," Andrew Óg said. "We'll take ye inside as soon as ye're ready."

"Dinna ye have to stay out here?" Catriona asked.

"Nay." Rab shook his head. "Our clans will mete out his punishment. Neither Óg nor I am tasked with it. Our greater concern is for our wives."

Rab and Andrew exchanged a look over the women's heads. Neither wanted their wives in the crowd, knowing how volatile public executions could become. They knew both women were aware since they'd each witnessed them during their tenure at Stirling Court, but they'd never participated in one. Andrew led them to where a pile of stones lay beside a stretch of inner wall that was being repaired. They each found a stone and made their way back to the crowd. They watched as people used their clothing to carry their rock selections. Maxwell shifted nervously as he tried to watch everyone. It wasn't long before the crowd encircled him. He opened his mouth, "Heavenly Father—"

"Keep yer prayers for God's ears only. Nay one wants to hear them," Caelan snapped. He tossed a rock in his hand, pretending to weigh it and test his hold.

"Maxwell Douglas, ye are sentenced to death for the deaths of each MacFarlane and MacLaren who died during the feud ye caused. Ye will die with the same lack of mercy ye showed those ye ordered killed. May God have mercy on yer soul because we willna." Andrew Mòr decreed before nodding his head. The first wave of rocks pelted Maxwell, knocking him to his knees. Catherine and Catriona threw theirs, striking him in the head. Rab and Andrew Óg followed suit, Rab's striking Maxwell's left cheekbone while Óg's struck Maxwell's left temple. The men shielded the women as they pushed through the gathering, steering the women into the keep. Catherine looked around, shocked to find the Great Hall empty until she realized everyone was in the bailey.

"I canna summon a bath for ye, Catriona, until the servants return." Catherine frowned, thinking about how much she wished to enjoy a bath too.

"We will bring the tubs up and the hot water," Andrew Óg offered. "Cat, I'll take ye to our chamber."

"I'll take ye to ours," Catherine said as she took Rab's hand. The two couples moved abovestairs in silence, all four lost in their own thoughts. It wasn't long before Andrew and Rab brought tubs to each chamber and then buckets of hot water to their wives. The water was cold in each tub by the time the couples climbed out of their respective baths. Both pairs of newlyweds drowned out the sounds from the bailey by creating melodies of bliss in their own chambers.

CHAPTER 20

*C*atherine swept her gaze over the MacLarens who'd rushed into the bailey when the bells tolled, announcing their laird's and tánaiste's return. They stared, mouths agog, as the MacFarlanes followed the MacLarens within Edinample's barmekin. Lady Nessa MacLaren hurried down the steps, headed toward her husband, her arms outstretched, until she recognized Catherine. With a squeal, she veered toward Catherine and Timber. Catherine tossed her leg over her saddle and slid to the ground, engulfed immediately in Nessa's embrace.

"Catherine, sweet lass," Nessa whispered.

"Nessa," Catherine breathed, as she returned the embrace. She found the same comfort in her mother's-by-marriage embrace as she had in her own mother's and her Aunt Aveline's. She clung to the woman, finding strength she hadn't realized she lacked. She shifted when she felt Nessa release one arm, then Rab pressed against her back.

"Mama," Rab said, before kissing Nessa's cheek. "Kitty and I—"

Nessa squealed again as she pulled the couple in for another embrace. "Do I have another daughter?"

"Another?" Rab and Catherine asked. They pulled away and found Douglan and a dark-haired woman with a rounded belly watching them. Catherine's belly clenched as she came face-to-face with the woman who'd shared her bed with Rab for two years, the woman who'd thought to trap Rab into marrying her. From Rab's stillness, Catherine could tell he didn't know what to do either. When his arm slid around her waist and drew her to his side, almost as though he intended to shield her, she glanced up at him. She expected to find him watching Douglan and his former leman, but Rab fixed his attention on her.

"Ye dinna need to meet now if ye dinna wish," Rab whispered. He tilted his head an inch toward where his mother and father stood talking to both Andrews and Catriona, knowing they were being watched.

"Better now than drawing this out." Catherine swallowed as she pressed her lips together.

"Lady Catherine." Douglan stepped forward with a clearly uncomfortable bride at his side. "Rab."

"Douglan," Catherine said with a forced smile. They'd talked little while they were at Inveruglas since she and Rab spent most of their time in her old chamber. She finally met Katherine's gaze, and she felt a moment of pity for the woman. She watched how Katherine watched Rab, watched the realization sweep over her when the former leman heard the shared name. Catherine didn't perceive any anger, regret, or love. Just shock. She watched as her could-be rival turned toward Douglan and rested her head against his shoulder. Douglan wrapped his arm around the woman's shoulders.

"Kitty," Rab started but was unsure how to proceed.

"Aye," Catherine breathed, steeling herself to say more. "Katherine, it's nice to meet ye. I see I come as much of a surprise to ye as learning aboot ye came to me. But I also see that ye and Douglan are clearly a couple nay longer in hiding. I wish ye happy."

Katherine blinked several times before dipping into a curtsy. "Thank ye. I—I—" She glanced helplessly up at Douglan. "I'm sorry. We're sorry."

"Brother," Douglan said and waited.

"Mayhap we can take this inside, since people are staring," Catherine suggested. The two couples walked up the keep stairs, aware the entire clan watched them, and the MacFarlane entourage was curious. Catherine wished she were still embracing Nessa, preferring to catch up with her mother-by-marriage than have the most awkward conversation with her brother- and sister-by-marriage. They went to Caelan's solar, where Rab shut the door behind them.

"Douglan, I'm nae angry at ye or Katherine. I wasna vera honorable with Katherine, even if I thought I wasna doing any harm." Rab studied his brother and his former mistress. He felt nothing toward the woman, and his brother only mildly irritated him. The overwhelming feeling was still relief. "It's clear that ye love each other. And it's never been a secret how I feel aboot Kitty. The Lord has seen fit to put the right couples together."

"But can ye forgive us for lying to ye? For me trying to trap ye?" Katherine blurted.

Rab glanced down at Catherine, realizing she wasn't as prepared to forgive and move on as he was. "I am because I'm married to the right woman. Can ye forgive me for using ye?"

"Aye. Douglan explained it to me. I wasna living under a rock. I kenned aboot ye, Lady Catherine, but I didna realize—I didna want to accept—that the only reason Rab sought me out was because he wished to pretend he was with ye."

"I canna imagine how that makes ye feel," Catherine offered. "Thank ye both for doing the right thing."

"We handfasted that night, Rab," Douglan spoke up. "We'll marry in a moon once the priest's read the banns. We wanted ye here for it."

Catherine's eyes narrowed as she watched Douglan, who turned bright red.

"I mean, we wanted ye to be part of our happiness and to ken we're making our future together," Douglan added.

"We canna both be called the same thing," Catherine spoke up.

"Should we call ye Kitty?" Douglan asked.

"Nay." Catherine and Rab answered together. Catherine explained, "I'd prefer only Rab to call me that."

"I go by Kate in the village," Katherine offered. Rab, Catherine, and Douglan nodded. "Lady Catherine—"

"Catherine. Ye're a lady now too. Ye married a laird's son, which makes ye and yer bairn nobles. It will only get tiresome and confusing if ye use ma title when we are peers."

"Thank ye. I need ye to ken that I love Douglan. I was fond of Rab, but I love ma husband."

The two couples stood staring at one another, neither certain what else to say. There didn't seem to be much else to say. Catherine leaned against Rab, suddenly exhausted despite having slept in her chamber at Inveruglas the night before. With an awkward parting, Douglan and Katherine left for the croft they now shared. Catherine and Rab found Nessa and Caelan and Catherine's relatives waiting for them in the Great Hall. A few more awkward smiles and a reassuring embrace from Nessa eased them into sitting around the table on the dais as the new arrivals ate. It wasn't long before

Catherine struggled to keep her eyes open. She was dozing by the time Rab carried her to their new chamber, but she roused herself to look around.

"Do ye ken how many nights I've dreamed of bringing ye to our chamber, of undressing ye, then making love to ye on this bed?" Rab asked.

"The same number of nights that I dreamed of being here," Catherine replied. She cast her gaze over the bed, which was wide enough for at least four women to fit but seemed just the right size for Rab. "I hope ye dinna lose me on that."

"I'm nae letting go of ye, wife." Rab pulled at the ribbons that laced Catherine's gown in the front. He peeled it back from her shoulders after she unfastened the brooch at his shoulder. Neither hurried as they undressed, pressing soft kisses as they exposed new patches of flesh. Rab kneeled before Catherine as he rolled her stockings down to her ankles and peeled them off her feet. He breathed cool air against her heated petals before sweeping his tongue along her seam.

Catherine's moan was tortured pleasure. She tilted her head back and closed her eyes, but she soon grew lightheaded as Rab's ministrations stole her breath. She grasped his shoulders as she swayed. When the tip of his tongue pressed into her core, she feared her knees might give out, but she had no intention of stopping him. She forced her eyes to open and focus as she watched his dark head press between her thighs. She was uncertain what mesmerized her more: the sensations he stirred within her, or the sight of him stroking his rod as his fingers joined his tongue. She cupped the back of his head as Rab continued to elicit one moan after another.

"I want to touch ye, too," Catherine panted. "I canna reach."

Rab rose to his feet, kissing her neck and trailing his tongue over her collarbone. Catherine wrapped her hand around his length and stroked. It was Rab's turn to let his head fall back. She watched his Adam's apple bob as he swallowed. He whispered, "Kitty," over and over as he kneaded her breasts.

"I want to be inside ye, but I also want to draw out this first time with ye in our chamber." Rab brought his mouth to Catherine's. They savored the moment before climbing onto the bed.

"I want the same, but I dinna think I can last." Catherine inched beneath Rab as he guided his cock into her core. With a hard thrust, he seated himself inside her as her nails bit into his biceps. "It can be slow next time or the time after that. Nae now."

They moved together as their bodies grew slick with perspiration. Catherine's hands roamed over Rab's shoulders and chest as the muscles bunched and flexed. She pressed her heels into the mattress and lifted her hips to meet each surge, the passion and need dragging them away like an undertow that threatened to leave them adrift. They clung to one another, each other's lifeline in the tumultuousness of their desire. There was no finesse. No gentleness. Just a consuming hunger to show and be shown the rightness of their coupling.

"I love ye, Kitty. I love ye so damn much I dinna ken how to say it."

"Just keep showing me because I dinna ken how to say it either. More, Rab." Catherine encouraged him to lose control as she moved with him, contracting her inner core until the muscles spasmed with release and held Rab captive as his seed jetted from him. They gazed into each other's fathomless blue eyes, a sense—an intuition—that their coupling had been more than passionate love play. Catherine reached between them at the same moment Rab did, resting her hand on her belly with his covering it. "Do ye think we did?"

"I dinna ken, but something makes me think we did." Rab brushed a soft kiss against her lips. "But even if we didna, I willna forget this moment together."

"Neither will I. I'm finally home."

"Where ye belong."

They nestled together, Rab's arms wrapped around Catherine as she rested her head at the crook of his neck. They were asleep only moments later.

"I canna believe all this," Catriona said as she and Catherine made their way back to the dais, out of breath from the country reel.

"I didna think they would welcome us with such an extravagant feast," Catherine said as they took their seats and watched the dancers in Edinample's Great Hall. "And I have a bone to pick with ye. Why didna ye tell me that how serious ye felt aboot Óg?"

"Likely for the same reason ye didna confide in me that ye were sneaking around with Rab. Neither of us kenned what the future held, and it was too painful to discuss."

"Aye. Ye ken it was never for a lack of trusting ye, Cat." Catherine rested her hand on her friend's arm.

"I ken. The fewer people who kenned, the fewer people who could interfere."

"Has Óg ever told ye that I encouraged him to speak to yer father?"

"He did last night. Did he tell ye that I wasna best pleased with him when I kenned he warned ye away from Rab?"

"Nay. But I canna blame him for being concerned. Ye have ma thanks for trying to help us. I ken that couldnae have been easy when things were uncertain between ye."

"Aye, well, he's stubborn. He needs someone to tell him some sense." Catriona leaned forward to look past Catherine to where Rab and Andrew Óg stood chatting. They looked at ease, but both women knew their husbands were constantly alert to any changes in the mood in the Great Hall. The truce was too new to trust. "He's a lot like Rab in that way. They need us."

"Blessed saints, dinna they? Cat, one day it will be the four of us leading our clans. I count ma blessings that we're friends. There will be times when our husbands may nae see eye to eye. I dinna want us to lose our friendship over it, and I ken they may need us to guide them. I canna think of a better woman to be Lady MacFarlane. Our clan is fortunate to have ye."

"I can say the same for the MacLarens. Caelan and Nessa will nae be with us forever. I've kenned ye nearly as long as I have Rab and his family. Ye will be good for yer people here."

"What are ye two gnash gabbing on aboot?" Rab asked as the men joined the ladies.

"How bluidy lucky ye are to have us," Catriona stated. Catherine raised her chalice, waiting for Catriona to do the same before they toasted one another.

"Everyone seems to be enjoying themselves," Catherine observed.

"Aye. Kenning who was responsible for what's happened over the years, and kenning it wasna any of us, has done much to ease the tension." Rab's cool fingers stroked along the back of Catherine's neck as they watched their clan's merrymaking. "I think it's helping to have the MacFarlanes watch us welcome ye and for them to ken we arenae rejoicing in yer loss. I hope they return to Inveruglas and tell their clansmen and women that we didna want the feud any more than they did."

"They will," Andrew Óg chimed in. "Yer clan has been gracious to our men since we arrived."

"Because we understand the pain a handful of Mac-Larens caused ye. That isnae us as a clan, and we want yer people to ken that. Pride kept the feud going when it wasna being fueled from the outside." Rab raised the chalice Catherine had placed between them. "We are more alike than we are different. I would toast to the day when we share both blood and wine."

Andrew raised the chalice he shared with Catriona as Catriona stared at Catherine, who could only shrug and smile bashfully. Catriona cocked an eyebrow and smirked. Catherine's eyes widened to saucers. She mouthed, "Does he ken?"

Catriona shook her head. "Nae yet."

"Nae yet what?" Andrew asked.

"I feel like I ought to hold yer cods at sword point, Cousin," Catherine warned, but her smile was irrepressible. "Someone needs to defend ma friend's honor."

"Hush!" Catriona giggled. "I rather like his cods. And since I ken they work, I'd like to keep them that way. I dinna want to have an only child. I want a large brood."

"Wha—" Andrew's face drained of all its color, and he appeared to sway in his seat.

"Óg?" Catriona cupped his cheek.

"Ma father is going to geld me," Andrew mumbled. "When he realizes we coupled without handfasting and that I might nae have asked for yer hand... He's going to geld me."

"I was hoping for felicitations," Catriona teased. "I'll protect ye."

"I will gladly accept." Andrew shook his head as a

smile stretched from ear to ear. He lifted Catriona onto his lap. "Are ye certain?"

"Fairly. I havenae had a midwife check me, but I realized it while I was with ma clan. I thought it was nerves that were turning ma belly over. Then I counted back." Catriona gazed at Andrew. "Are ye genuinely happy? Ye dinna think I did this on purpose, do ye?"

"Got with child with a mon who ye rightly may have feared wouldnae get up the nerve to demand he marry ye? Nay. I dinna think that was yer intent. But I canna say I regret it either, Cat. I love ye and our bairn."

"I love ye, Drew." Catriona rubbed her nose against Andrew's. Neither noticed she'd used her own diminutive for him. Rab led Catherine back out to the dancers as the other couple enjoyed a private moment together.

"I never imagined finally having peace without a battle," Catherine confessed.

"Neither did I. It all feels surreal, but I dinna want to say it aloud too often for fear of tempting fate. If Catriona hadnae ridden out to tell us, we likely wouldnae be feasting together. I'm nae sure if Óg and I could have kept our fathers at bay."

"We owe her a great debt." Catherine pretended to grimace. "And we paid it by giving her Óg."

"I dinna think she minds." Rab jutted his chin toward the dais, where Catriona and Andrew were locked in a passionate kiss that soon led to them fleeing the raised table and flying up the stairs to their chamber.

"Let us enjoy this peace. We're finally where we belong, and our clans arenae at each other's throats. Mòr and Caelan look as if they've been friends since the cradle." Catherine pointed to where the two lairds challenged each other to one dram of whisky after another. "They look like they could be brothers, dinna ye think?

Dark hair. Same build. They both remind me of a bodach."

"I dare ye to tell either of them that they remind ye of a cantankerous auld mon."

"Mayhap another time." Catherine twirled in Rab's arms before they settled back into the steps that kept them together. "I think they are far more alike than they wanted to admit. But I hope that means they'll also find it easier to be allies than enemies."

"I think so. I think they could have been friends if there hadnae been tension between our clans since they were lads."

"I hope they can be. I dinna think the MacGregors will take well to learning our clans are now allies. Caelan might even come around to getting along with Brodie."

"Kitty, I wouldnae be so quick to believe that. I dinna ken that we'll ever call the Campbells allies if they expect us to accept the MacGregors onto our land. Brodie suggested ma father pay fealty to him as an overlord for them supporting us against the MacGregors. I dinna ken if Father will ever accept that, and after what we justly owe yer uncle, we canna afford to pay them aught."

Catherine sighed, but nodded. "If nae friends and allies, then at least nae enemies. Naught's resolved with the Buchanans and leaving half a score of them dead isnae likely to endear either clan to the Buchanans."

"I havenae even had time to tell Father aboot that."

"I dinna think Óg's told Mòr yet either."

"I dinna ken if I should do that now while they're three sheets in the wind or wait until tomorrow."

"When they have sore heads?" Catherine giggled. "Mayhap now and pray they forget."

"Or mayhap yer cousins had the right idea." Rab swooped Catherine into his arms to the cheers of those around them. Since they arrived married, no one suggested a bedding ceremony the previous day or as part of the feast. The couple made their escape as they had the evening before, retiring to their chamber where they made love throughout the night.

"I wish ye didna have to go so soon, Uncle," Catherine said as Andrew Mòr nearly swallowed her whole in his embrace.

"Lass, we've been here nigh on a fortnight. We canna overstay our welcome."

"Nay such thing, Mòr," Rab said as he and Andrew shook forearms. "I ken I can speak for ma father when I say ye and yers are always welcome here."

During the past ten days, there was much healing between the two lairds and their people. The MacLarens accepted the MacFarlane warriors in the lists, training alongside the MacLarens after the first few days of wariness. Caelan and Andrew discussed clan politics across Scotland, the ongoing troubles along the border, and how they should handle the inevitable summons back to court after their offspring left without permission. They reminisced over several tots of whisky, recalling fighting alongside the Bruce and Brodie's father. Caelan explained to Andrew why the MacLarens and Campbells might not become allies, hoping it kept Andrew from feeling caught in the middle.

Nessa's hospitality, ensuring everyone had their fill of food and ale, helped the MacFarlanes feel accepted outside the training field. She encouraged the musicians to tune their instruments early and to begin the dancing as soon as the servants cleared the last course. The MacFarlanes watched how she doted on both

Catherine and Catriona, her sincerity obvious. It even surprised the MacFarlanes to witness how paternal Caelan was to both ladies. He was no longer the ogre they had painted him for so many years.

Andrew Óg and Rab admitted they liked one another now that they were no longer representing feuding clans, and Rab was no longer a clandestine suitor, while Andrew was an overprotective relative. They accepted Douglan into their midst, and it appeared as though nothing was ever amiss between the brothers. The transition wasn't so smooth for Catherine and Kate. They skirted around one another until the day Kate tripped going down the keep steps. Catherine was approaching from a storage building where she'd gathered a basket full of turnips. The root vegetables went flying as she dashed to catch Kate as she pitched forward. They barely kept their footing, but Catherine kept Kate from taking a nasty fall. With hearts pounding and relief coursing through them, the women embraced. Stunned, they backed away and stared at one another. Something passed between them that neither could describe, but it put the tension between them to rest. Catherine wasn't certain they could become fast friends, but neither felt uncomfortable after that.

"If the weather holds, I invite ye and yer parents to Inveruglas during Christmastide," Andrew Mòr offered.

"Aye!" Catriona chirped. "I shall challenge ye to see which one of us can still eat the most sweet chestnuts."

"Nay," Rab snorted. "I ken ye can eat more, and I'll end up ill. Ma mother still reminds me of that bet when we were weans whenever she warns me aboot overindulging."

"I shall take up that challenge," Catherine chimed in.

"Nay competitions between ye two," Andrew Óg

shook his head. "I willna feel right rallying behind one of ye and nae the other."

"Vera well," both women said. Catriona wrinkled her nose at her husband. "We challenge ye."

"Bluidy hell," Andrew grumbled.

"Dinna fash, Cousin. I'll let ye win like I did when we were weans," Catherine said with a wink.

"I think it's time we're on our way. I dinna need ma wife and ma cousin conspiring against me anymore."

"Aye." Rab stretched his neck from side to side. "We're still sore from ye convincing ma mother we should help ye organize the attic. Help. Bah."

"And I showed ye I was grateful." Catherine laid a smacking kiss on Rab's cheek. Catriona did the same on Andrew's cheek. The couples exchanged embraces before Andrew helped Catriona onto her horse. Catherine accepted a last embrace from her uncle before the MacLarens watched the MacFarlanes ride out.

"We will have to return to court, Kitty. We canna ignore the king," Rab whispered as he slid his arms around her waist and pulled her back against his chest. "We will make our appearances, accept whatever he has to say, then we'll be home in time for Christmas. After that, we'll go to Inveruglas."

"I ken. I'd rather travel with them than go to court," Catherine admitted.

"Ye and me both, *mo chridhe*. We shall leave in the morning and be back before the first snow."

Rab hoped he was right. The weather had changed during his newly extended family's visit. Autumn was rapidly giving way to winter. He didn't want to travel with Catherine even while the weather held, and he was especially disinclined to do it once it started snowing. However, the king's missive that arrived two days earlier was clear that King Robert expected both Rab and Catherine to appear. Everyone wondered what the

Douglases told the monarch since no such summons arrived for Andrew Óg, not directly from court or by way of Inveruglas.

"I dinna even care aboot aught I left behind. The other ladies can have ma gowns. I just want to have done and be back here. I'm far happier with Nessa than I am with the queen. I'm even growing to like Kate, as odd as that sounds. I ken why ye—"

"Kitty, ye dinna have to explain yerself. She's a nice lass, and I hope ye can be friends with her since we're all kin now. But I'd rather we never speak of that past. I dinna need to think of a time when it wasna ye. It's a dreadful reminder to me of how painful those years were. I dinna think back with any fond memories."

"Fair enough. I'm trying to be understanding, but I feel the same. Thinking aboot it only reminds me of why... Reminds me of how I nearly wound up with the wrong mon, and how I spent ma nights crying maself to sleep. The past needs to remain there."

"Good." Rab and Catherine waved one last time as the last of the MacFarlanes faded from sight. With a parting kiss, Rab went to the lists, and Catherine went to the kitchens to seek Nessa. Catherine found Nessa filled the void left by her mother's and aunt's deaths. Nessa was unassuming and kind, which is what Catherine's fragile heart needed. She enjoyed spending time with the maternal woman as she learned her way around Edinample and the 'keep she would one day run. The day passed in a blur, keeping Catherine busy. The night wasn't nearly long enough when Rab and Catherine finally agreed they needed sleep more than they needed to make love again. When morning came, they dragged themselves from their bed and prepared for their journey.

Everyone in their party appreciated Rab insisting that the ground was far too cold for Catherine to sleep on while they traveled. They indulged and spent the nights at inns, allowing even the guardsmen to sleep inside the tavern's main room or the stables. However, the journey felt too short when Stirling's town gates came into sight.

AN OLE DAME THE EDINBURGH COURT

in which they traveled. They jostled and shook the night air and, although even the exhaustion to sleep their awakened, made rough or the Castle. However, they hadn't felt the short with a slight enough night? came to light.

" $\mathcal{B}$ ut—"

"Enough, Buchanan," King Robert bellowed. "Your sister repeated what she said to Lady Catherine. Three other ladies already told me what Lady Agnes said. Your sister is no fool. She knows the good fortune she had that Lady Catherine only slapped her. Even if I were a lady, I don't know that I would have Lady Catherine's restraint."

"Your Majesty," Dennis Buchanan tried again.

"I'm uncertain how you are not understanding me, Buchanan. But you are certainly testing the last wisps of my patience. Your sister was in the wrong. There is naught for your cause. Lady Catherine and Rab owe you naught. If aught, you are mighty lucky that Lady Catherine isn't demanding an apology before the entire court. And you're even luckier that Rab hasn't called you out for your sister's vile comments. Count your blessings while you still have any."

Dennis Buchanan glared at Catherine with such venom that she reached for her dirk, and Rab angled himself to shift easily in front of Catherine. He trusted Dennis not at all. He hadn't addressed the Buchanans attacking them while they traveled, Dennis having cut him off when the Buchanan heir bewailed how Catherine treated Agnes. King Robert had sat with his mouth agape before bursting into laughter at Dennis and Agnes's expense. That only further infuriated Dennis. Catherine and Rab felt not an ounce of sympathy or remorse.

"Yer Majesty," Rab spoke up. "There is the matter of the Buchanans attacking us and chasing us onto the Grahams' land."

"What?" King Robert held up his hand when Rab made to respond. He locked eyes with Catherine. "You explain."

"Your Majesty, we crossed onto Buchanan land while we traveled, but we kept to ourselves. One of my husband's guards spotted a party of Buchanans who followed us. We broke camp and rode farther north before stopping for the night. We thought we'd put enough distance between them. The next day, they attacked while we were riding. My cousin found us at the right moment. Between the MacLarens and the MacFarlane bowmen, we were the victors and hastily made our way onto Graham land." Catherine stood with her hands folding in front of her, her courtly accent back in place before the king. It rankled after weeks of not having to hide her brogue, but she sensed the refined speech benefited them.

"Could the Buchanans have known aboot your spat with Lady Agnes?" King Robert asked.

"We don't believe so. They chased us without provocation. Or rather, being MacLarens was their excuse." Catherine kept her eyes on the Bruce, but she knew where Dennis stood in relation to her position beside Rab. She doubted she would have sounded so confident if her husband weren't there to bolster her confidence. She found Dennis even more intimidating than she had when he cornered her in the passageway.

There was something more feral about him as they stood in the Privy Council chamber. He seemed desperate.

"Declan, come forward," King Robert called out. Declan Douglas, Catriona's oldest brother, joined the group, standing between Dennis and the MacLarens. "Share what you told me just yesterday."

Declan appeared decidedly ill at ease. Catherine thought he even seemed tempted to tug at his leine. He glanced at Dennis before turning to face Catherine and Rab. "My uncle, Maxwell, sent a messenger to the Buchanans the moment we suspected you left court. It was before Andrew Óg knew you ran away. Uncle Maxwell recognized the MacLaren guard wearing a MacFarlane plaid. It made him suspicious. He figured if you headed toward Edinample, you would pass through Buchanan land."

"And what was his goal?" King Robert prompted.

Declan shifted his weight before he caught himself. "He wanted Lady Catherine dead, so my sister could marry Rab."

Catherine felt Rab stiffen, but he said nothing. The culprit was already dead. There was no bringing him back to execute him again. Rab had to take solace in Maxwell's demise, and how he would never pose a threat to Catherine again. It surprised Catherine when Declan took a step closer.

"I traveled home with ma uncle, brothers, and Catriona. I was the one who saddled Catriona's horse that day and told her to go. I did what I could to delay my father and uncles, so she could reach you. Neither my father nor uncle told me what they discussed with Laird MacLaren and Laird MacFarlane. I was too far back when we met you in the meadow. Is she safe?"

Catherine offered Declan a gentle smile. "She's very safe. She and Óg handfasted and will marry right after

Christmas. The Black Douglas knows Óg intended to marry her. He said Maxwell was her dowry."

"He traded his brother for that bi—" Dennis gasped as Declan's hand wrapped around his throat. Declan moved so quickly none of the guards reached him before he yanked Dennis onto his toes. He was half a head taller than Dennis and far more muscular.

"Finish that thought," Declan dared. "Call my sister that word, and I will challenge you. Your clan will be short an heir before the sun sets."

"Settle down," King Robert commanded as though he spoke to a group of rowdy children. "Buchanan, go home. Take your sister. You have both caused trouble here too many times. Tell your father that your marriage to Lady Sarah Anne will take place at the start of the new year. Your sister will marry Laird MacDonald of Keppoch. You will keep to yourself and cease antagonizing the MacLarens. I will not come to your defense if you rile them, and the MacFarlanes ride alongside them. From the sounds of it, at least some of the Douglases stand beside the MacFarlanes now too."

Declan shoved Dennis away from him, but his expression promised retribution once they were away from the king. Catherine wondered if Dennis would make it to the altar. She believed Dennis and Sarah Anne deserved one another, but she wasn't eager to have either as her neighbor. Declan glanced at Rab, a message passing between them that Catherine suspected confirmed her guess that Dennis would never make it to his wedding.

"Lady Catherine, Rab, you will stay. Everyone else, leave." King Robert leaned back in his chair as people filtered from the chamber. He didn't spare Dennis a glance when Declan followed him from the chamber. "I cannot say I approve of your secrecy and conspiracy, but I understand. MacLaren, I know you wouldn't have asked for me to intercede given what brought you to court. But once I knew—once my queen pointed out— you still shared feelings for one another, I would have sanctioned the marriage. I would have eased the restitution I ordered."

"Yer Majesty, we owe those reparations to the Mac-Farlanes, regardless of how things turned out. We may have ended our enmity, but our marriage doesnae undo the wrongs already committed." Rab kept his voice quiet but unwavering.

"Be that as it may, I see little point in paying the restitution if you are receiving Lady Catherine's dowry. You are hardly facing hardship now."

"I told ma father to decline the dowry," Rab stated.

"You what?" King Robert spluttered.

"The point of yer sentence was to see us brought low. Accepting the dowry eases the burden and defeats the point. Besides, ma father and I agree that we've taken enough from the MacFarlanes already. I never wanted Catherine's dowry, only her. I didna marry her for it. Our marriage may have brought the feud to an end, but I married Catherine because I love her."

"How romantic," King Robert noted, the disdain clear. "However, love doesn't fill a mon's trencher, nor does it care for a widow and unwed daughters. You will neither accept the dowry, but neither will you pay the full restitution. You will send the livestock but keep the coin." He steepled his fingers as the heels of his hands rested on his belly. He watched the couple, waiting to determine if the silence unnerved them. When he realized they would likely wait him out, he nodded. "Had it come to it, I would have backed a claim that you pre-contracted all those years ago. MacLaren, you said you'd both expressed your wish to marry one day before that fateful gathering ended. Your marriage is good for the Highlands."

Catherine and Rab listened to King Robert, not convinced everyone believed that as they recalled Maxwell Douglas and Dennis Buchanan. But they had no intention of contradicting the monarch. They prayed the declaration held true.

"Thank ye, Yer Majesty," Rab said with a bow. Catherine dipped into a deep curtsy.

"Lady Catherine, the queen wishes to offer her felicitations. You will find her in her solar."

Catherine and Rab took that to signal their dismissal. They left the chamber in silence and remained quiet until Catherine pulled Rab into an alcove. They embraced as their kiss reassured them that they'd survived their time in the lion's den.

"Say yer farewells, Kitty. Ye've packed yer trunks, and the men will load the wagon in the morning. We can be on our way back to Edinample before the sun wakes."

"I'd leave today if we could," Catherine mused. She canted her head and raised an eyebrow as she studied Rab's expression. "Dare we?"

"Nay one has told us we must stay." Rab shrugged. "We havenae even had the midday meal. There's nay reason to dally here."

"Vera well. I'll see the queen, and we can depart by the nooning." Catherine sighed as she leaned against Rab. "And with a wee touch of luck, I willna have to sound like a Lowlander ever again."

Not even two hours later, Cullen and the other guards loaded Catherine's two trunks onto a wagon. The MacLarens left Stirling castle and the town of Stirling without a moment's temptation to look back. Despite how she'd spoken and dressed, Catherine had always felt as much like the outsider that the courtier accused Rab of being. She focused her gaze on the true

Highlands and their home, knowing that she and Rab were returning to where they belonged. Together.

"Race ye," Catherine called as she spurred Timber forward. Both rider and horse knew Rab and Bolt would easily beat them, but the warrior and his trusted steed took their place beside the lady and her mare. Their matching MacLaren laird's family plaids flapped in the breeze as they distanced themselves from Stirling and raced toward a future that began seven years earlier in an apricot orchard.

EPILOGUE

"Can ye see them yet?" Catherine bounced on her toes as she stood beside Rab on the battlements.

"Ye ken I canna." Rab grinned down at his petite wife. The past three decades had been kind to Catherine, and her cornflower blue eyes held the same mischief that he'd spied the day he met her. Gray now laced her hair, and laugh lines crinkled beside her eyes. But she was still the most breathtaking woman he'd ever seen.

"Ye're nay even looking, *mo ghaol*. What's the point of having such a tall husband if ye arenae looking for them?"

Rab's chest rumbled with laughter as he lifted Catherine off her feet, bringing her eye level with him. "Do ye see them?"

"Well, nay. But Clyde said they'd be here soon."

"And they will be. Our son didna exaggerate. Yer cousins are in as much a hurry to arrive as we are to have them here." Rab grinned as he tried to contain his own excitement that Andrew Óg and Catriona were soon joining them for the summer solstice celebration. "Look, the lads are riding out to greet them."

Rab and Catherine watched their three sons, Clyde, Arran, and Logan, and their one son-by-marriage, Angus, ride through Edinample's gate. Just before the four young men crested the first hill, a swarm of horses charged to meet them. Catherine and Rab waved as Andrew and Catriona came into view. They hurried down to the bailey, Rab calling the stable hands to greet their guests.

"Cat!" Catherine exclaimed as her best friend and cousin-by-marriage reined in and leaped from her horse. The women collided in an embrace that was still as wild and merry as it had been when they were lasses. Rab and Andrew embraced, pounding one another on the back as the breeze lifted their gray heads of hair. A babe's cry pierced the air, soon followed by two more. Catherine and Catriona pulled apart with happy tears streaming down their cheeks.

"Elsie had her bairn a fortnight ago," Catherine explained the first babe's cry.

"Our Melisandre and Kiersten sound like they wish to greet their wee cousin." Catriona turned toward her family as her sons escorted their wives forward. The women each carried a bairn strapped to their chest with their arisaid. Catherine gleefully kissed the women's cheeks before brushing a kiss on each babe's head. The childhood friends stood together as they watched their husbands and sons greet one another.

"It's a miracle any of them still have teeth in their heads the way they go on," Catherine mused. "Come inside. The nooning is aboot to be served. Let's get ye all fed and cooled off."

Catherine accepted Rab's outstretched hand as the two older couples led the way for their broods of children. Catherine pointed to seats as everyone took their places. She and Rab took their spots in the laird's and lady's chairs. A tapestry fluttered against the wall, drawing Catherine's attention. She recalled the day Nessa ordered it hung in the Great Hall. It was the first time the MacLarens and MacFarlanes gathered after Catherine and Catriona gave birth to their last children. She remembered how Nessa gave thanks for the opportunity to enjoy the two clans gathered. It was the last time they gathered while a member of the older generation was still alive. Catherine offered her own thanksgiving as she watched her children and their children.

"We've made a wonderful life together, Kitty. I couldnae ask for aught more, except mayhap more time with Da and Mama. Even more time with Mòr. It went too fast."

"It did. But ye ken they're watching us. Nessa is likely trying to get Caelan and Mòr to behave while Aunt Aveline encourages them. Ma parents are with them and have been. They've all guided us at one point or another. We're blessed beyond measure with the family we have here today and the family who awaits us in heaven."

"It's hard to believe Óg and I have been lairds for nearly a score of years," Rab murmured as he looked down the table at his closest friend besides Douglan. He glanced at Douglan and Kate, who sat to his right. Their daughters, Esme, Vaila, Morven, and Rona, sat at the table just below the dais with their husbands and children.

"If our family keeps growing as it is with grandbairns, there willna be room in the Great Hall for the clan," Kate mused with a grin.

"Aye." Catherine's eyes crinkled again. The first year had been difficult for the two women, but once they were both mothers, neither thought about the pasts they shared with Rab. It was far too obvious that the best matched couples had formed. Douglan doted on his wife and daughter as much as Rab did his wife and son. As both couples added more children to their expanding family, Catherine and Kate relied on one another out of necessity then eventually friendship.

"When do ye think the first clan will arrive?" Andrew asked from across the table.

"This eve. Brodie and Dominic are bringing their herd of sons."

"Eleven between the two of them," Catriona crowed. "And nae a one of them will win a race."

"Mama, dinna go gloating again," Arran said to Catherine as she nodded her agreement with Catriona. "Ye ken the Sinclairs are coming. They didna make it last year because of the flooding right after they planted. But they'll be back this year. Nay one but them ever wins."

"Speak for yerself, Brother," Elsie said as she patted her daughter's back. "I held ma own against Ainsley, even if her mama is Mairghread Mackay. We tied in the knife throwing."

Arran opened his mouth to argue that it was luck that allowed Elsie to tie, but his wife kicked him under the table. Logan, unmarried, with no one to censor him, wasn't so wise. He pretended to hide behind his older brother Clyde when Elsie twirled her eating knife. Her husband, Angus, playfully pulled it free from her hand.

"Ailish Sinclair is just as likely to win as her cousin. In front of her father, she swears it's Tavish who taught her to throw those knives. But I remember her mother, Ceit, from when Catherine and I competed. Ailish has her mother's dead aim." Catriona elbowed Catherine. "Remember how it surprised everyone else to learn Ceit was a spy for the Bruce?"

"It was nay surprise to us when we saw her hunt with only a *sgian dubh*." Catherine grinned. She watched her youngest son, Logan, as Catriona continued teasing.

"Ailish is of an age to marry."

Everyone laughed when even Logan's ears turned crimson. "I'm nae interested in having Tavish Sinclair as ma father-by-marriage. The mon is a berserker."

"Then make sure he's fighting on yer side, lad." Andrew quipped. Everyone at the table chuckled. It was no secret among the family that Logan was taken with young Ailish Sinclair, but the girl never took notice of Logan. Catherine shot her cousin a warning glare. She'd seen Ailish exchanging glances with Ewan and Allyson Gordon's son, Leith. She didn't want her son to get his hopes up for nothing.

The meal continued as the MacLarens and MacFarlanes swapped stories as well as shared memories from previous holidays and gathering spent together. Catherine leaned against Rab, who draped his arm around her shoulders, while the servants cleared away the meal's remnants.

"Are ye happy, *mo piseag?*"

"How could I nae be? I have ye and our weans and their weans. Our family is here to celebrate with us as we host this year's Highland Gathering. We've enjoyed prosperity and peace for the past dozen years. We have created a wonderful life together. Thank ye, *mo chridhe.*" Catherine and Rab ignored the grumbles and snickers as they shared a kiss that was as heated as the ones they shared when they reunited in Stirling. Nearly thirty years of marriage had done nothing to dampen their love and their passion. Instead, it had grown deeper and richer, taking root in the land they ruled together and in the home they built with their children.

"I love ye, *mo piseag.*" Rab whispered in her ear before nipping the tender flesh behind it.

"I love ye." Catherine cupped Rab's jaw before

pressing a tender kiss to his lips. "Thank ye for bringing me where I belong. Where we belong together."

The couple shared another kiss, forgetting the world around them like they so often did when they were locked in each other's embrace.

THANK YOU FOR READING AN OUTSIDER AT THE HIGHLAND COURT

Celeste Barclay, a nom de plume, lives near the Southern California coast with her husband and sons. Growing up in the Midwest, Celeste enjoyed spending as much time in and on the water as she could. Now she lives near the beach. She's an avid swimmer, a hopeful future surfer, and a former rower. When she's not writing, she's working or being a mom.

Subscribe to Celeste's bimonthly newsletter to receive exclusive insider perks.
Subscribe Now

www.celestebarclay.com

Join the fun and get exclusive insider giveaways, sneak peeks, and new release announcements in Celeste Barclay's Facebook Ladies of Yore Group

THE HIGHLAND LADIES

A Spinster at the Highland Court

BOOK 1 SNEAK PEEK

Elizabeth Fraser looked around the royal chapel within Stirling Castle. The ornate candlestick holders on the altar glistened and reflected the light from the ones in the wall sconces as the priest intoned the holy prayers of the Advent season. Elizabeth kept her head bowed as though in prayer, but her green eyes swept the congregation. She watched the other ladies-in-waiting, many of whom were doing the same thing. She caught the eye of Allyson Elliott. Elizabeth raised one eyebrow as Allyson's lips twitched. Both women had been there enough times to accept they'd be kneeling for at least the next hour as the Latin service carried on. Elizabeth understood the Mass thanks to her cousin Deirdre Fraser, or rather now Deirdre Sinclair. Elizabeth's mind flashed to the recent struggle her cousin faced as she reunited with her husband Magnus after a seven-year separation. Her aunt and uncle's choice to keep Deirdre hidden from her husband simply because they didn't think the Sinclairs were an advantageous enough match, and the resulting scandal, still humiliated the other Fraser clan members at court. She admired Deirdre's husband Magnus's pledge to remain faithful despite not knowing if he'd ever see Deirdre again.

Elizabeth suddenly snapped her attention; while everyone else intoned the twelfth—or was it thirteenth—amen of the Mass, the hairs on the back of her neck stood up. She had the strongest feeling that someone was watching her. Her eyes scanned to her right, where her parents sat further down the pew. Her mother and father had their heads bowed and eyes closed. While she was convinced her mother was in devout prayer, she wondered if her father had fallen asleep during the Mass. Again. With nothing seeming out of the ordinary and no one visibly paying attention to her, her eyes swung to the left. She took in the king and queen as they kneeled together at their prie-dieu. The queen's lips moved as she recited the liturgy in silence. The king was as still as a statue. Years of leading warriors showed, both in his stature and his ability to control his body into absolute stillness. Elizabeth peered past the royal couple and found herself looking into the astute hazel eyes of Edward Bruce, Lord of Badenoch and Lochaber. His gaze gave her the sense that he peered into her thoughts, as though he were assessing her. She tried to keep her face neutral as heat surged up her neck. She prayed her face didn't redden as much as her neck must have, but at a twenty-one, she still hadn't mastered how to control her blushing. Her nape burned like it was on fire. She canted her head slightly before looking up at the crucifix hanging over the altar. She closed her eyes and tried to invoke the image of the Lord that usually centered her when her mind wandered during Mass.

Elizabeth sensed Edward's gaze remained on her. She didn't understand how she was so sure that he was looking at her. She didn't have any special gifts of perception or sight, but her intuition screamed that he was still looking.

THE CLAN SINCLAIR

His Highland Lass **BOOK 1 SNEAK PEEK**

She entered the great hall like a strong spring storm in the northern most Highlands. Tristan Mackay felt like he had been blown hither and yon. As the storm settled, she left him with the sweet scents of heather and lavender wafting towards him as she approached. She was not a classic beauty, tall and willowy like the women at court. Her face and form were not what legends were made of. But she held a unique appeal unlike any he had seen before. He could not take his eyes off of her long chestnut hair that had strands of fire and burnt copper running through them. Unlike the waves or curls he was used to, her hair was unusually straight and fine. It looked like a waterfall cascading down her back. While she was not tall, neither was she short. She had a figure that was meant for a man to grasp and hold onto, whether from the front or from behind. She had an aura of confidence and charm, but not arrogance or conceit like many good looking women he had met. She did not seem to know her own appeal. He could tell that she was many things, but one thing she was not was his.

PIRATES OF THE ISLES

The Blond Devil of the Sea **BOOK 1 SNEAK PEEK**

Caragh lifted her torch into the air as she made her way down the precarious Cornish cliffside. She made out the hulking shape of a ship, but the dead of night made it impossible to see who was there. She and the fishermen of Bedruthan Steps weren't expecting any shipments that night. But her younger brother Eddie, who stood watch at the entrance to their hiding place, had spotted the ship and signaled up to the village watchman, who alerted Caragh.

As her boot slid along the dirt and sand, she cursed having to carry the torch and wished she could have sunlight to guide her. She knew these cliffs well, and it was for that reason it was better that she moved slowly than stop moving once and for all. Caragh feared the light from her torch would carry out to the boat. Despite her efforts to keep the flame small, the solitary light would be a beacon.

When Caragh came to the final twist in the path before the sand, she snuffed out her torch and started to run to the cave where the main source of the village's income lay in hiding. She heard movement along the trail above her head and knew the local fishermen would soon join her on the beach. These men, both young and old, were strong from days spent pulling in the full trawling nets and hoisting the larger catches onto their boats. However, these men weren't well-trained swordsmen, and the fear of pirate raids was ever-present. Caragh feared that was who the villagers would face that night.

The Dark Heart of the Sea **BOOK 2**
The Red Drifter of the Sea **BOOK3**
The Scarlet Blade of the Sea **BOOK 4**

Leif BOOK 1 SNEAK PEEK

Leif looked around his chambers within his father's longhouse and breathed a sigh of relief. He noticed the large fur rugs spread throughout the chamber. His two favorites placed strategically before the fire and the bedside he preferred. He looked at his shield that hung on the wall near the door in a symbolic position but waiting at the ready. The chests that held his clothes and some of his finer acquisitions from voyages near and far sat beside his bed and along the far wall. And in the center was his most favorite possession. His oversized bed was one of the few that could accommodate his long and broad frame. He shook his head at his longing to climb under the pile of furs and on the stuffed mattress that beckoned him. He took in the chair placed before the fire where he longed to sit now with a cup of warm mead. It had been two months since he slept in his own bed, and he looked forward to nothing more than pulling the furs over his head and sleeping until he could no longer ignore his hunger. Alas, he would not be crawling into his bed again for several more hours. A feast awaited him to celebrate his and his crew's return from their latest expedition to explore the isle of Britannia. He bathed and wore fresh clothes, so he had no excuse for lingering other than a bone weariness that set in during the last storm at sea. He was eager to spend time at home no matter how much he loved sailing. Their last expedition had been profitable with several raids of monasteries that yielded jewels and both silver and gold, but he was ready for respite.

Leif left his chambers and knocked on the door next to his. He heard movement on the other side, but it was only moments before his sister, Freya, opened her door. She, too, looked tired but clean. A few pieces of jewelry she confiscated from the holy houses that allegedly swore to a life of poverty and deprivation adorned her trim frame.

"That armband suits you well. It compliments your muscles," Leif smirked and dodged a strike from one of those muscular arms.

Only a year younger than he, his sister was a well-known and feared shield maiden. Her lithe form was strong and agile making her a ferocious and competent opponent to any man. Freya's beauty was stunning, but Leif had taken every opportunity since they were children to tease her about her unusual strength even among the female warriors.

"At least one of us inherited our father's prowess. Such a shame it wasn't you."